A Matter of Temperance

ICHABOD TEMPERANCE

ISBN-10: 149744750X
ISBN-13: 978-1497447509

The Adventures of Ichabod Temperance

Volume One: 'A Matter of Temperance'

Volume Two: 'A World of InTemperance'

Volume Three: 'For the Love of Temperance'

forthcoming:

Volume Four: 'A Study in Temperance'

TABLE OF CONTENTS

ACKNOWLEDGEMENTS

It is with a humble heart that I gratefully acknowledge gaining the storytelling art from my mates in professional wrestling. Thanks go out to my wonderful karate dojo friends, and my Aetherweb pals.

Special thanks go to Mr. Wolfgang Metzger for generously providing the silhouettes, and to Sergeant Turk for designing the gorgeous cover.

Also, I would like to thank the fates that allowed me to meet the charming cast and crew of the movie "Engines of Destiny," who generously allowed me to be apart of their world, and opened me to this lovely genre.

Finally, of course a special thanks and acknowledgment go out to the beautiful Miss Persephone Plumtartt for her invaluable assistance and inspiration without which this story would not have happened.

CHAPTER 1 – ADVENTURE!

Ichabod

The rumbling purr as of an impossibly big cat thrums through my body. Titanic engines vibrate this colossal ship. Wheels the size of four story buildings mercilessly paddle the Atlantic Ocean into submission.

It is the middle of the night; the ship is dark and quiet. Lying on the deck, I can sense the dark expanse of the ocean depths spreading out below, while at the same time, a bright ocean of stars bursts outward above. I feel as if I am tumbling through the aether of space, swimming in a celestial ocean.

An ocean of unexpected phenomena inhabit this wondrous, astral void.

Our world became even more wondrous nearly six years ago with the coming of the Revelatory Comet during that fateful Summer of 1869. Unreported through history, this fiery white snowball entered our unsuspecting solar system. It made a pass around the Sun and then, racing along its elliptical trajectories, the magical inter-galactic meteor crossed the path of Earth's orbit. Many astronomers feared a collision between the heavenly bodies, but Mother Earth traveled safely through the Comet's tail. It has only been a short five and a half years since the Earth crossed the Comet's sparkling wake.

On this day, March 16, 1875, the world is a greatly changed place. It seems that the Comet has had a strange effect upon our planet. Everywhere on Earth, tens of thousands have become strangely affected by its passage. Not all people, but many, find that any natural talent they already possessed has been greatly enhanced. Tinkerers began to sprout up like wildflowers in spring. The changes were subtle enough that people may or may not have been immediately aware of their amplified aptitudes. Soon, however, the world came to accept this state of being. Nowadays, you can't swing a bucket without hitting some sort of tinker, engineer, musician, actor, acrobat or Doctor of unusual expertise. Most apothecaries have a laboratory of some sort, with bubbling cauldrons, smoking thuribles, and tangles of complicated glass tubing. Every barber has a wall of assorted fiendish-seeming, gleaming, glistening, never before seen devices for the grooming of the hirsute man. Not all men have the courage, stout will and constitution to face down these gleaming apparati for just a fresh haircut and a smooth shave.

For years, the power of steam has been harnessed to serve man's ingenuity. Rail lines spread like kudzu across our land, and others, giving platforms for great steam locomotives, but in recent times, the power has been tapped for many inventions, great and small. Horseless carriages powered by steam are becoming more commonplace. A blacksmith shop can, nowadays, manufacture almost anything the mind can conceive. One hears of certain smiths, more affected than most by the Revelatory Comet's passing, who have built entire horses, mechanical horses.

Astounding devices with wound springs bring inanimate objects to life, large objects and small. From tiny, but intricate, clockwork playthings, they include also full size, mechanical people. I am given to understand that gyroscopic attenuators maintain the balance of this new breed of person.

Airships, great and small, prowl the skies around the world. The flying wonders come in such a variety! Single operator balloons share the skies with small and medium blimps of many sizes. I understand that a capacity for steering and propulsion grants these cigar shaped ships the all important status of dirigible.

Floating fleets of majestic Zeppelins proudly spread the prestige of their home nations.

First private, then military, and now many commercial craft have arisen as well. Even groups of air pirates have made their aerial presence felt. It is a changed world, but it is still a very dangerous one.

Then we have the marvel of this magnificent ship on which I voyage, this mighty, eight wheeled, ocean paddler. My gracious, she's quite a miracle of human achievement! Imagine a Mississippi riverboat, but grown to fifty times her normal size. Four wheels on each side propel this amazing ship ever forward. A heavy steel keel runs her length. Steel ribs support her wooden hull and decks. Extra steel reinforcements support her mammoth engines and drive wheels, amidships.

A Sol Furnace powers this ship's mighty steam boilers.

The Sol Furnace is the greatest invention to arise in this flowering of ingenuity that has taken the world.

The power of the Sun itself, has been captured, and harnessed for the the use of Mankind, by Professor St. John Entwhistle Plumtartt, an eminent physicist (who is reputed to be an initiate of several arcane orders). By a process that is understood by only a very few, he has developed a technology capable of generating a seemingly endless source of energy.

This ocean paddler is on her return trip to England, completing her maiden cruise. I feel a special attachment to this ship, and to her furnace. Little ol' me, Ichabod Temperance, just an Alabama knockabout, count myself as one of the many from around the World affected by the Revelatory Comet's passing. I was fourteen years old that summer of '69. My family had a small place in Jefferson County. I didn't realize the change at first. Little ideas would pop into my mind. After the idea, the formula for bringing the idea about would similarly materialize in my mind like a flower quickly spreading into bloom. I swiftly developed quite a knack for design and engineering solutions to problems, especially goggles. I crafted a pair of goggles for Professor Plumtartt himself in his work with the dangerous elements involved with his manufacturing process.

This brought me a bit of notoriety, which has led to other commissions.

That is the errand I am upon now. My most precious invention to date are my "Green Beauties." I hate to let them go! Last year, I sent Professor Plumtartt his goggles. Professor Plumtartt's "Elemental Protectors" got to enjoy the ocean voyage to England. These marvelous goggles are likewise commissioned by a British client. This year, I have decided to not send my marvelous new goggles to my esteemed client. Instead, I shall deliver them myself! Why should *they* have all the fun? The "Beauties" are destined for adventures in darkest Africa. For the first time in my life, I have left Jefferson County, Alabama, USA, to cross the Atlantic Ocean, and to visit jolly old England. I never would have dreamed that one day I should make a journey to the legendary city of London, herself!

What great fun this is!

This is the greatest adventure I have ever known!

Chapter 2 - Nocturnal Disturbance.

Persephone

"I am a Plumtartt and I must gain control of myself!"

I awaken in a cold panic. Tremors shake my body, and tears form in my eyes.

It is the same terror I felt in Father's laboratory at the time of the accident. The atmosphere of evil that filled the room on that tragic fateful night, when I thought we had banished these horrors forever, has returned.

"Persephone Plumtartt, get a grip on your senses, girl."

I command myself to still the core-rattling vibrations that shake my body, but the cold rebellious fear disobeys my orders.

I pull my knees to my chin and covers to my face. This great house, the palatial Plumtartt Manor, is so hugely empty. I have always felt as if I were surrounded by family. Father, and "Uncle" Victor, our long-time family retainer, and dear Michael, the stable boy, these were my family. They, the rest of the staff, and the whole bustling estate, made for a happy place to live. Now they are either dead, have fled, or I have ordered them to leave for their own safety. How I wish I had someone here with me now. I am in the grip of a mounting terror and I know not why. I have never before been afraid to be alone, not in the least. However, this moment, this night, is different. I can feel it. Dreadful solitude and loneliness solidify in my heart.

Oh, my. I have the most ominous sensation.

There is a commotion from the lower forty. The dogs are worked into a terrible fit. The fearsome brood of the estate's canines are tearing into something, a few hundred yards from the buildings. Far from what would be expected, they make the most heartrending cries I have ever heard. This pack is a ferocious group, yet the stout canines are whelping like frightened puppies. The great pack of mighty canines can be heard to retreat from our estate; yelping, whining, and with tails presumably between their lowered haunches.

An unnatural quiet engulfs the grounds. A terrible silence that should not be. I feel as if my hearing has been greatly amplified as I am acutely aware of the tiniest sound. What on Earth could have scared away that fearsome pack? How is it that I know that it comes for me?

Now the horses in the barn have their turn to panic. They thrash and scream in complete terror. Kicking and fighting in their comfortable stables, incredibly, those beautiful, gentle horses are kicking their way free of their stable captivity to escape that which approaches Plumtartt Manor.

Now, once more, a silence grips the estate, uncanny in the wake of all the tumult. Something has frightened away the fierce pack of dogs that reside here. They would have given their lives in my defense, but unimaginably, they have fled in terror. So too have the other livestock managed to join the exodus. The barnyard is disturbingly quiet, after the beautiful horses have fought their way from their stables and taken flight from the peaceful estate.

That ominous sensation washes across me again. Something terrible is coming for me; I can feel it. I want to flee as the animals of the estate have, but I am trapped by a paralyzing fear that has me secured within my boudoir.

An intuition tells me that something oppressively large and foul is on the property and it means to get in. A thing of loathing slowly, steadily approaches and then touches the house. Somehow, I know evil is in contact with the old building. A presence, big and heavy, is pushing against the North wing of Plumtartt Manor.

I hear a creak.

I hear it again, but stronger this time. I am locked in my room, but I can tell from the sounds that what I hear is the magnificent stained glass window from the end of the long hallway. Saint George, slaying the dragon, is beautifully rendered in lead and coloured glass. Capping the wing on that side of the house is the great, circular, historic window. It sits a full twenty feet off the ground, yet somehow a massive weight is pressing against it.

Slowly, one pop and snap at a time, the pride of our family home is giving way. Shattering cracks signaling the failure of the distressed glass comes faster and faster. More than a hundred years old, the intricate pattern of coloured glass shatters, raining down shards of myriad color. With a huge reluctant creak, followed by a large crash, the famous old window has been pushed in. A disconcerting thud resounds along with the crash of breaking glass.

Evil is in the house.

The noises I hear coming to me are unidentifiable. There is a sucking pop, followed a heavy plop. The disgusting sounds repeat, again and again, as something large and unthinkably heavy slowly makes its way down the hall. The hateful sound gradually comes closer. My heart races. I want to scream. I want to flee. I am paralyzed with fright. Hair rises on the back of my neck.

A pale, green glow shows around the edges of my bedroom door. I clutch my sheets all the tighter to my throat as something touches the heavy wooden entrance. The oak creaks with tortured resistance, as a tremendous weight is inexorably pressed upon the portal. I push myself against the wall, atop my pillows.

The door gives way!

"No!" I cry, the plea bursting from within.

An enormous amoeba pours through the failed aperture. Its grotesque, jellied form, pushes and then pulls itself into my bedchamber. With deliberate effort, the shapeless blob slowly maneuvers itself towards my canopied bed. Pseudopodal limbs crawl up over the bedrails.

I scream with unbridled terror, but an unexpected grunt cuts off the aural outburst.

"Unh!"

A warm tingling passes through me. Something has been triggered within. An electrical charge builds inside me. The impossible form reaches out for me.

"No!" I shout again.

I feel an intense bolt of organic lightning pulse through my innermost core.

A powerful and intense burst of energy blasts from my body and from my outstretched hand towards the terrible murderous amoeba.

A brilliant red light fills the bedchamber.

KAH-WAH-BUH-BOOM!!!

The creature is atomized in the thunderous explosion.

I collapse and know no more.

CHAPTER 3 - LONDON!

Ichabod

London!

What a wonderful city, and I really do mean, full of wonder. The city's skyline has changed. Along with St. Paul's, Buckingham Palace, and London Bridge, now there are also elevated railways, with trussed supports connecting important buildings. Mooring towers grow from various structures, that they may be serviced by aircraft. Fantastic ships of the latest construction and design sit upon the Thames.

A strange wave has passed over this city. It is as if the five thousand pounds of clockwork in Big Ben's tower has spread like algae on a pond. More often than not, it is in cities that the Revelatory Comet's effects are most pronouncedly prominent. Throughout this urban sprawl, modern marvels insinuate themselves into the fabric of busy life.

The streets are still full of the most elaborate and beautifully appointed carriages the world has ever seen. Two wheeled Hansoms and four-wheeler carriages of quality and luxury, crafted of the most exquisite woods and leathers, abound in this busy English metropolis. However, they occasionally have to share these London streets with steam-powered lorries and trams. Double-decker passenger wagons, a wonder in themselves, are now pulled by steam powered land locomotives. I spot the occasional mechanical horse, but one sight that nearly floored me was the sight of an Auriental Rikshaw. What made it even more remarkable was that there was a steam-powered, clockwork man in the traces!

I was unprepared for the fashions worn by modern day city dwellers. As I am a young man from Alabama, I hope you will forgive me for not being as up to date on the latest fashions as you may be, but in this city, the apparel boggles my mind. "Fancy" is not a sufficient description, for these are some dandified gentlemen, indeed. Ties and pins bring sparkle among the lacy collars along with all sorts of accoutrement. Self-tipping hats seem to be very popular this year.

I am feeling pretty good right now, so I attempt to be friendly with my English cousins.

"Howdy, my good man." says I with all my charm and manners. "How are you all doing tonight?"

I receive some dubious appraisals.

"Cheerio, y'all." I sportingly call. "This fog's somethin' else, ain't it?"

Disapproval is all I'm getting, so I move along.

My attention is drawn to the fairer sex.

My head's a spinnin' at these pretty women. Each girlie is gussied up like a peacock at the Bird's World Fair.

These cosmopolitan British gals and their intricate dress designs are as pretty a sight as I've ever seen. I did not know so many colors and styles existed in dressmaking. The variety of design and shapely contours dizzy me.

And good grief, the ladies' hats are marvelous, sometimes wide and tall, or sometimes tiny, and compact. Most of these fancy chapeaux are packed with enough bird plumage to give flight to the Tower of London.

I hope that I am not out of line if I mention that these

lovely English ladies in their suggestive bustles, sometimes tend to make me quite light-headed.

What's more, there are endless varieties of shoes and boots, fans and parasols, purses and handkerchiefs. These accessories, combined with the whole outfit, and the shapely beauties within, threaten to overwhelm this poor observer.

CHAPTER 4 - A NEW ALLY.

Persephone

What was before a lively courtyard, bustling with creatures great and small - cows, horses, and goats; geese, chicken and ducks - is now lifeless and desolate.

Drained from the events of the night before, I leave this melancholy scene. With no horse in the stable, I set out to walk to the Elderberry Pond train station. The events that led to this sad moment play in my mind.

It began a few months ago, just after Father's tragic death. I cling to the hope that the foul forces he had used to complete his experiments have departed as well. Alas, no...

As Uncle Victor and I are cleansing the laboratory of the disgusting sigils father had scrawled over floor, wall, and ceiling, the beloved family retainer is attacked in a vicious assault I am powerless to stop. I know it is something not of this world, something unclean and unnatural. It draws the very life force out of Uncle Vic and drops his used husk. A hideous thing is formed, something I do not want to remember. I fly from the abomination in terror. I run into Michael the stable boy. He has heard me scream and come to my aid. The monster comes! Michael cannot see it! I can, but he cannot! Run, child, run! Alas no, I think his teenage infatuation with me has led to his wanting to protect me. He is a tragic, would-be gallant, slain in a wasteful manner.

Father had always been a man of the strictest scientific disciplines. After the passing of the Revelatory Comet, it was Father – with his already brilliant mind amplified by the Comet's effect - who discovered the inner workings of atoms, leading to his discovery of the nature of the Sun's power: nuclear fusion. I remember the night when he showed me the equations, which he said had "come to him" as if in a dream. Even then, his excitement seemed a bit alien, yet I was enthralled by the concepts he presented.

He knew that if he could make use of his new understanding to replicate this series of reactions, Mankind could harness the power of the stars themselves to provide incalculable energy. Energy enough to power the world.

Yet for all of his knowledge, for all of his precise and brilliant equations, he could not recreate the necessary conditions through scientific means. Where before the Comet's passing he would have accepted this dispassionately, the changed man Father was could not contain his almost-frightening zeal. It was then that he succumbed to the temptations of dark magic to bring about what he could not, by science alone. It was as if the Revelatory Comet's effect not only amplified his intellectual prowess, but somehow warped his character, weakening his resistance until he became capable of misusing magic in such a way. Father Summoned... and Something came. Now that Something has returned to our home.

After last night's attack on Plumtartt Estate, I know that evil forces are loose in our fair land.

I have been in contact with a newspaper reporter. Normally, I would eschew such an ally, but this is a man of resolve and grit. He has seen much in this world, and could very well be the man to help me tell my story to an unsuspecting country.

I have been walking for some time, when a wagon

approaches. It is from the Plumtartt Factory, home of the Sol Furnace.

"Miss Plumtartt! You are needed at the factory. We had two more deaths overnight. Horrible things. Some men are refusing to enter the plant. Other employees know the importance of the operations and want to continue. Please come at once!"

"Take me to the train station." I command the wagon driver. "Then return to the factory and have it closed until further notice. I appreciate the men's loyalty to the factory and the important projects we have contracted, but no further loss of life is tolerable."

The Plumtartt Factory wagon drops me at the station, the driver returning to carry out his previously unthinkable duty of closing the factory. That means stopping production at Plumtartt shipyard. We are close to launching the *Dreadfulle.* She is destined to be the greatest Battleship afloat, and the Flagship of Her Majesty's Navy. Three more Battleships are under construction. They are considered a vital part of the England's and our allies security. Though still a few months from my twentieth birthday, I have always taken an active part in the oversight of these massive factories and shipyards. The supervisors will not be happy about it, but my wishes will be respected and my orders will be followed. Governments from around the world will not be happy about the factory and shipyard being shut down.

It is with a heavy heart that I leave my country home.

I arrive in London, and eventually my hotel, still a bit shaken.

The loss of the Plumtartt stables has made me late for my appointment. I hurry to 'Clubbe Mandrake' for the chosen meeting, for it is deemed socially acceptable for two persons of opposite gender to meet there without word of our private tete-a-tete raising eyebrows amongst the leaders of London society?

My destined meeting is with the famous reporter and adventurer, Sir Henry Stanley!

He is the very same reporter who successfully searched darkest Africa for the lost Samaritan, Doctor Livingstone. I am afraid he is perturbed at my tardiness, but he tries not to let his disapproval show. In fact, he is so charming, and kind, that he convinces me that the best course of action is to lay the whole story out for him, from beginning to end, leaving out no detail. He gives me the sense of being a worthy confidante, and soon, the whole sordid tale gushes forth. Though I normally bear myself with the utmost composure, I am, admittedly, in a weakened state for the nonce. I sob just a little on his sympathetic shoulder. It is a welcome moment of release, after the loneliness and heartache I have suffered of late.

"The sooner we can awaken Britain to these hideous dangers the better," says this stalwart, and handsome man. I am actually relieved at being able to tell my tale to this heroic figure.

With this man's help, we shall open England's eyes to her peril, and defeat the scourge that threatens our country.

Chapter 5 - The London Journals.

Ichabod

I'm as perky as a white-tailed doe in February!

I do not want to stand out as a foreigner; therefore, I attempt a camouflage. I celebrate my arrival in Europe at the same time by allowing myself a small purchase: a genuine, London Derby. What a handsome hat! I feel myself blending in already. Sophisticated English society, here I come!

And now it's time to catch up with what's going on in the world.

Several papers' exclamatory headlines catch my eye.

The Britannic Observer

> **S.S. *TRIUMPH* SETS ATLANTIC CROSSING RECORD!**
>
> "Sol Furnace-driven marvel conquers the Atlantic."
>
> "Great Britain's place as the leading shipbuilder in the world is secured as the *S.S. Triumph* shatters the Atlantic crossing record."

Amazing! I was just on that ship, and a part of her historic crossings.

The Evening Comet

> **PARLIAMENT CONSIDERS SAPIENCY DECREE**
>
> "The 'Animal Sapiency Alliance' pushes forward with bill to allow rights to

> animals able to prove an elevation in intelligence to the courts."
>
> "Humanists vow to fight for the dominance of Man over Beast."

How about that! I'm not sure how I will react if I ever meet a talking horse. The idea intrigues me, for I have always had a fondness for, and a talent with, handling animals.

The London Sun

PLUMTARTT SCANDAL THREATENS NATIONAL SECURITY

I purchase this paper. Not only is this article written by my client, with whom I have an appointment, but it concerns the family Plumtartt, with whom I have a relationship.

> "The proud name of Plumtartt, which has brought so much fame and recognition to our country, has now fallen into a pit of shame, and wallows in disgrace. After the recent, untimely death of Professor Plumtartt, eminent scientist responsible for developing the great "Sol Furnace," the factory, shipyards and estate have fallen to his unfortunately demented daughter, Miss Persephone Plumtartt. In an interview, she reveals a belief in "Evil Forces" at large in the country. She believes that they are the nexus of "ghost" attacks in the areas. In the ridiculous story she relates, her father was stymied in his efforts to capture the Sun's energy. He turned to arcane

methodology, combined with the latest in scientific application. The Plumtartt girl claims to have been at her father's side throughout the process, until he entered this occult avenue. Upon entering her father's inner sanctum of experimentation, she interrupted a grand process, an 'Evocation', the mad girl claims. A violent explosion ensued. Miss Plumtartt claims to have been "bathed in an elemental beam, that wrought a change within me."

In the past two weeks, several more deaths have followed upon the heels of her father. Now, the girl claims to be attacked by hideous monsters. She related that last night, a microscopic creature, an amoeba, miraculously grown to the size of a haystack, attacked her home. She even claims to believe the accident she suffered in her father's laboratory gave her the ability to combat the giant jellyfish.

This reporter reveals that it was all I could do to keep from shouting with laughter in the face of this deluded girl. That, however, is where the amusement stops. Since then, she has closed the vital Plumtartt factory and shipyard. Only two passenger ships have been completed, the *Triumph*, and the *Victoria*. Miss Plumtartt attributes several recent deaths at these locations to these same 'Evil Forces' summoned by her Father. Four battleships are in the middle of construction, and she has stopped their progress just because a few clumsy workmen have managed to get themselves killed. The hysterical girl needs to realize that accidents are a part of business. Our nation's pride and dignity are at the whimsy of this dangerously unbalanced woman, who obviously is not up to the rigors of industrial command decisions. The Plumtartt factory, in the middle of constructing more Furnaces, is, unfortunately, likewise shut down.

These institutions are of National concern. The critical nature of these ships is what will propel Great Britain on to rule the Seas for years to come. One psychotic débutante is standing in the way of World commerce and progress.

It is this reporter's conviction that Miss Plumtartt must be locked up in Bedlam Asylum, for the public good and safety."

Chapter 6 - Stanley's True Colours Revealed.

Persephone

Oh! What I fool I have been to trust that traitorous reporter. He has made me a laughing stock! Worse, he places our country in danger, not to mention my own freedom.

Sir Henry Stanley has brought shame and ruin down upon the good name of Plumtartt, with my unwitting assistance.

I cannot allow myself to to be concerned with my own personal misfortunes. There is something larger at stake, and I am even further behind in my efforts to awaken my unsuspecting countrymen.

My eyes are drawn to other papers. "Ghost" attacks continue around the country. Horribly dessicated corpses, followed by terrible stories of violent attacks by invisible creatures. Many suspect that local constabularies are attempting to keep the stories quiet, as not to start a panic.

My worst fears are realized.

Evil runs rampant through the nation, while my fellow countrymen obstinately remain reluctant to come to grips with the reality of the menace that threatens us. I am helpless to stem the tide of danger inexorably rising around the unseeing eyes of my country.

Chapter 7 - MisAdventure With A Scoundrel.

Ichabod

I am excited about and eager to keep my appointment.

A meeting with Sir Henry Stanley! What a fine fellow he must be!

With my "Green Beauties" safely ensconced atop my new Derby, I faithfully keep my appointment at the wonderful Strand Hotel. (I am entranced by its opulent beauty, luxury, and charm. It is a shame that they will never let me return.)

I find Sir Henry in the dining room. I exercise the opportunity to observe this famous gentleman before introducing myself. I admit to being let down in my expectations as he is apparently enjoying a liquid dinner tonight. Sir Henry is unsteady in his balance, and belligerent in attitude toward the staff. Smug waves of arrogance, ripple from the intoxicated Knight as he rudely berates his waiter and insults his chefs efforts. He is an obnoxious avalanche, cascading down a mountain of rude behavior.

I am still nonetheless anxious to engage this man in conversation. He is famous throughout the world as a fearless adventurer.

He appears to be delighted to see me, though I suspect he could be having me on, for I suspect Sir Henry of being just a little bit condescending towards me. I hope that his patronizing tone is just my imagination.

He hungrily eyes the goggles residing upon my hat.

"Please tell me how you intend to use my lovely

inventions," I beg of the notorious reporter. "I have grown attached to these goggles like no other I have created."

A leering grin spreads across his red, flushed face.

"They are for my next African excursion. The jungles of the wild lands are not for the faint of heart. It takes an iron fist to conduct a safari and a rigid constitution. It's best to let the Darkies know that a White man has taken charge!" laughs the English Knight.

(!)

(I sense a warning exclamation point go off in the back of my cranial bucket.)

"You have to let the natives know who is the master. With my marksman skills, I dominate everywhere I travel. Elephant, tiger, and lion. I destroy all before me. The Darkies have certainly learned to fear my approach. Like some great white God, if I can find you in the sights of my rifle, then you belong to me." A bit of drool appears at the corner of his mouth. "With these goggles, that allow sight in dark conditions, I shall rule the night, as well!"

(! ... I can almost hear a tiny 'plinck.')

With revolt in my stomach, I realize that this horrid man intends to use my wondrous invention for indecent purposes! Subjugation of the African populace is not what I had intended for my device. This man callously murders defenseless folks without a second thought. I decide that a switch in conversation is necessary as I sense myself getting upset. I attempt to change the subject with a slight swerve in conversation.

"I read your interview with Miss Plumtartt. The poor girl. I have heard nice things about her and how clever she is at the running of the Plumtartt assets. I don't think she would have closed the factories unless she was sure there was a serious problem. Do you think she is getting a fair shake from your article?"

Sir Henry sprays our table with spittle as he explodes into guffaws of mean-spirited laughter.

"That hysterical little high bred wench? Ho, ho, if only you could have seen how easily I manipulated that buxom bird. I can trick a little twist like that into doing my bidding any time I want. This is a man's world, boy. Even a silly little American like you should be able to see the folly of halting production at a vital industrial resource such as the Plumtartt facilities. That high breasted pigeon lets her inferior feminine intellect interfere with what's good for her."

He grows more repugnant. I can see him envisioning Miss Plumtartt in his mind. He gives me the impression of enjoying an inappropriate imagination.

"That uppity little chick is off her rocker."

(! ... I was brought up to be courteous to a lady.)

"A rooster in the henhouse is what she's wanting."

(! plinck !... I might be getting upset.)

"What a mewling little quim like that needs is a bit of the Ol'..."

That is as far as Sir Henry gets before I plow my fist several painful inches into his face.

The deed is done before I even cognitize what I have perpetrated.

"That is no way to talk about a Lady," I shout across the scandalized restaurant to Sir Henry, as I am forcibly escorted from the premises. "I choose to default on the commission, Sir!"

Chapter 8 - Disturbance At The Queen's Hotel.

Persephone

A bellboy of the Queen's Hotel brings me todays newspapers from across the lobby.

With this fresh information, and what I have already learned about the ghost attacks, I attempt to find a pattern to the perils troubling our nation.

"Unh!" I am seized by a horrible sense of revulsion, just like last night.

It is the same loathsome sensation as in the laboratory and in the attack on Plumtartt Manor.

How can this be? This is the heart of a major metropolis! Surely the horrors that pursued me in the quiet countryside of Elderberry Pond are completely out of place in this modern city! I have never known an evocation to summon something on this order. It cannot be the result of Father's conjuration, or can it?

There is a disturbance outside the front doors. I hear a commotion and sounds of struggle. Now, there is shouting. The staff of the Queen's Hotel hurry to ascertain the trouble. A bellboy ducks back in: "Old Tom's having a fit!"

Indeed, the distinguished old doorman, who was so charming on my way in a few minutes ago, is in some sort of turmoil. I cannot see well from my vantage point, yet I can see that the struggle grows in intensity. The old fellow is fighting his fellow employees, now.

"My word!" I exclaim at the next sight I behold.

In an unnatural display of strength, the old doorman grasps, and raises one of the bellboys above his head, and bodily throws the poor lad through the ornate front doors!

The dangerous doorman enters directly behind his improvised missile. But this is not the same man who greeted me so charmingly in the minutes prior.

Something is in possession of the wretched fellow's body.

He looks upon me with sightless eyes.

The enraged entryman screams, and lurches towards me, like a clockwork automaton whose brain gears have lost their ratio.

With a certain knowledge that the possessed doorman intends to kill me, I bolt from the lobby. The terrible, wrath-filled intelligence controlling Old Tom's body is in a determined pursuit. I run straight through the palatial dining room and into the kitchen. Behind me, I hear the the uproar caused by the gentlemanly greeter's reckless chase trailing at my heels. There is a relentless uproar of anger, amidst the screams and bellows of outrage surrounding my pursuer. His hands are as claws, slashing into wreckage table, chair, and dinnerware. Though I am just able to elude his grasping fingers, I push through the confines of the kitchen and out the back door into an alley. Heedless of any direction, I blindly run, bursting out into a busy thoroughfare.

Miraculously, I am not run down by horse or carriage in my headlong flight.

I risk a look back.

The stricken doorman has stopped. A heartrending howl is torn from the poor man, the first human sound he has made since being ridden by the foul spirit.

He shakes.

He rises...??? ...

A green miasma issues from his mouth.

His depleted body falls.

The thick smoke coalesces into a form I can hardly fathom.

An unthinkable creature that has no place in our world, forms.

It drops to the street, and it comes for me.

Chapter 9 - A Stroll In The Park.

Ichabod

Punching a newspaper reporter in the nose is probably not the wisest thing I have ever done.

I sometimes act before I think.

A stroll through this lovely English park, and a tug on my old clay pipe, is just what I need to settle back down.

Standing on the curb of 'BirdCage Walk', opposite to the entrance of the neatly laid out urban refuge, the sign informs me that this manicured meadow is Saint James Park.

"What's this?"

A terrible cry disturbs the frenzy of traffic, filling the busy street.

The source is an old gentleman in the fancy coat of a hotel doorman is in the middle of the road. Horses rear up in fright from the tortured howl. It is the worst sound I have ever heard from a human.

He holds the unearthly scream long after he should have run out of breath.

He violently spasms, with severe convulsions.

And slowly levitates! ? ! ?

An icy hand grips my heart to see this man suspended in the air. I almost lose consciousness at the unreality of the sight.

A thick, green, and oily smoke pours from his body, leaving a desiccated corpse to fall to the ground.

Green mist churns in the roiling tumult of a small emerald thunderstorm, localized just above the fellows remains. For a fraction of a second, it seems to coalesce into a horrible nightmare. A creature from beyond imagination is briefly glimpsed in reflective silhouette, and then suddenly it is gone.

Or is it? In a trick of the light, or my eyes, I seem to be able to catch partial, and fragmentary glimpses of shadowy movement towards the park.

The horses certainly see it! They are all going out of their minds!

The sight of the apparition has turned my legs to jelly.

Then a woman's scream cuts the night.

My legs have re-solidified and are already running in the direction from which came the scream before I realize what I am doing.

CHAPTER 10 - NO ESCAPE.

Persephone

"No!" I cry.

A chilopodal worm of enormous size, and moving with alarming speed, makes straight for me.

I dash headlong into a city park that lies before me and across a long bridge in the middle of the erstwhile sanctuary.

A high speed, mechanical tapping makes me turn and look back.

The monsters countless legs, work in an unearthly coordination, tapping a blood-curdling rhythm, as insectlike appendages propel the centipedal horror. The grotesquely grown grub seems to glide across the masoned bridge.

I cannot outrun it! Within seconds, the massive and wrongful form is upon me.

The Creature strikes!

CHAPTER 11 - THE GHOST.

Ichabod

Swift on my feet, in spite of my heavy 'Mud Pounders,' I am off like a shot.

Many of these English dandies kit themselves out with some interesting hardware. Derringers slide from out of their sleeves on spring-loaded delivery platforms. Sly devices appear from their shiny vests. A fancy walking stick may double as a rifle, sword, or flask. I can't help but think that those elaborate top hats may hide some nefarious device.

I augment my defenses with a '72 Colt .45 revolver.

The farther I run into this park, the further I get from the gaslights that line so many London streets. It is hard to see and I don't know which direction to search. I fear that I have lost the path of the poor woman and her horrible pursuer.

Wait, my "Beauties!"

Spinning up the generator behind the left ear, I pull on the unusual goggles.

Saint James blooms into an eerie, phosphorescent green meadow. Under the "Green Beauties'" view, it is impossible not to see the hideous monster. What was invisible to me before, now glows with a sickly luminescence. I am very nearly unable to comprehend what I see. Perhaps the size of an overgrown pig, but with hundreds of insect legs, a creature that does not belong in our world is running through this London park.

Flying along at an alarming pace, the monster kicks up a clickety-clackity ruckus from the paving like that of an automated typesetting machine. The appearance of the creature and rapidity of its hundreds of legs mesh oddly with the sounds echoing from the passage of the grotesque horror over the long bridge spanning this urban artificial lake.

I pour all my efforts into catching and dispatching this outrageous worm, for even though I dearly love most all of our Earth's creatures, this disgusting bug definitely does not rate consideration.

No! I am too late! It has overtaken a woman and I won't be there in time!

There is a blinding flash of red light! A sphere of intense crimson energy has burst from the girl. This burns brightly for a moment, expanding out in all directions to swiftly collapse back into a scarlet bubble that surrounds the young woman.

With this thin shield she seems to hold the beast at bay.

Whatever the power is that emanates from the victimized girl, her strength wanes as the creature becomes more enraged.

I have drawn my revolver by this time. I am a fair shot, and I put a round through the creature's head. (By head, I mean the end with the mouth: the circular, row upon row, daggertooth lined mouth, that seems equally bitey/suckey. This opening can be found beneath the two large hemispheric protuberances that are so overcrowded by innumerable visual receptors.)

My pistol shot has no effect! The monster does not even take notice. The fanged aperture continues to push its way through the protective energy bubble in a persistent effort to bite and devour the girl.

I put five more rounds square into the creature's head

with no result.

This is no time to be disheartened, for the lady can barely keep the creature from latching hold.

Drawing my Bowie knife, I pounce on the monster's back, going into a frenzy, stabbing the foul, armoured, larva.

Again, my weapon has no effect. The knife passes through the chitinous plate like air.

The paramount parasite is bent on devouring this poor girl, and there is nothing I can do to stop it!

The disgusting, mouth/nozzle of the oversized demon prawn begins to apply a terrible suction towards the poor girl. I stab again and again without effect. In fact, I realize it is my hand, not the hilt of my Bowie, making contact with the foul beast. I drop the blade - it falls through the monster to the ground - and begin to pummel the brute. I jump off and kick that son of a gun as hard as I can.

That gets its attention!

So I lay in some more with all the pepper on the shelf. This is enough to break off its attack against the young lady.

My new pal turns its attention on me.

My blood runs cold and my heart is filled with a nameless dread as thousands of fractal eyes focus upon me. I can feel an inhuman intelligence push itself into my mind and I almost lose heart.

Then it springs. Either I am lucky, or just blessed with good self-preservation instincts, but I am able to roll out of the way of the leech's launch. The creature twists after me as quickly as I can scramble away. Scrabbling to stay ahead, I get to my feet and run. It is on my heels. Zig-zag, jump, dodge, bounding over deck chairs, the filthy larva is just at the back of my legs. Vaulting into a gazebo at full tilt the monster is my shadow. I aim low diving under the rail and the 500 pound leech passes over my head. I barely get to my feet when the monster has already turned on me. I leapfrog the beast in a grotesque version of the way children play. I grab hold of something growing from the beast's back as is passes between my legs mid-leap. Could it be hair, or a prehensile horn? I don't know what I have a hold of, but despite the flip following the leap, I hang on tight.

It is a dang sight safer riding on this monster's back than having it at my heels.

This monster is mad and full of fight. It twists and turns and chases its tail like a dog. It can't get to me on its back. It tries to roll me off, but I ain't having it. I stick to that Hellish armadillo like a Tennessee tick.

Then it makes a break. Have you ever seen a centipede run? Those are some busy legs!

Well, we take a tour around the park and then hit upon a lane towards the entrance of St. James. We are causing quite a stir at this point. Some boys take up a pursuit. They can almost keep up. They think I am flying somehow! I remember that they cannot see the creature, just me floating over the ground by about five feet and traveling faster than they can run.

My invisible stallion carries me out St. James Park and into a crowded with sophisticated, evening, traffic, Birdcage Walk, carrying fashionable folks to dinner and theater. Every horse on the ridiculously named thoroughfare begins to scream and panic. No driver can control his terrified equine for even if they cannot see it, every horse knows there is an abomination on that street. Nothing will keep them there. My own horrid mount turns Eastward. All the carriages, carts, four-wheelers and hansoms are backed up at Great George Street. My worm and I smash full tilt into a gorgeous hansom, exploding the two wheeled carriage into splinters. I fall from my steed and my goggles are knocked loose. I can no longer see the monster! I scramble for my "Beauties," getting them back on in time to see the creature rise up on its hind(?) legs and leap upon me. I barely get my hands to its ugly face to keep that disgusting sucker/mouth from clamping on my head. The legs seem to ripple, as each leg begins to move just after the previous one did, like fingers on a piano. In this manner, with machine-like efficiency, knitting appendages propel me towards the intake chute.

I cannot allow it to bite me!

I kick and fight for all I am worth but cannot release my grip lest I feel those awful teeth. I isolate one of the creature's forelegs with my feet. I get it locked out against its own joint, and then kick. One insect leg does not work with mechanical efficiency anymore, since it is at a right angle to the others. The mammoth roly poly shrieks in an unspeakable alien rage. Risking the release of one hand from the creature's face, I tear the stricken limb from this hungry HellSpawn. With all the strength of a man who would not be a meal, I plunge the serrated, chitinous limb as far into the alien cranium as my arm will reach.

Succumbing to a violent series of tremors, the beast shudders with a few last death throes, before expiring with insectile ignominy.

Chapter 12 - Aftermath at the Queen's Hotel.

Persephone

Blind with tears and half out of my wits, I stumble away from the ravenous horror. I have to get away from the repulsive segmented worm. I fear for the gallant cavalier that came to my rescue, but I am too done in to help the man. I feel a craven sense of cowardice for the relief I feel when that horrible consciousness is turned from myself to that unwitting victim.

Though blinded by fear and emotion, I manage to stagger out the North end of St. James.

My heart breaks again as I hear scores of horses go mad with terror on the far side of the Park. Kind hands catch me as I slump to the ground.

Helpful young gentlemen assist me in gaining conveyance back to the Queen's Hotel. The streets are congested with onlookers trying to discover the source of the troubles wrought by the brain-fevered horses. General confusion and disarray make for a slow and tedious ride through a crowded throng. Many carriages are damaged, and the horses still nervous, but the disturbances seem to have subsided. I catch snatches of conversation moving through the crowded street. No one knows why, but every horse on BirdCage Walk, for a few moments, went mad with terror.

I overhear snatches of rumour that some claim to have seen, momentarily, a monster of some kind. Two young boys claim to have seen a flying man, wearing goggles that “glowed like two, small, green lanterns.”

When I arrive back at my hotel, I find it a sombre shambles. The front doors are smashed, the lobby is in disarray, and the dining room, along with the kitchens, are nearly destroyed. Yet it is grief over the death of their beloved, gentlemanly old doorman that has overcome the hotel staff. I am simultaneously relieved and ashamed, that no one realizes I am to blame.

Chapter 13 - A Smoke, a Bit of Contemplation, and a Decision...

Ichabod

I fall back in exhaustion, disentangling myself from the hated legs of the creature. The unnatural glow of the worm subsides, and simultaneously, the shocked faces of those around me show recognition of the dead leech. Interesting that, although it was invisible in life, apparently, all can observe it in death.

I remove my goggles, momentarily blind as my eyes adjust to the change in light condition, but there lies the horror. The monstrous beast is now visible, but gets noticed by only a few people as Birdcage Walk is a shambles. Every hat, purse, fan, and corsage that was present now blankets the street. The wreckage of smashed carriages and misused citizenry litters the scene The horses are still trying to climb over one another to vacate the premises.

A steam begins to rise from the worm. Cracks appear in its shell, and then widen. The foul crawfish is dissolving before my eyes. A thought strikes me. Once again, I find myself following my instincts before I have a chance to think about my actions. Spotting a miraculously unbroken bottle of champagne, I pop the cork and pour out the contents. Using the shattered remains of another bottle, I scoop the quickly evaporating goo that was my former adversary into the emptied bottle, and then seal it with the cork.

Then I remember the girl, the catalyst of the past few minutes' events. I fly back to the park, but she is nowhere to be found.

I gather my lost items. My trusty tinder box ignites my old clay pipe to resume my smoke. The girl, or should I say, young lady, was quite striking. And familiar, somehow... perhaps in a photograph... Miss Persephone Plumtartt! Of course! Her newspaper image does not do her justice! For though I barely got a glimpse of her, this is an amazing woman to behold.

As I ponder my encounter with the beast that was attacking Miss Plumtartt, I am overcome with deep feelings of chagrin and shame. I was amused at the "Ghost" stories I had read. Now their reality is all too well proven to me. A double dose of shame for doubting the remarkable Plumtartt family.

I have a tendency to quick reaction. There have been many instances in my life where I have reacted to a situation with blinding speed. You, my dear reader, have already witnessed a couple of those episodes.

Some might refer to this as going off half cocked, or shooting from the hip; maybe acting without thinking.

I tend to think it is a willingness to trust in my instincts.

More than just good versus bad, or smart as opposed to stupid, I tend to find my guts lead me towards right and wrong.

I sure did spoil the deal with Sir Henry Stanley tonight, though.

Oh well, I really did not wanna give up my 'Green Beauties' anyhow.

Miss Persephone Plumtartt. Wow. I barely got a look at her, but I could see straight away that she is as amazing in her beauty as she is in her character.

It sure was a good thing that I happened to be there in the park, tonight. Miss Plumtartt would've been a goner for sure.

I have a hunch that I am about to make a fateful decision.

I feel a stubborn tenacity overcome me. A sensation washes through me, as if I am a fragile teacup, balanced on the razor's edge of a high mountain ridge, filled to the rim with a beverage of possibilities.

Was it fate that had me bop Sir Henry on the horn?

('Slosh,' sloshes the tart tea of fate.)

Could the hand of destiny be at work?

('Slosh,' sloshes the swirling sweetener of destiny.)

If that jumbo sized satanic shrimp was one of the ghosts that's a running 'round here, then maybe this girl ain't outta the chipper yet.

(Slosh!)

I think that last slosh sent my teacup over the edge.

I jump up and shout out loud:

"I shall find and help this damsel in distress!"

Let's see: the initial disturbance seemed to arise from the South East end of St. James Park. I search that area for a trail to follow. It does not take long to find the front doors of Queen's Hotel being repaired. I make my way in and find the lobby being made whole after some sort of disturbance.

Inquiring at the desk, I confirm that a Miss Persephone Plumtartt is indeed, in residence.

(! *plinck* !)

Feeling it inappropriate to approach the sophisticated lady at this late hour, and in such a disheveled state myself from my previous exertions, I depart.

I spend a restless evening in my more frugal digs, at the 'Spotted Richard Respite,' and return to Queen's Hotel again first thing in the morning.

I scribe a note and the clerk has a bellboy deliver it. Shortly afterwards, I am stunned at my reward.

Chapter 14 - On What I Learned While Perusing the Daily Papers.

Persephone

I awaken somewhat recovered from the prior evening's traumatic events. Not wanting to see the damage done to the lovely Hotel, or face the saddened staff, I take my breakfast and papers in my rooms.

There is an account of the strange occurrences in:

The Morning Calamity

HARRIED HORSES HEAP HEAVY HAVOC ON HAPLESS HEADS

"For unknown reasons, scores of horses on Birdcage Walk went completely berserk, wrecking dozens of carriages. Many of our finer citizens were quite put out of sort. Most witnesses were at a loss as to a cause for the frightened animals. There were a few who suspected that they had seen the mysterious "Ghost" that is leaving gruesome corpses across the countryside. These witnesses and others describe the "Ghost" as a just barely visible, flickering shadow. There were even a couple of young boys who insisted that they were witness to a flying man and a horrible monster."

The Gadfly Gazette

QUEEN'S HOTEL IS SCENE OF ELDERLY TERROR

"Beloved doorman of the Queen's Hotel

> suffered a severe fit while on duty at the exquisite lodgings. During his departure from this World, the kind, gentle, dear old fellow managed to throw several colleagues about the premises in his compulsively violent death throes. 'Ol' Tom' then proceeded to wreak havoc on the lobby, and to cause thousands of pounds in damage to the crystal enhanced dining room before expiring."
>
> 'He will be missed.'

Ominously, there are accounts from around the country of horribly dessicated corpses and terrified citizens.

Amazingly, there is one story that brings me a smile. It almost makes me laugh.

> **NATIONAL HERO THE VICTIM OF COWARDLY ASSAULT**
>
> "In an outrageous display, a crazed brute has assaulted famous explorer and reporter, Sir Henry Stanley. The noble countenance of this worthy gentleman may be forever altered. The scoundrel responsible is thought to be from the United States. Citizens are urged to keep watch for this 'Mad American'."

There is a knock at the door. A bellboy has a note:

Dear Miss Plumtartt,

I hope I was not presumptuous, interfering with your activities at St. James Park.

May we meet?

Respectfully yours,

Ichabod Temperance.

Good Heavens! Is this the marksman that came to my aid? Could that foolhardy soul have actually survived?

I cannot recall an image of the brave man, for I was in such a shocked and beaten state that I had not the capacity to observe my hero. He must be a great and fearsome beast of a man. Only a man with a stout heart and valiant soul would or could have faced the challenge of that unnatural fiend. I am suddenly thrilled at the prospect of meeting this no doubt, robust, and dynamic example of English Manhood.

Upon entering the hotel lobby, I am directed to a gentleman on the far side of the room. At first, I must admit that I suspect there has been a mistake. I am a bit let down in the fellow, for he stands staring at me from across the room with his mouth agape. He is not the muscular champion that I was expecting. He is just a thin little chap; his jaw and face have an unfortunate slackness to them and his general expression is all agog. He suddenly seems to shake himself awake and I realize that he was merely under some sort of enchantment by my own femininity. His place in the world, I think, has not been such that he would have encountered many young ladies.

"Mr. Temperance?"

"Uhb."

"I say, sir? Mr. Temperance, are you quite all right, sir?"

"Uhb, ... uhb, oh, Ma'am! Yes, Ma'am, I beg your pardon. Gee, I sure am glad you're okay, Ma'am."

He seems an innocent young man, and he is very shy and bashful in my presence. My first impression of the young man now changes. Though he is thin, I detect a wiry strength in the young tradesman. Topped with sandy brown hair and hazel eyes, as soon as he speaks, he betrays his American origins. He is desperately, if not wholly successfully, attempting to conduct himself with exaggerated courtesies. His clumsy etiquette is poorly formed, but sincere in its intentions. His accent is of a soft melodious tone that I infer he developed in the Southern regions of our former colonies. Mr. Temperance is familiar with my sad story through the libelous newspaper account from recent editions, but I must know his!

"How were you able to see what others could not? Until that time, it was my impression that these horrors were invisible to all but me. Your pistol shots were spot on the creature's head."

"Oh! It was because of my 'Green Beauties!' These are a specialized set of goggles of my own design."

The young man is suddenly very excited and animated. He forgets his quaint exaggerated manners as he eagerly describes the inventions of which he is so proud.

"I was havin' a stroll when I heard you call out. I responded without really thinkin'. I used my 'Beauties' to find you. When I cranked 'em up, that big ol' worm shone out like an emerald lantern. Last year I built a pair of goggles for your father, the 'Elemental Protectors.'"

"How marvelous! The goggles you built for my father were quite extraordinary. How fortuitous for you to be at hand and that the ability to see these other worldly terrors was then realized in these, your latest fantastic invention, Mr. Temperance."

"Quite by accident, actually, Ma'am." He looks down, in his self-conscious, modest, manner.

How he flushes with a crimson blush! How sweet! I hope that I am not blushing as well, for now that he is becoming more relaxed, so too does he reveal himself as a most attractive young gentleman.

However, now is no time for indulgence in matters of the heart. Our lives - and perhaps the lives of countless others - are at risk.

I fill in the chilling details of my story, beginning with fathers laboratory and the tragedies suffered there, the factory shutdowns, and the attacks upon my own person. We are in agreement that the danger is growing. Indeed, it is probably growing exponentially by the day. Mr. Temperance is determined to assist me, but I am loath to put this impetuous young man in danger.

It is painfully evident to us both that the problem is bigger than just ourselves: England Herself is in peril.

I reluctantly accept his help.

The first order of business I think is to visit one of father's closest confidantes. I require knowledgeable guidance.

"Yes, Ma'am, seeking wise council and advice is always a good idea, but if you don't mind, I've got a little errand I'd like to run first."

CHAPTER 15 - CHEMYSTS.

Ichabod

An idea has occurred to me. Remembering how my pistol and knife failed me, I do not want to find myself in such a predicament again, for I have a feeling I am not done with the inter-dimensional varmints.

The city of London is as heavily populated with those affected by the Revelatory Comet's passing as any other, if not more so. Miss Plumtartt and I visit a neighbourhood of Apothycists, Chemysts, and Doctors of Alchemycal bent. I possess a fantastic navigational sensibility, and though new to the city my innate abilities help us find the help we seek. Perhaps I have just the tiniest fragment of magnetized iron in my nose. It seems to give me an uncanny sense of direction. I find a union hall of sorts, sulphorous vapors in the air. A tangle of chimneys betrays the location of many individual furnaces. This appears to be a rather dirty place of production and I do not want Miss Plumtartt to soil her fine clothes and be subject to the strong scents of industrial enterprise.

"Miss Plumtartt," I ask of the aristocratic young lady, "I would feel better if you did not leave the carriage. I'm gonna see if these fellas can be of any help to us. I shouldn't be too long."

"I am not the delicate flower you seem to think I am, Mr Temperance," she answers with a casual acceptance, "but if it will make you feel better, I acquiesce to your request."

Going down a flight of brick stairs, I enter to find a low-ceilinged room lined with tables, and laden with chemycal apparatti.

It is difficult to determine if the foul odors arise from the workbenches, or the workmen. None seem eager to be of assistance. Some are quite rude! I thinks my American accent has put these boys on an offensive footing. There is a little bristling of proprietorial trespass. We might be on the verge of a little dust-up here...until Miss Plumtartt walks in. Silence falls over the dirty crew of smelly chemysts.

The likes of Miss Plumtartt does not often enter this odorous establishment.

"Are you getting the assistance you require, Mr. Temperance?" she asks.

Suddenly the whole workshop is my friend and they fall over themselves to be of service. Miss Plumtartt explains to the best of her ability, the adventures of last night, and our reasons for being here. Namely, we aim to gather what intelligence we can from our bottled treasure, and to determine if a weapon can be fashioned to combat the creatures should they manifest themselves once again. Then all are awestruck by the unusual qualities of the contents of my champagne bottle. I relinquish only a few tiny drops for their experiments and examinations.

Several different teams of scientists work on their tiny samples with varied approaches to fathoming its secrets. Cold and heat are applied. Oxygen is deprived.

One of the fellows, after experimenting with several electrical applications, happens upon a process that hardens and crystallizes his precious drop. His fellow chemysts roundly ridicule him, and condemn the poor fellow for ruining his sample.

It gives me an idea, though...

Chapter 16 – Homecoming.

Persephone

There is some disagreement amongst the scientists. It would seem that one chemist has ruined the small, precious sample that Mr. Temperance shared with him. His fellow chemists voice their dismay.

Mr. Temperance is actually quite intrigued with what the old fellow has hit upon. In fact, he appears to be thoroughly pleased at the old gentleman's accidental discovery.

My American friend quickly fashions himself a simple, but effective, device, using the elderly chemist's formula.

I must say, there is a definite element of ingenuity to the prize with which we leave this guild of Apothytical Arts. Although the chemysts did not hold great affection for him at first sight, Mr. Temperance is now leaving with many friends and well wishers. I am heartened by this small spot of good fortune.

I require advice and guidance and so turn to one of my most influential tutors. I bid Mr. Temperance deliver us to Charing Cross from whence we secure railed transport to my college at Cambridge, but not before sending a wired telegraph ahead.

I am conflicted. Still stinging from my embarrassing experience with Stanley, I am apprehensive about putting my trust into young Mr. Temperance. Yet something about my impetuous companion pulls at my heart. Where Stanley was all disingenuous charm, Mr. Temperance is...simply himself.

Arriving at Cambridge's train depot, my tutor and

mentor, Sir Arthur Helmsley, greets us with relief. However, one look into each other's eyes conveys the dread weight of our meeting. I am dismayed to find the professor in a terribly agitated state. Something beyond our knowledge, or even comprehension, seems to be developing. An evil dew covers our fair land. The scholarly knight knows of a rare relic, or document of sorts, that was in possession of my father, a dark and foul thing that I shudder to think resides at our honored family estate. Sir Arthur will not utter the name of the hated relic, telling us only that it is some sort of scroll. He then tasks Mr. Temperance and me with retrieving the unclean document, feared to still be at the family dwelling. We are to take it to a respected author and translator, my lifelong friend Stanislas de Guaita, in Paris, for advice. It is hoped that there will be vital information within the evil text that will give us a way to stop the spread of these atrocities.

A foreboding sense of urgency sends us quickly on our way.

Disembarking our train at Elderberry Pond Station, we hire a horse and cart to carry us to Plumtartt Manor. Dusk falls and darkness gathers as we pass through the iron gates of my grief stricken home. It is an ill wind that heralds our arrival. The rising atmospheric signs of a coming storm, adds to the already forlorn aspect of the Estate. The long, tree lined drive is lifeless and desolate. It is difficult to believe this was a happy place, not so long ago. The many chimneys of the great estate are cold and unused. Plumtartt Manor has always been so bright and cheery, a festive place. Now, the empty windows seem to peer at me like sad and accusing eyes.

Mr. Temperance and I enter the melancholy manor through the unlocked front door. I hurriedly light a candle and move swiftly toward the North Wing of the house, to a hidden cache where our family has traditionally protected our most valued secrets. Two hundred plus years old, this wing is the oldest surviving part of the Manor. Seized by a sense of urgency, I rush to the family chapel. Pulling the heavy door open, I hurry into the place of refuge. I know this to be a secret place of hiding for the family going back for generations of Plumtartts. I carefully remove several relics from the altar. A painting depicting the Sermon on the Mount is removed. A small cabinet is revealed to be built into the wall. Opening this hidden compartment, I see its solitary possession, a small, iron chest. I know with certainty that this is the terrible artifact of which Sir Arthur had spoken. Reaching for the metal box, I hesitate. I know not why, but I cannot bring myself to touch the dreadful thing. I bid Mr. Temperance to take the iron chest containing the disconcerting artifact.

At that moment, a certain knowledge of evil's presence clutches my heart.

This is confirmed by the cry of terror from our poor cart horse.

CHAPTER 17 - TRAPPED.

Ichabod

I am somewhat comforted by having a means of combat, even if its effectiveness is still unproven. Miss Plumtartt seems certain that we are to confront more of these abominations. It would sorely comfort me to have a functional firearm.

"I do beg your pardon, Mr. Temperance," the lovely girl asks me, "but I have a sudden, unexplainable revulsion to touching this object. May I prevail upon you to carry it for me?"

"Yes, Ma'am," I reply. Miss Plumtartt is so pretty and such a fine girl. If she asked me to carry an armful of angry pit vipers, I would not hesitate.

As I step forward to get the strong little chest, Miss Plumtartt snaps her head toward the door. A wave of despair passes over her sculpted countenance.

At the same time I hear our horse scream out in mad terror.

I reach into the hidey hole and retrieve a small, iron-bound chest. Tucking the mysterious box inside my vest, I grab Miss Plumtartt by the hand and deliberately pull her from the chapel. Miss Plumtartt led the way in, but with my sense of direction and urgency, I have decided to lead the way out. We fly to an outside door. I hurriedly unlock it and pull.

The door opens an inch.

I put my boot to the wall and pull with strength. The door slowly opens another couple of inches, but stops. Some horrible glue-like substance holds the portal fast. A thick, sticky, organic rope-like substance criss crosses the doorway in many places from the outside and refuses to let the door be swung inward. We can hear rapid movement outside and upon the house. It seems to shuttle about the mansion with inconceivable speed. Dashing to the front entry hall, the way we came in just a few minutes prior, we find the exit in the same condition as the other door. The thick sticky ropes hold the great double doors shut against us. I ram my shoulder into the barrier in an attempt to force it open, but it stubbornly refuses me. It is amazing, and impossible to conceive, but something has bottled us up in the house. We have been wrapped up like a Russian papoose in only a few short minutes. Taking up a heavy bust (that of King George III, I think) and with a running start, I heave the weighty object through a window. Impossibly, it sticks, halfway through. The marbled Imperial Monarch seems to sputter, 'what? what? what?' as he realizes himself in such an undignified and strange position. The windows are sealed against us.

We hear the sounds of something heavy enter an upstairs hallway. Something big has come through the open aperture of the stained glass window Miss Plumtartt told me about. I put on my "Green Beauties." The rapid and terribly stout tapping of impossibly fast footfalls quickly reveals our antagonist.

I blanch and nearly falter at the sight. Bigger than a grand piano, is our uninvited guest. This creature is very different than the crustacean from evening last. Putting a few of his too many legs on the upstairs rail, the grotesque aberration looks down upon us. Several clusters of eyes, much like bunches of grapes, seem to spin with happy and dizzy thoughts of yummy consumption. Many pairs of slathering mandibles work and click in fevered expectation. What appears to be an enormous, slavering Black Widow spider props itself up on the rail of the landing. It looks down upon us with delight, for all the world like some horrific family pet. Despite the creature's bloated size, it leaps to the ceiling of the grand entrance hall, scurries across the wide expanse, and drops its bloated weight upon us.

CHAPTER 18 - STEP INTO MY PARLOUR.

Persephone

A horrifyingly huge arachnid-like creature hits the marble floor where Mr. Temperance and I stood a fraction of a second prior. Unlike the amoebic, and then centipedal predecessors, this is some type of enormous spider, but of unearthly size and foul origin. The poison-dripping fiend clearly means to devour us. I cannot be sure which one moves the faster, this wrongful monster or my own Mr. Temperance, for I fail to be able to keep up with the blurred actions of either.

We fly back into the depths of the mansion. My would-be protector takes up a heavy halpern. Swinging the pole-armed axe in a wide arc, Mr. Temperance means to cleave the bulbous bug in twain. The blade enters and passes completely through the monster without effect, contact, nor loss of momentum. The wooden pole, however, makes solid contact and vibrates out of the user's hands. Mr. Temperance then attempts to slow the horror by throwing obstacles in its path. Several heavy suits of armor would seem to get in the insect's way, but the frightful apparition runs directly through the steel protectors as if they were not there. It does not knock them aside; rather, the beast runs through the objects without interacting contact, as light passes through sheer fabric material. It is as though, to the creature, the iron or steel does not exist. It is apparent that metals are as nothing when attempting to strike or otherwise harm these "inter-dimensional" terrors. It is as though, to the creature, the iron or steel does not exist.

Reaching the chapel we narrowly are able to shut ourselves in. The giant insect tears into the heavy wooden door with a ferocity the portal was not built to withstand.

The oaken door quickly disintegrates.

Pulling a large chair into a place beside the door, Mr. Temperance draws his weapon and positions himself by the failing frame. The obscene creature pulls itself into the room, only to have a crazed American drop upon its loathsome body with fell intent. Mr. Temperance is in a killing frenzy! He needs his berserker rage in order to dispatch the creature, which would seem to have an equal amount of ferocity. I scurry to stay clear of the frenetic fight, which bounces and scrambles around the room. The desperate spider cannot get this tenacious foe from its back.

Eventually, the alien arachnid slows its struggle. It tries to climb back out of the chapel but this has proven to be its death room. Mr. Temperance finally completes his dispatching duties as he finalizes his insecticidal victory.

The emerald device works! The blade that Mr. Temperance and his Alchemical allies have forged functions with deadly efficiency.

My hero has slain the Dragon!

Chapter 19 - A Trip in the Country.

Ichabod

P.E.R.K.

Petrified Ectoplasm Resin Knife.

I am out of breath, and a bit done in at the conclusion of my pest control efforts, but I happily manage, "the P.E.R.K. worked, Miss Plumtartt!"

"Why yes, Mr. Temperance," my beautiful and aristocratic companion exuberantly agrees. "Rah-thah! I should say so. Well done! Good show."

In my experience, it is a rare problem that is solved on the first iteration. With most ideas a fellow has to try and fail, then make an adjustment, then try again, and maybe fail again before stumbling on the perfect solution. Most field tests are failures. Fortunately for Miss Plumtartt and myself, this one was a success. The hardening process that I worked out with the stinky old chemysts has proven itself. So has my hope that these monsters' own juices may be turned back against them. The hastily prepared mold of my Bowie knife worked perfectly to pour the refined ectoplasm into. The curious old Chemyst added a hardening agent, along with an astoundingly powerful electric charge, to create a most formidable, inter-dimensional monster-killing blade.

I cannot help but feel proud of the cleverly constructed knife.

"Mr. Temperance! I cannot convey the sense of pride I feel at your having developed such an effective weapon.

Congratulations, sir!"

"Dang, I mean, shucks, Ma'am. I'm just glad it worked out for us." I feel myself blush, in spite of my already flushed state from the spider fight. I can feel my bashful side coming through whenever Miss Plumtartt flashes her electric blue eyes upon me.

"However, my clever combatant, we have no time to waste. Let us hurry back to the train station so that we can make passage to the continent."

'Yes, Ma'am."

We set out for our train station, a few miles down the road. The poor horse that pulled our cart out to the Manor is long gone and we are forced to walk.

About halfway to the station, we hear the now altogether too familiar, and disheartening cry of a panicked horse. This one sounds like it is behind us by less than a mile. We hasten our pace. Many dogs in the area take up the alarm. Another panicked horse whinnies somewhere off to our left, maybe a little closer this time. We continually increase our pace. Soon, we are running for the little village of Elderberry Pond. From disparate areas we hear a growing tumult of frightened animals.

We come to the outskirts of Elderberry Pond, home of our train station, but it is still on the other side of town and I hear the whistle blowing.

Miss Plumtartt is about done in. Just then, the dangdest bicycle I ever saw comes around the corner. Two people are riding on the vehicle: two wheels, two seats, one bicycle. I charge, hitting the driver amidships. The pedaled transportation device is upset by my broadside shoulder tackle. The pilot and his girl go flying. I snatch up his two-wheeled, two-seated marvel and prompt Miss Plumtartt to board this most serendipitous conveyance.

"Sorry folks! I'll leave her at the station!" Outrage flashes in Miss Plumtartt's azure eyes.

"The bicycle, not you, Miss Plumtartt," I hastily add.

"Eyes forward!" the harried girl commands, as she has to bunch her skirts, and ride, not sidesaddle, but actually pedaling like a man!

I know there are bloomers on display, but I keep my mind on business.

"Faster," she implores, for it seems that we are being overtaken, even at the heady speeds of this bicycled conveyance.

"Unh!"

Miss Plumtartt cries out! There is a red flash, to my right! And now another, to the left! It would seem that Miss Plumtartt is able to dispatch a couple of the horrors herself, utilizing some red-hued bolts of destruction! She had said that a laboratory accident had apparently bestowed this astounding power, and now I see it proven once again.

We take a tumble onto the train platform just as the train is pulling out. Up we scramble, dashing headlong for the train. I pull on my "Green Beauties." A one-hundred and fifty pound tentacled leech is catching up to us. I drop back a step to give this fellow a 'PERK' to the hilt in the midst of his octopusy grabbers.

My wondrous companion and I are narrowly able to catch our train.

CHAPTER 20 - ELDERBERRY POND STATION.

Persephone

Although we have managed to board our train, we are not out of danger. I feel the approach of several more horrors. Mr. Temperance commandeers the rear car of our train, strongly urging everyone out. It is not difficult to get people to flee a well-armed man, especially one with his deadly earnest countenance. That helps us, and I also believe that the frightened passengers of this train car may have a sense of the horrors that pursue us. I have never seen my fellow countrymen move faster.

After emptying the last train car, we follow our fellow passengers towards the next car forward. Turning, and with some effort, namely some very deliberate stomps and kicks, my ever-resourceful friend unlocks the coupling mechanism between this penultimate car and the one recently vacated. The terrific speed of the creatures is chilling. Only I and my goggled defender can see the aberrations catch up to and board the now empty last carriage. Mr. Temperance's efforts succeed in freeing us from the contamination that has managed to climb aboard. Several creatures make a headlong plunge after us, but we are just out of their grasp.

We are bound for Ipswich.

We arrive in Ipswich without further incident, but

there is an overwhelming atmosphere of foreboding in this English Channel port. The instant we step onto the platform, and then out into the street, we feel a sense of panic. Even the atmosphere of this lively city is astir. There is a tangible taste of fear and confusion in the mood of Ipswich. She feels to be edgy and nervous. Her citizens stand together in small bands murmuring of the 'Ghost' assaults and possible sightings.

Excited boys hawk their newspapers full of accounts of attacks from around the country.

'GHOST PLAGUE SWEEPS BRITAIN'

'GHASTLY CORPSES IN GREATER OCCURRENCE'

It is no longer considered a joke or source of amusement; rather, the public consider these phenomena some kind of supernatural plague.

Mr. Temperance hires a cab and strongly encourages the driver to hurry us to the docks.

Our plan was to go to France, but I feel as if we are fleeing for our lives. The dynamic of our mission has changed. It is not until this instant that my understanding has developed and I can see a larger picture. All of these supernatural events, the nation over, are solely designed to destroy... me. But why?

"Oh!" This pops from my mouth without prompting from my own conscience, for I suddenly have a dreadful sensation wash through me.

"They are here, Mr. Temperance!" I unequivocally inform my trusted new friend.

The horrible sensation of an unclean horror is

overwhelming. I suddenly feel as if this entire area is saturated with the presence of my enemies. The disturbing presence feels to be roiling up out of the Earth itself.

How can there be such a great concentration of evil throughout England? There are so many sources of the terror materializing so quickly.

The horse of the Hansom we are in rears up. Screaming in unbridled terror, it is in a mad panic, just as every other animal in the city is suddenly going berserk.

I see a phosphorescent cloud bloom above the heads of a cluster of pedestrians! And now it is followed by another green miasmic cloudbloom in the streets before and behind us.

The panicked horse of our two-wheeled conveyance bolts in a maddened panic. It does not take long for the poor creature to wreck the Hansom, wedging it against a building and post. Mr. Temperance takes me by the hand and pulls me out of the trapped cab and after him. He and I then make a desperate dash for the city's channel docks.

We are attacked by foul monsters that appear to hail from an alien dimension. Similar to the creature of St. James Park, these loathsome, scuttling bits of nastiness have a nightmarish, aquatic insect stylization. Faster than my mind is able to process, Mr. Temperance has an uncanny ability to dodge and flee the monsters, while pulling and pushing me along and ahead. When unable to dodge, he successfully defends us by bladed attack. The docks are a short two blocks away.

"We can make it!" I gush.

"Ah!" bursts from my lungs unbidden.

I am caught! A detestable tentacle has grasped my

ankle! Mr. Temperance cuts me free, but now he is caught by the creature...

Great Heavens, what a monster!

A most squidlike creature fills the street opposite. Such a nightmarish creature I could have never imagined.

Mr. Temperance is putting up a jolly good fight, until he looks at the monster. That seems to dampen his fighting spirit.

My word, the monster seems to be affecting Mr. Temperance in a psychic assault. Unthinkably, this misplaced massive aquatic seems to be bearing down on the young man with a crushing weight of intelligence. Barrel sized obsidian eyes bore into the little American lad.

"Break away, Mr. Temperance!" I call, but he does not hear me. He is caught in the horror's thrall.

"Mr. Temperance!" I plead. My heart jumps to see the earnest chap endangered.

He has quite given up his fight. The monster means to devour the dear man!

"Mr. Temperance!"

No! Not my dear Ichabod!

"Ichabod!" I call. "Ichabod!"

Please hear me, my sweet!

"Ichabod!" I scream as loudly as I can manage.

He stirs!

"Ichabod!" I scream again with a touch more hope in my strained voice.

He rouses himself. He is back! That's it.

Fight, Ichabod!

My Ichabod seems to awaken from a deep slumber, but quickly rallies his stuporous senses. He now fights as a man possessed. Mr. Temperance cuts first himself, and then me, free from the horrible squamous appendages. He catches me up into his arms and bears me to the docks; I am too weak with relief at our narrow escape to protest.

My companion's faculties have apparently made a sudden recovery for he is able to quickly ascertain which vessel has her steam up and is ready to launch. We unceremoniously board this Channel Launch.

"Here ya' go, boys." Mr. Temperance calls, tossing me into the arms of a group of seamen on the deck of the boat.

The captain of the vessel is not amused at our uninvited boarding of his ship.

Before he can have his crew throw us back off, he is distracted by a commotion on the docks. The docks themselves are being wrecked. Invisible forces smash crates, boats and the piers themselves into splinters.

Mr. Temperance passes the captain his goggles and then draws his large American pistol. With three quick but deafening retorts, he unerringly shoots the mooring cleats off the boat. I credit this action for our escape.

The captain's face goes slack with the vision he is presented with through the goggles and then he roars at his crew to push us from the cursed dock.

I thank providence that Mr. Temperance had the presence of mind to disengage our boat by means of firearm. Otherwise, we would have been too late, overrun by the pursuing mobbe of monsters.

Ipswich is aswarm with our aberrant adversaries.

I feel as if I am a leaf in a hurricane, no longer in control of my own life and destiny. I am blown about by terrifying forces beyond comprehension. A howling gale continues to rise about my ears. This foul wind sends me from my English island home. These storms that have steadily picked up all night seem to blow us off the isle, just a breath ahead of our adversaries, as if the great gaping maw of an enormous beast has just missed snatching us into its abominable gullet.

Chapter 21 - We Arrive in Paris.

Ichabod

I am uneasy carrying the dread scroll in its heavy iron chest, but I am bound to carry the unwieldy burden upon me at all times. During the Channel crossing, I secure a short piece of lead pipe. Using steel tongs, I remove the hated relic from its chest. With a second pair of tongs I tightly roll the dreadful artifact and shove it into the pipe. Two caps are cinched onto the ends, giving it for all the world, the appearance of some mad anarchist's improvised incendiary device.

The wind has followed us to the Continent. It howls around the rail car, and nearly snatches my prized Derby from my head when we disembark the Coast Express to the City of Light. I steady my lovely companion as she steps to the platform of Gare Montparnasse.

I feel an eerie sense of familiarity to disembarking the train in Ipswich, the night before. Paris, too, is caught in the supernatural panic. A sensation of tension, combined with a growing anxiety, exacerbated by the mounting storm creates a grim apprehension in the sensitive souls of many Parisians. I get a taste of copper in my mouth. Electricity seems to be in the air. Newsboys excitedly hawk their papers:

"MONSTRES CONFIRMÉS"

"LA MORTE VERTE"

"TERREURS EN ANGLETERRE"

We brook no delay making for our destination. The sense of urgency from which we enjoyed a brief respite during our English Channel crossing, has returned. An expert of things 'occult' is our best source of advice, we hope. The leading man on the subject appears to be a Stanislas de Guaita.

Traveling by hired coach to the Northern parts of Paris, Miss Plumtartt directs us to his clubbe on the Rive Droite. It looks to be a pretty swank place, so I am sure to knock all the mud off my boots before we walk up. We enter the posh establishment of the Da'ath Clubbe. From what I can gather, I presume it to be a hoighty-toighty herd of high society occultists. I can tell the entry staff are not happy about letting me into their fine digs, but Miss Plumtartt has an amazing charm that is difficult to resist.

"Miss Persephone Plumtartt! How charming to have you in the Clubbe tonight, Mademoiselle!" Miss Plumtartt is approached by a tall and dashingly good looking young coloured gentleman. He gives a courtly bow and a chivalrous kiss to Miss Plumtartt's hand.

Dang! I wish I knew how to be so sophisticated!

"Trevor Aeon, my dear, how wonderful to see you again my good friend! It has been too long! I am, however, on urgent business. Please tell me, is Monsieur Stanislas de Guaita in the residence tonight?"

"Oui, Mademoiselle, as a matter of fact, he is. I shall escort you to him and your friend may wait for you in the kitchen."

"Oh, but Trevor, dear. I should really like for Mr. Temperance to accompany me."

The handsome mahogany features attempt to refrain from assuming a sour expression.

"I really shouldn't, but I shall relent and allow him to

enjoy the atmosphere of our comfortable lobby."

Miss Plumtartt raises a questioning eyebrow.

"Persephone, darling. You know that if it were up to me, I would not hesitate. Any friend of yours, normally, would be openly welcomed. We do, however, have certain standards that must be enforced. I am sure your friend would not mind waiting."

"But Trevor, my dear, it *is* up to you. You are in charge."

"Oh, my. But Persephone, just look at the little specimen." The cultured gentleman sweeps a hand up and down to encompass and indicate me. "He is clearly not 'Da'ath Clubbe' material."

"He is not applying for membership, Trevor, and we shall only be here for a short while."

Trevor casts a dubious and despairing examinatory eye over me again.

"Oh, I am sorry, Persephone, but I just cannot allow it."

Miss Plumtartt touches the touchy manager on the sleeve and batts her lengthy lashes.

"Oh, Trevor, darling, please?" {batt, batt, batt}

"Very well," Trevor relents with a weary sigh. Those lashes are hard to resist. They could probably gain entrance to the Bank of England.

Mr. Aeon's dark features darken further as I am perused from head to foot once more.

"I'll be good, Mr. Trevor, sir."

"That's Aeon."

"Yessir, Mr. Aye-yawn, sir. Y'all ain't gotta worry 'bout me none, I promise. You all won't even know I'm in the house."

"Mmnnyyeesss, well. Please leave your armaments at the

desk, young man."

"Yessir." I leave my pistol belt and knives at the lobby desk.

Our reluctant host ushers us to a splendidly laid out and exquisitely appointed parlour. Mr. Trevor gives me one more disapproving once over before going to find the man we are here to see.

I locate a big comfy chair and pull out my clay pipe. I think back on our desperate flight last night through Ipswich. It was a near thing indeed, that we made it to the docks for there was a bushel of nasty kritters that wanted to do us in. I think I am proving to be fairly adept at this slash and thrust sort of thing with the new emerald blade. I was doing pretty well against the wormy insects, up until... hunh... Things faded out for a bit. I feel as if there is a span of time that I have lost from memory. Did I dream it, or did Miss Plumtartt actually call me by my Christian name? I have a vague impression that she did. Miss Plumtartt's distinctive and lyrical voice calling my first name. 'Ichabod.' In fact, Great Scott! I took that incredible woman in my arms! I held her and carried her! I had almost quite forgotten! The last thing I remember before this is running through the streets, making for the now smashed Ipswich docks. There is a muddy blur in an indistinct temporal hole. What could have transpired that I would gain such an intimacy with the beguiling girl, only to forget it immediately?

At this time a gentleman enters the parlour. He is of stout girth, fancy dress, and an arrogant attitude. I can tell straight away he is not the man we are to meet. Rather, he is quite a rude fellow with a German accent.

He dismisses me as being beneath his contempt, barely giving me a glance before he is all over Miss Plumtartt.

Like black on coal, like white on rice, like stink on a Junebug, this Teutonic Lothario is putting himself forward against Miss Plumtartt.

I ain't liking this a bit.

But I promised to be good.

This slimey son of a gun has not stopped staring at Miss Plumtartt, his eyes roving over her figure, and I am getting hot.

But I promised to be good.

"Mein scrumptious strudel! You have zee pleasure of meeting," (Brightly shining booted heels sharply click together.) "Herr Doktor Rudolph Himmel!"

Herr Doktor Rudolph Himmel tries to impress Miss Plumtartt with a long list of family titles, scholarly credentials and enough following initials to start a new language with.

"So, Fraulein Plumtartt," drools the passionate Prussian. He wedges a thick monocle into position to get a better look. He is leering at Miss Plumtartt in a most inappropriately familiar manner! "normally I would be staunchly against allowing der female entrance to mein clubbe, but for a delightful Leibchen as yourself, I vill happily make zee exception, Ja."

"Chah-ming, Herr Doktor, I am sure, but you see, I am a founder of this clubbe. One might say that you were in '*mein*' clubbe, sir."

The randy count is not pleased at Miss Plumtartt's oneupmanship. I can almost see the salivating fangs of the Hessian Wolf as he backs Miss Plumtartt up against a table and then presses himself against her until you couldn't get a piece of butcher's paper between them.

"Persephone!"

A small young fella stands in the doorway from which he has called. He looks to be barely a teen, but has an adult's authoritative presence. There is also a frailty about him; he is out of breath from his short travel to this room.

"Stanislas!" Miss Plumtartt calls back to the youth as she ducks beneath Herr Doktor Himmel's grasp. It is so good to see you, my dear!"

She runs to and warmly embraces the little gentleman.

"My dear Persephone, I can tell that you are deeply distressed. Please tell me what concerns you so."

"Yes, of course, Stanislas, but in private, if you don't mind."

"By all means, dear Lady."

"But Fraulein," cuts in Herr Doktor Himmel very brusquely and without regard to me or Monsieur de Guaita, "I was in the middle of mein own conversation vith you, und I vaz not finished."

"Really?" Miss Plumtartt regally arches a single eyebrow. "I think that we are quite through. However, I am sure Mr. Temperance will keep you company while I am away. Thank you, gentlemen."

With that, Miss Plumtartt and Monsieur de Guaita swiftly whisk away.

I don't like the way he's eyeballing her bustle.

This continental Casanova is not treating Miss Plumtartt with the respect she deserves.

But I promised that I would be on my best behaviour.

"Good evening, sir," I say, vainly trying to break his

fanny-focused attentions. “My name is Ichabod Temperance.”

I am completely ignored by the thwarted German Gigolo.

“Excuse me, sir? That’s Herr Doktor Himmel, isn’t it?”

He looks as though he has just tasted something sour. This boy is having to dig deep to come up with the good manners to speak to me. In his opinion, I am obviously beneath his notice.

Once the bustle in question turns out of sight, he finally acknowledges my existence with a dismissive snort.

I try my hand at high-brow small talk.

“Some weather, eh?” I attempt. “Looks like we might have a spot of rain.”

Herr Himmel has returned to not even acknowledging me.

“I like your clubbe, Herr Himmel,” I try again. “Very posh indeed.”

A small flicker of distaste crosses the single lens enhanced face.

“Any ‘Ghost’ attacks in your neck of the woods?“ I inquire.

He snaps his focus on me. I feel like a bug under his glaring monocle.

“Why yes, my little American,” leers the beastly baron, “we do have zese ‘Ghost’ attacks in mein country. Quite horrible they say.”

Then why do you grin when you say it, you creepy Kraut?

“These will run their course in due time,“ he muses.

What does he know?!

A cuckoo in his hat alerts him that he has an

appointment to make.

Checking the many amazing clockwork devices hidden about his wardrobe, he makes to depart. He taps my shoulder with his cane.

I suspect this device to be of dubious design.

"You and zee young lady. You are intimately involved, are you not?"

Is he questioning her virtue?!

(! plinck !)

I promised....

"Herr Himmel, it is my understanding that Miss Plumtartt is of the highest moral character." I strongly inform this horrible fellow. "Our relationship is of the most honorable sort."

"Yes, vith you, I can imagine. Well, you never know with the English women zees days," he sneers. "Interesting, though, for she is most comely, for a common quail!" Himmel looks up and into his own downward-plunging thoughts. "I have a goal to achieve, but it strikes me there may be an alternate route to achieve this aim." I can almost see the crude imaginations passing through his eyes. "Ja, a most delightful way to derail this girl."

"What was that, Herr Himmel? I don't think I like your insinuations."

He had forgotten me for the past couple of moments.

"Oh, yes. Fraulein Plumtartt's little American friend." He steps back and looks me up and down. "Do not send a boy to do a man's job. You are obviously inadequate to satisfy Fraulein Plumtartt's requirements. Do not take offense; you just lack the proper breeding to rise above your station."

I promised her I would behave... I promised. I promised.

“A few minutes with zee pride of Dusseldorf and this maiden will no longer be eligible for her destined role.”

(! plinck !)

“Ja! Of course! I merely have to de-flower this English virgin hen.”

(! PLINCK !)

CHAPTER 22 – NO HUMAN HAND.

Persephone

Stanislas and I hurry from the parlour containing Herr Doktor Himmel and Mr. Temperance. I deplore forcing that awful man upon my friend, but desperate times call for desperate measures.

With a surprising grace given his mere fourteen years of age, Stanislas leads me to his private parlour, on the floor above my father's chamber.

I am pleased to note that young Stanislas has been accepted into the clubbe despite his extreme youth, but, to their credit, occultists of our Post-Comet generation are somewhat more inclined to accept members based upon their abilities and not their gender or age, and in any event, young de Guaita is a prodigy by any standard. However, I find myself discomfited at his obvious nervousness - clearly, he has not yet learned to cloak his emotions as rigorously as other males of our time are required to do. For all of his prodigious abilities, he is still little more than a child.

I am thankful for the transparency of his emotions, but am distressed at the anxiety he reveals – it confirms my own assessment of our position. Our subsequent conversation removes any doubt that Mr. Temperance and I are in the most dire circumstances imaginable.

Still, I am somewhat distracted during the early moments of our meeting: I confess to having formed an instant dislike for Herr Doktor Himmel, whose dismissive and denigrating treatment of Mr. Temperance roused my ire to a surprising extent. Arrogantly, he was obviously making a clumsy attempt to insinuate himself into my affections, as if I should be flattered that he was condescending to offer the dubious delights of his - ahem - "charms" to my person.

At that moment, Stanislas breaks into my distasteful musings with a chilling train of thought that restores my focus to the urgency of our situation.

"Persephone, I believe that you are in the gravest danger. Beware of the "great" Herr Doktor, for he is not all that he seems."

"Indeed, Stanislas, I concur."

"I could almost see two faces superimposed upon each other: a rather handsome, if florid, outdoorsman, and something...something dark and amorphous, not...not human..."

"I am sorry to admit that I have thought the same thing, my dear" Stanislaus admits. "Worse still, it is my belief that Herr Himmel is at the center of the dark events surrounding you and your Mr. Temperance."

"'*My*' Mr. Temperance?"

"Persephone, you are as a sister to me. I must speak as I feel; if you wish to upbraid me for my forward speaking, you may do so."

"I could never upbraid you, my dear friend, for your honest opinion...even if I find it...uncomfortable. But now let us turn our attention to these dangers you have mentioned...and that I have somehow known existed, though I could not tell you how."

"That is because, Persephone, you are like Herr Himmel in one way - and one way only: you too are far more than you appear, or than you realize, but your hidden depths are to the good, and not of the darkness."

He pours me a snifter of the finest Cognac - knowing that I eschew those vapid alcoholic beverages typically allowed to respectable females - and turns to the large bay window overlooking the small mews at the side of the Clubbe.

"I believe that we must consult the cards for more information," he says, and without further ado, he reaches for his cloth and his Tarot deck.

Quietly, Stanislas lays out the cards for me:

1. The General Situation: Le Monde (Reversed)
2. What crosses this for good or for ill: La Maison Dieu
3. The root of the problem: Le Bateleur (Reversed)
4. What crosses this for good or for ill: L'Diable
5. The next steps for us:

L'Amoreux

Le Chariot

L'Eremite

6. What surrounds me, and what I must do: La Papesse

crossed by La Lune

7. What surrounds Mr. Temperance, and what he must do

Le Fou

crossed by Le Pendu

8. The outcome predicted at this time:

La Roue d'Fortune

9. What are the most likely scenarios, given that the last card was ambiguous:

Either La Morte

or

Les Etoiles

Stanislas quickly explains:

"I drew the cards as I felt compelled and into a new configuration I have not yet used. In sum, the World itself faces an unprecedented catastrophe; the cause of this is an evil Magus who is in league with something diabolical; you and Mr. Temperance (and here I blush, for the card so clearly representing us was "The Lovers") must take a long journey and meet with a wise counsel. You must trust this advice and follow it to the letter, for there is much you do not know.

In regard to you, Persephone, for your whole life, you have had certain hidden abilities, abilities which make you a woman of a certain power. As a Plumtartt, you inherited a secret, millenia-old trust, as well as this power. The accident in your father's laboratory has amplified those abilities, much as the Revelatory Comet has affected my own abilities. Yet much darkness surrounds the truth of these abilities. I know not what they are. I know only that they relate to the foul scroll that your companion carries. You have done well not to touch it, for its proximity to you is pernicious to your very health. The presence of the Moon here also indicates that there are hidden dangers that will try to obscure the truth from you, and even to harm you in a grievous manner.

For Mr. Temperance, however, the situation is somewhat different. Though he is brave, honorable to a fault, and undoubtedly loyal to you, he is still a boy - an innocent - and that boy must become a man. He must do this through making a sacrifice...a sacrifice that may involve the loss of his life."

"When I drew the Wheel of Fortune as the outcome card, I realized that the future is still mutable...there is an element of chance. The end result of your efforts will lead either to the death of much, if not all, that we have known as a species, or to a renewed hope for a future free of this darkness. You and Mr. Temperance are indeed spinning the roulette wheel, but you must make the effort. It is all up to you."

"As to the scroll itself, I cannot myself translate it. Just as the Plumtartt family has been entrusted with the document itself, so others – a very select few – have taken upon themselves the task of uncovering the scroll's history, and understanding its contents. You must consult..."

Before Stanislas can say more, we hear a loud altercation taking place in the parlour we had so recently vacated. I can hear the gruff, guttural voice of the obstreperous German, and a strange, but somehow familiar, angry voice in riposte to the Prussian's. Then the sounds of a scuffle become unmistakable. We rush downstairs to see Mr. Temperance being dragged out of the clubbe by main force, and the odious Herr Doktor Himmel lying in a fetal ball upon the floor, clutching his own person in a most unseemly manner.

Stanislas and I rush past the excruciated Doktor and catch up to where the many staff members have tossed Mr. Temperance out of doors.

I make hurried apologies to the officers of the Clubbe, but they seem more concerned over the reputation of their establishment rather than of Herr Himmel's present condition. Likely enough, he has not been the most pleasant, nor the most popular, of members. Once I make a few discreet murmurings about Herr Himmel's unwarranted attentions, my friend, Monsieur Trevor Aeon, assures me that I am welcome to return at any time.

"But if you bring your American friend," he adds, "Mr. Temperance must learn to restrain his...boisterousness." Trevor attempts to remain stoically stern; however, his exquisite ebony expression reveals a trace of bemusement as a tiny smirk is allowed to find its way onto his debonair countenance. I think Trevor has wanted to do exactly what Mr. Temperance has done for a long time and is secretly delighted at the isolated violent disturbance.

As we leave the Clubbe, I cannot help but notice that the line of dark clouds above has grown heavy and ponderous. The atmosphere is leaden and unnaturally oppressive. Clearly, the weather mirrors my inner turmoil and growing sense of a storm about to strike. A storm consisting of Something else... Something heavy...waiting...hidden. But where? And what?

Stanislas brings Mr. Temperance his knife and gunbelts.

"You may very well need these and much more, Monsieur Temperance, before your tasks are complete."

My American friend is obviously embarrassed and deeply chagrined at his actions.

"I sure am sorry about whoopin' up on the 'Dok' in your nice clubbe, Mr. De Guaita."

"Do not trouble yourself over tonight's unpleasantness, Monsieur Temperance." The young prodigy attempts to console the regretful combatant. "No doubt the odious Doktor had that and much more due to him. I confess to being envious of your forthright actions. May they see you through your coming trials."

"Yessir, thank you." Mr. Temperance answers, shaking

the youth's hand. "We'll try an' do that."

We are then directed by young de Guaita to this translator, a man of great reputation. I caution Mr. Temperance that we must keep this man's identity secret. Mr. Temperance hires us a Parisian-style Hansom cab to carry us on our lengthy journey. Leaving the Rive Droite and crossing the Seine at Pont d' Austerlitz, we arrive at our destination: the Arabian Quarter, located in the Gobelin Arrondissment. By the time we reach Mr. Bin-Jamin's building, the rumbles of thunder are maintaining a steady roll, and the skies are alight with great flashes of lightning, giving the streets a surreal aspect.

We knock upon the scholar's door. After what seems an interminable wait, we hear a slow, shuffling tread, and a series of furtive, careful slidings and scrapings. At last, the door opens but only by a few inches, obviously secured by a thick chain inside. "Who is this, please?"

"Mr. Bin-Jamin, I am Miss Persephone Plumtartt. My friend, young Stanislas de Guaita, recommended you as an expert translator in obscure languages."

"Miss Plumtartt?" The door opens a bit wider. I can see glimpses of a wizened face through the aperture.

"I am but an humble scholar. Perhaps you are at the wrong destination."

The wrong destination? What can he mean? Why all of the trepidation? And then I recall my father once telling me that certain scholars were quite reticent to discuss certain topics without a type of verbal "pass-key".

"Monsieur Bin-Jamin, my father, Professor Plumtartt, asked me to convey a message to you. It is of a personal nature, but it relates to one who seeks Utnapishtim?"

A few moments of silence follows, then, we hear the sound of a chain disengaging, and the door opens. Yet, as we step into the tiny foyer, we still see little more of our host than shadow. "One test remains, Miss Plumtartt. Even were it Gilgamesh himself who stood before me, he should be required to submit."

He waits for my reply.

Sensing no malice from the man (nor, thank Heavens, any green miasma), I accede, whereupon he passes a small crystal in front of Mr. Temperance. I cannot tell its color in the near-darkness, but it begins to glow a sunny gold as the scholar tests my companion. Apparently satisfied, he passes the crystal in front of me.

Iridescent crimson light fills the air! In the eerie light, I see his hands shake violently, causing him to lose his grip on the crystal. What can it mean? Have I failed?

"You...have come. It was inevitable, I suppose. You have brought...the scroll?"

He lights a small lamp, and then a second one. The room, comprising a typical scholar's farrago of scrolls, codices, inkstands, and various odd specimens in glass jars, reminds me strangely of my mother's old studio. Mountains of books grow in precarious pillars about the room as the shelves are far past overflowing.

I nod to Mr. Temperance.

"Lemme loosen one end of the tube, sir." Mr. Temperance says as he then produces a matched brace of adjustable 'simian' spanners from his constant tool supply, breaks the tightly cinched seal, and then hands the lead pipe containing the scroll to Mr. Bin-Jamin. Something moves me to speak:

"Sir, I should be careful in touching it. I confess I

cannot abide to do so."

"Indeed, you could not. It is inimical to your very nature. But no child of the Light could hold this particular text without taking certain precautions." He slips two oddly-embroidered gloves onto his hands, and clamps a thickly-lensed pince-nez onto his nose. He handles the dread document with two thin rods of wood. Holding the sticks in one hand and using them in conjunction with one another, the old scholar manages the pair of sticks with amazing dexterity in the Auriental manner of food utensils.

He points to two chairs by the window. "Please be seated. I fear I know what I shall find...but I must have total quiet for concentration. With such things, one must be absolutely sure."

Mr. Temperance and I wait for some time while the elderly scholar reads through the nauseous scroll. He appears to be making his way through the incomprehensible scratchings with surprising speed, given his obvious caution. Impelled by a morbid curiosity, I look at the document from time to time with growing unease; somehow, the convoluted symbols strike a chord of memory deep with me. A memory that I do not wish to remember. As we wait, the storm continues to increase in intensity as it makes its approach on Paris. The ancient apartment seems to vibrate with the reverberation of the thunderclaps, which seem to be getting closer, and more frequent.

At last, the old scholar speaks.

"It is as I feared, my child."

"The text your family has guarded for so long...we had always assumed it to be a translation into Arabic, or perhaps, at worst, Sumerian. If it were, things would be less dire. With every subsequent translation, more and more of the original text was lost, you see. But this is no translation."

"The document I now hold is the original Eye of the Forbidden Gate!"

The Eye of the Forbidden Gate!

That name! A frisson of atavistic fear runs through my body.

I have heard rumors of a text stored in a small, North American university, supposed to be the remnants of a medieval-era Arabic translation of a Sumerian grimoire, but its provenance has always been dubious. Yet when Mr. Bin-Jamin mentions the name, I feel a strong shock of recognition that this lies at the root of the evil currently besetting Northern Europe.

"Sir, the...*original* Eye of the Forbidden Gate ?" I ask, but secretly fear I know the answer.

He sighs. "The document stored in the American university is a pale copy, containing many errors which weaken its power: though, make no mistake, it is still quite dangerous. Indeed, the Enemy has created quite enough horror with another such copy. This document is the original."

"Is not the Eye of the Forbidden Gate designed to summon some terrible demon to feed on mankind?"

"Not precisely. This document is designed to summon Something utterly Other, Something that does not belong to this universe."

I feel my gorge rise. Surely...?

"And this particular document was written by no human hand."

"They saw the end coming, you see. These abominations were from some place incomprehensible to us. They could not interact with our world fully. Metals and certain gases were useless to them, but they needed access to these materials for their dark industries. They could "possess" life forms, but the brains and nervous systems of our existing animals were too simple to serve as vehicles for their aims. Thus, they attempted to...meld...with and adapt tissues native to Earth. They used their black magics and their twisted sciences to create living creatures of the matter of this universe, but these mongrel creatures failed to serve as adequate vehicles for the monsters' ambitions. The result led only to life forms that were little more than clockwork factory workers, quite capable of seemingly complex tasks, but with no more power to decide than a slime worm...yet they could remain, when their masters were banished by another alien race, one from our own universe."

"A guardian race?"

The elderly scholar shook his head in negation. "They were guardians only in the sense that a man might avoid stepping upon an ant. Although they were beneficent enough to our world, they were to our world, it was only to serve their own goals and to defeat their own enemy."

His tone bids me interrupt no more.

"Working in secret during the last months before their defeat, the abominable masters used their misshapen servants to write down a means by which they could be summoned from their entrapment. They knew a time would come when the incongruity between our universes would lessen to the degree that they could come through the portal in their original might."

"For millions of years, these twisted servants preserved this knowledge. When our species emerged, the monstrous shepherds watched quietly, as their masters had created them to do. As humanity rose from the savannas to the ziggurats, the dark scribes prepared the alien knowledge in a form our minds could understand. By the time of our first civilizations, many men had become all too ready to worship at the altar of any evil if it would slake their thirst for power. It was a simple matter for the servants to pass this information to credulous and evil humans, though few human minds could fathom this utterly alien language; thus, the translations began. The Sumerian name became attached to it, but only because its true name cannot be spoken. Acolytes began work and dark rituals were enacted. And now, the time approaches out of the unfathomable past such that the congruency of our universes grows close enough for their return."

"The Eye of the Forbidden Gate cannot be destroyed by humans; thus, wise men have taken the last scroll written in the hands of their servants to keep evil men from summoning these abominations. You are the latest in the long line of scroll protectors, as I am the latest of its loremasters. It is a sacred trust, and one upon which everything that exists...depends. That is why we cannot fail. We cannot let this document fall into the hands of the enemy. If we fail, the Portal Dweller will open our world to them so that they can return to conquer this universe utterly."

I am not a woman accustomed to vapors, but I feel the room moving far away, and the distressed voice of Mr. Temperance calling for me. He steadies me in those surprisingly strong arms and we take our leave of Mr. Bin-Jamin.

I hear Mr. Bin-Jamin give Mr. Temperance some last instructions, but their words come as from the bottom of a well.

As we leave the apartment, I am still not quite myself. I had suspected that these dark forces were after me, and I had feared incipient megalomaniacal tendencies. But now I know that it is true: they are after me, because I hold this key... and because, somehow, I am a key. Worse, I now know, beyond any doubt, that my father betrayed a millenia-old trust to use the filthy document in some way to complete his design. The sigils in Father's laboratory, once incomprehensible to me, I recognize all too clearly now. They came from the inhuman language of the Eye of the Forbidden Gate! I am shaken to my core.

I stumble slightly on a cobblestone. My heart sinks to hear a familiar, Deutsch Doktor's voice...

CHAPTER 23 - THE DOKTOR RETURNS.

Ichabod

Black smoke pours from her double stacks. Gleaming copper, brilliant brass, and lovingly varnished wood delight the viewer. Deep, rich, maroon upholstery, no doubt smelling of Corinthian leather, comfortably caresses the operator's backside as he mans the controls. The wheels are a composite. A wire spoked chromium treated rim is surrounded by a new invention called the 'tyre.' Constructed from an amazing, tropical, organic substance, known as 'rubber,' these "tyres" are inflated as balloons, giving the craft remarkable stability. Her steam is up, giving promise of great energy on store. She is a wondrously appointed mechanical carriage! I have seen quite a few examples of commercial and privately maintained vehicles, but this carriage is a true phaeton! A land torpedo, she is built for speed! I am familiar with the abundance of many new steam-driven horseless carriages, and I had heard of such a marvel here in metropolitan Europe. So sleek and dynamic, this ostentatious creation is a gorgeous sight to behold!

Unfortunately, the sight of this wonder is marred by the insouciant pose of its owner, lounging against it. Herr Doktor Himmel has somehow followed us. He grins at us evilly.

"Guten Abend, Fraulein Plumtartt."

Miss Plumtartt and I are plumb struck by the unexpected sight of the dastardly Doktor.

"You like the Steamer? Beautiful, eez she not? Horseless, as you can see. I have found that in years, zaht my presence makes horses nervous. I am sure I do not know why."

We are transfixed. I snap my mouth shut as I realize it is hanging open.

"My little American with the big boots. You have struck a superior. A superior being of a superior race. You are in possession of that which will fulfill my destiny. I shall have untold power over this world, and I shall eat the likes of you for mein lunch."

"And my Dear Fraulein Plumtartt. All the portents indicate you as the one who could possibly be a threat to our plans. I assume that you are still in possession of your maidenhood, ja? It is the delightful little chore of relieving you of that burden that will seal my fate to rule this plane!"

He chuckles. He laughs. He bubbles up with maniacal laughter.

Miss Plumtartt gives a frightened start. At the same time, I hear horses in the vicinity whinny their displeasure.

Knowing what this usually portends, I quickly pull the 'Green Beauties' into place and spin up the generator.

Miss Plumtartt looks up with a start. Gasping, she falls back a step.

I turn to where she is looking only to see two fluttery, batlike creatures: batlike, but more insecty. I want to feel pity for the unfortunate beasts, but they seem so happy to be evil. Awkwardly flying to us over the rooftops, they come to circle above a young couple who have stopped to gawk at Herr Himmel's golden conveyance and his outlandish behaviours. The Parisians are oblivious to their danger as the winged crawfish are unseen by all but myself, Miss Plumtartt, and the insidious Doktor Himmel.

With an unsettling insect squeal of joy, the buggies drop,

alighting upon the heads of the unsuspecting onlookers.

The stricken couple struggle and scream vainly as the obscene, and to them invisible, monsters absorb themselves into the skulls of the strollers.

A rigid tightening of muscle and tendon seizes the young Parisians. An internal vibration throttles the couple into a morbid Saint Vitus Dance. Horribly violent convulsions wrack their tortured bodies. Onlookers first step in to assist, but then stumble back in horrid fascination as the victims slowly levitate. Thick plumes of dark smoke pour from these victims of horror. The roiling clouds coalesce into two iridescent green scarabs. These are gopher sized beetles with a few extra legs, and sets of mandible pincers.

These beastly bugs fall to the sidewalk with excitedly clicking prongs and scurrying legs.

Instinctively I draw, squeezing off a .45 calibre shot into each one as they fall to the ground before I remember the proven ineffectiveness of the lead bullets.

The big insects, moving with blinding speed, are immediately upon us.

I say us, but no, the arthropodal horrors make straight for Miss Plumtartt.

I run forward and kick the first one into the stone lion guarding the entry to the apartments. I have to twist and then fall flat out, to barely but painfully catch the other by its serrated leg. The emerald scarab is just a hair's breadth from snapping a chunk out of Miss Plumtartt's leg.

I pull back on the determinedly murderous Palmetto bug as the slavering mandibles continue to snap, just short of their target. I use its surprisingly heavy weight to pull myself up, while concurrently spinning, somewhat like a gyroscope's self-balancing inertia and momentum. This centrifugal force allows me to fling the creepy-crawler back at its companion, just as it is regains its senses from impact with the lion. I endeavor to push my advantage by running up, and kicking one of 'em as hard as I can right in the middle of his ugly face.

"Dang!"

Now my boot is stuck on his blasted mandibles!

I yank out the green knife and stab at one of the fiendish cockroaches, while trying to shake the other off my boot. The ever-lovely Miss Plumtartt valiantly, if ineffectively, gives the one on my boot a severe thrashing with her parasol.

This causes that devilish Deutschman to laugh even more uproariously.

(! ! !)

My blood's a' boiling now, and no doubt about it.

I am caught up fighting these persistent pests, but I get a flashing impression from out of my peripheral vision. The Doktor's cane shoots out and hits Miss Plumtartt behind the ear. I turn as she goes down. Miss Plumtartt has been struck and knocked into unconsciousness by the Doktor! Herr Himmel is several feet out of reach even with the cane: how did he strike her, I wonder? I am sure he has not moved. I kick the one on my boot against the steps and try to pick a soft spot to stick the other. There is another flash of movement in my peripheral vision. The Doktor is now holding the unconscious Miss Plumtartt in his arms! He hasn't moved! How did he do that?

"Aufweidersehn, you little American bug," he chortles.

"Zee girl ist mein!"

"Hahahahahahaha!"

He places Miss Plumtartt's innocent self in his steam driven speedster.

"Mwuhahahahahahaha..."

They speed away.

"Ahahahahahahaha..."

(! ! !)

This is intolerable!

In exasperation I try to reason with the ugly fellow still clinging to the end of my boot.

"Make up your mind! Either chew your way in, or let go and get off my dang foot!"

Fighting giant, beetle, cockroach monsters from another dimension is bad enough, but I feel pretty silly with a giant bug yanking my foot. The other is quick and vicious. I want to stomp him, but I can't as long as I've got the other at the end of my appendage, disrupting my equilibrium. I try to get a fix on the monster trying to bite me, while the critter trying to get away from me keeps pulling my leg.

"This ain't gonna work."

Tinkerers mostly build, but when we are not building, we dismantle. I believe this is what is called for in this situation.

I tango my toe-bound partner to the sidewalk. Keeping the one on my boot between me and my harasser, I locate a spot behind boot boy's head and shove in my emerald knife. Quickly, but with great effort, I pop the body from the head, granting myself balance and maneuverability.

The other is too big to squash with my boots in the conventional manner. I do manage to stomp down and pin one of its legs, though. I use my free hand to grab one of the mandible pincers trying to pinch me. As I dismantle the monstrous insect, I try not to notice that the thick, horrid bug goo within reminds me of Key Lime Custard. That will no longer be one of my favorites, I suspect. I am quickly in pursuit of that German laughin' hyena, and my dear Miss Plumtartt.

You'd think my old mud pounders had wings on 'em the way I fly down Rue Cruelebarbe. When I clatter out into the expansive Boulevard des Gobelin, the horses have a bad reaction to the beetle head, still stuck on the front of my right boot. Apparently it is now visible to the naked eye.

I pull the 'Beauties' out of the way.

These Parisian boulevards are big. They are crowded, even with the storm starting to hit. I look quickly left and right.

There! The path of the speedy steamer is easy to spot. Horses are giving it a wide berth.

I run for all I'm worth but they gain distance. The steamer is a sleek, and built for speed. Passing all horse drawn transportation, it appears to be the fastest conveyance on the Boulevard.

I gotta commandeer a vehicle to maintain my chase 'cause I ain't havin' Herr Himmel to kidnap Miss Plumtartt.

Fancy carriages and Hansom cabs ain't gonna cut it. There are a few private, mechanical carriages, but ain't none of 'em in the same class as the Doktor's beautiful craft.

I run down the street, the now pouring rain mocking me as I watch Herr Himmel get away.

I continue my pursuit undaunted. The mounting wind pushes me along.

A constant, rolling thunder, accompanied by approaching lightning promises a massive storm.

Besides those already mentioned, the only other choices of transportation are commercial: trolleys, wagons, and a lumbering steam-powered coal wain.

(! ! !)

It was so big, I almost didn't see it.

Dominating the center of the Boulevard is a colossal, tandem, steam powered coal wain. With drive wheels taller than the size of a grown man, it makes pretty good speed. Catching the rear gate, I pull myself up onto the back of the gargantuan coal bin. Climbing the twenty feet to the top, I scramble in, dash the forty feet forward and jump across to the next wagon. I barely am able to catch the other side and pull myself up and in. Then it's across, and down, into the land locomotives own smaller coal bin. I jump down onto the engineer's platform. I rattle away to the startled engineer in English, and he angrily rattles away back at me in French, with equal incomprehension. Pulling my pistol, I use it to point first to him, the coal, and then the furnace. I repeat the procedure more emphatically, and he starts to shovel coal reluctantly into his locomotive's furnace.

I climb back over the tractor's feeder car and uncouple the coal bins. Many tons of coal and trailer are unburdened from the trackless train. The steamer does not exactly lurch forward, but it does noticeably pick up speed.

When I return, the engineer's platform is really warm. I indicate that I require more coal in the already glowing furnace. The French engineer refuses, pointing at the red lined monitoring gauges.

"I don't read French," I say.

The engineer is very angry and emotional. He begs me most tearfully to spare his beautiful machine, something a tinkerer like me can comprehend in any language. Normally I would be in agreement with the fellow, but the needs of a fair maiden in distress tips the balance against the machine this day.

I point my pistol. He blubbers a bit as he continues to plead. I cock the Colt. He is very disapproving as he shovels more coal into the furnace that is now turning from orange to white with heat. A gauge pops off. The glass of another cracks. The French engineer throws his shovel off the platform, and bares his chest for the bullet. I respect this man's love for his machine. This is his 'Lady' and I am not treating her with the respect she deserves. I indicate for him to climb into the coal feeder. The tractor gets a little faster as I uncouple the feeder car.

With a natural knack for things mechanical, I am able to quickly work out the controls of this leviathan. By the opening of certain valves, and then the closing of certain others, I am able to maximize the full power of the machine.

I lean out and look ahead for the Doktor's carriage. I am gaining on him.

The tearing rain hits broadside as the full force of the pent-up storm finally bursts against us. The wind, rain, and lightning that have chased Miss Plumtartt and me these past two days at last has us at its mercy.

Good grief, what a racket! The great engine of my commandeering is being pushed way past its tolerances. This brute was never intended to achieve the speeds that I exhort from it. The monster is so clattery that it barely touches the ground except in hops, skids, and skips. The tractor was built to be stabilized by its trailing cars. Without even her coal bin in tow, she has difficulty remaining vertical. The gigantic steel wheels chew up the stone thoroughfare. Sparks and gravel spew behind as smoke and steam billow to Heaven.

An Alabama Fury is driven inexorably forward.

I am an unstoppable juggernaut.

Another forty feet and I've got him, along with her!

Blast it! He has turned to see what is approaching him in so dread a manner and realizes his position! He makes to gain speed and thus escape!

Dang! The glass of the dials is starting to pop. The needles in the gauges are actually bent from being driven so far past the red line. A valve shoots by my ear! Rivets are popping. Scalding steam forces me from the controls.

The German's smaller steamer dodges obstacles on the wide Parisian street. My runaway locomotive runs over or through any obstruction. Carts and wagons explode as the rambling wreck crashes down the boulevard.

As the Doktor gains speed, the borrowed behemoth is shaking itself apart.

Herr Himmel will escape with Miss Plumtartt! I am close enough now to see that she has regained consciousness and is giving the Doktor what for! Atta girl, Miss Plumtartt. I don't know how much damage you're gonna do with that little ol' parasol, but I admire your gumption!

This poor tractor ain't gonna go no faster, and that's a solid fact. I gotta slow down that villainous baron.

Quickly tearing it in two, I wrap my hands in the Engineer's discarded shirt and climb out to the front of the disintegrating tractor. The twisted material of the rags protecting me from the red hot train. I draw a bead on the steamer. This rickety ride does not make for good aim. Timing the shot between bounces, I fire. I miss! A cloud of glass shards explodes as I have hit a safety lantern on the steamer, rather than the Doktor himself. The crystal clue alerts the shameless shifty chauffeur of sure shootin.' The Bavarian bully is outraged as he realizes he is under fire. I shoot again, hitting the steamer's body. The pressure tank for her boiler is punctured, forcefully shooting scalding steam into Herr Himmel's face. Gratefully, Miss Plumtartt is spared the heated release. The truculent Teuton screams in pain and rage as the steamer quickly loses speed from her pressure drop.

I, on the other hand, have quite lost control of my steed.

An angry hum brings my attention to the hub of the tremendous drive wheel behind me. It is smoking and whining in tortured defiance.

The wheel begins a drunken weave at unbelievable velocity. This disharmonic imbalance severely throttles the entire machine before the wheel releases its hold on the axle.

It is an unreal and sinking feeling to see one's own wheel pass one by.

The unlucky locomotive Leviathan unhappily flings its parts in all directions as it slowly tilts to its unsupported 'port' side. With a terrific crash, we fall to the left side of the tractor, the axle angrily rending and carving an ugly gouge deeply into the pristine Parisian Boulevard des Saint Jacques. The plunge of unforgiving steel into the immaculate stone fills the wide street with its tortured objections. The wrecked locomotive's whistle wails as if in mourning for her own sad death.

I am thrown clear. After a series of uncountable tumbling spins, somehow I am on my feet and running at top speed. My errant wheel maintains its pursuit of the Doktor's steamer. As the Doktor slows, and then stops, I see him grab the wrist of Miss Plumtartt, making to pull her after him. He is forced to release her and dive for his safety as the gigantic steel wheel from my locomotive crushes the steamer as flat as the Kansas prairie, making the once gorgeous mechanical carriage one with the street. Steam rises from the squooshed carriage. The sleek steamer is now as flat as a puddle of water. Like a penny that's been laid on the railroad track, and then run over by a train, she looks like a shiny steel puddle. Her tyres are forced akimbo, like a puppy that has lost its footing on a slippery floor. The villain and the heroine are now about fifteen feet apart, facing each other with the flattened steamer between them.

The howling wind and pounding rain will not slow me.

At a hundred feet, a sight that bends my concept of reality almost causes me to slow: almost.

From a distance that is too far for him to actually reach her, Herr Himmel reaches out to Miss Plumtartt. His arms stretch out in length. Further and further they extend, metamorphosizing into ghastly squidlike appendages. They have a squamous, boneless attribute. These articulate into a dozen tentacle arms that grasp Miss Plumtartt and lift her into the air with a crushing, viselike grip. I can just make out the Prussian cad's words, something about 'Nipponese fetishists.'

There is a terrific red flash! With Miss Plumtartt at its center, a sphere of crimson energy bursts out in a scarlet bubble. The explosive concussion knocks me on my rear.

Herr Himmel has been blasted back about twenty feet, and Miss Plumtartt also. I'm glad she was wearing her bustle!

While the concussion knocks me down, I barely touch the ground, as I am back on my feet immediately and running at top speed. I am intent on getting Miss Plumtartt to safety. Before either of them can recover, I have already snatched up Miss Plumtartt, and I'm making tracks in the opposite direction.

After the initial few steps, Miss Plumtartt takes over for her own running chores. I hang onto one of her delicate hands in an effort to increase her speed. The buffeting wind and rain blows us along with the same indifference as the newspapers around us.

There is a lot of Deutsch cursing, behind us.

"Schweinehund Amerikaner! Anmaßende Schlampe!"

(I hope that's not a language Miss Plumtartt is familiar with. I am sure Herr Himmel is not using polite words.)

Miss Plumtartt starts, as if gravely stricken. She has shown a propensity for awareness of unnatural occurrences and I gather by her terrified countenance that something enormously horrible has been triggered. Even I can get a sense that something basely evil has been released.

Pulling Miss Plumtartt along, we both look back to see a huge plume of phosphorescent green smoke pouring up from out of a narrow, tunnel entrance.

"No!" cries Miss Plumtartt, "not the Catacombs!"

A steady show of lightning illuminates the dastardly Prussian madman's outrageous features, accompanied by that dang maniacal laughter again.

"Oh, Mr. Temperance! I somehow know that this monstrous Herr Himmel has drawn upon the uncounted dead of Paris' ancient subterranean mausoleum for his horrible army. What can we do?"

"I'm doin' all I can, Ma'am."

Wind, rain, lightning and monsters chase us North, towards Rue de Enfer. More green puffs of smoke form and burst in that direction also. An overwhelming clacking closes upon us. I spin up the "Green Beauties." Maybe I shouldn't have.

The roiling miasma churning up out of Paris' catacombs forms into scores of hideous monsters.

Paris is alive with glowing green monsters under my goggles.

There are skinny ones, like praying mantis, or walking sticks. Others seem like a bottom of the ocean style of underwater insect. These are usually more of a bloated consistency. They all seem to have the same characteristic of possessing too many legs, eyes, and teeth.

I desperately try to help Miss Plumtartt along, but the futility of our efforts is becoming all too apparent. The overwhelming cacophony of insectile chitterings is maddening to my senses. I stalwartly defend this beautiful girl from the endless horrors in a maddened attempt to save ourselves. We dash northwards, vainly trying to avoid more monsters, but alas, we are completely surrounded. We have been encircled in an unthinkable ring of horror.

Thousands of giant, wrongful insects are forming and then making for us. I P.E.R.K. the first one to catch us in his cephalopodal eye. I slash the legs from a couple more as we dodge and scramble for safety. I give a few others a swift and meaningful kick.

Miss Plumtartt directs a red-hued energy blast at an

aquatic abomination. It is blasted to dangnation.

Miss Plumtartt collapses in an exhausted state, having expelled her defensive humours in that brief, crimson flash of defense. I am a fighting madman at this point. I do not know how many of the creatures I have killed, but I must defend Miss Plumtartt's defenseless form.

Legions of demon spawn make our position untenable.

The angriest storm to hit the Continent in many years hammers Paris with high voltage punches of destruction.

The light show is so steady, it is almost a blue-tinged daylight.

I fight to the bitter end and then fling myself across Miss Plumtartt's prone body to protect her from the murderous mandibles intent on devouring the beautiful girl. I cover her with my arms and torso, kicking at the hateful, hungry monsters.

{{{ BOOOM!!!}}}

A terrific explosion bursts in the air behind us. A dissipating cloud marking the point of ignition.

{{{ BOOOM!!!}}}

Another green cloud violently blooms on a rooftop!

Now there are more and more explosions! My ears ring and I cannot hear myself scream from the onslaught! The lightning storm has turned the fury of Mother Nature herself against my enemies. With an uncanny speed, lightning strikes seem to be finding every disgusting monster in Paris. Each hideous creature explodes with unbelievable energy! I am quite pounded by the proximity of myself to the exploding monsters. Fortunately, I have Miss Plumtartt covered, to protect her. The light overpowers my 'Green Beauties' so I hastily remove them. I no longer need the devices to see my enemies. Each bolt of lightning horrifyingly reveals its terrible target. This strike of meteorological might shows our foes in stark silhouette. Fiends of many legs, eyes and tentacles enjoy a fraction of a second's visibility before suffering a concussive demise. Hundreds of these horrors provide a pop-up picture show across the boulevards. Monsters that are caught out upon the tops of buildings smash great holes in roofs when slain in the electric combustion. The overpowering cacophony continues unabated for what seems a small eternity. Eventually, it tapers off into distant rumbles, as the high voltage cleansing drifts out across the city, and then the French countryside.

Miss Plumtartt!

She is pale, and seems at death's door.

"Miss Plumtartt!" I call.

Her lifeless body has no response.

"Miss Plumtartt!" I cry!

All life would seem to have left my beautiful charge.

I recall another manner of awakening a slumbering girl.

I tenderly raise her head and shoulders.

I kiss my princess.

I hold the sweet kiss for several, beautiful moments...

and then... a flicker?

"Miss Plumtartt?"

A flutter?

"Miss Plumtartt!"

Her eyes are definitely fluttering now.

"Per..! ... That is, I mean, Miss Plumtartt!"

She slowly comes to her senses, as if waking up from an afternoon nap. Calmly taking in her situation, she says to me.

"We really do seem to be getting on, Mr. Temperance."

I realize that I am being a bit forward and help Miss Plumtartt to her feet.

(I have the impression that she is having me on, a bit.)

We take shelter from the storm in the alcove of a nearby church. Doing what we can to wipe and shake ourselves dry, we start to laugh. Just a little at first, but then it grows and by golly, we really let it out in a burst of relief and wonder. By the time we have settled back down, the storm's front has passed through, and Miss Plumtartt suggests that we return to the Da'ath Clubbe. She seeks further advice from Monsieur de Guaita.

Surprisingly, the streets outside have resumed their normal activity, almost as if nothing had happened. These Parisians! Unflappable, they refuse to be impressed by anything! Then I remember that much of the activities concerning the monsters were largely invisible, up until the lightning storm, anyways. Many people could see flashes of the creatures before the storm hit, but everybody could see the monsters just for a fraction of a second before they exploded beneath the powerful lightning strikes. There are many people who are quite upset. Something very unusual has happened, and even these haughty French aristocratic folks know it.

There appears to be a look out for "un fou Américain," in reference to the coal wain débâcle.

We surreptitiously get a cab for the Occultists' Clubbe. I stay in the coach as Miss Persephone meets again with her young Occultist friend.

I spend that time prying that ugly roach head off my boot. It did not disintegrate for some reason. I might keep it as a souvenir of my visit to France.

Miss Plumtartt soon returns with bad news. Where we had hoped that this climactic show of lightning and power would signal the end of our harrowing adventure, Monsieur de Guaita thinks not. Rather, he suggests that the facts indicate instead that there are increasingly powerful forces moving against us. He believes we were extremely lucky with the arrival of the storm and its brutal power that was so strangely effective against our foes.

Miss Plumtartt says that Monsieur de Guaita is quite amused by my tendency to kick the brutes. He suggests a lesson in 'savate.' This is a way of fighting without weapons that these French folk have developed. He says I oughta do this before leaving the city, but leave it we must, and as soon as possible, for there is no time to waste. Our task, though I have not quite got a handle on it as of yet, still lies ahead.

CHAPTER 24 – FOOTSIE.

Persephone

"I was thinkin' of maybe keeping it as a souvenir of our trip to gay Paree, Miss Plumtartt."

"Lovely," I convey in a voice to indicate that it is anything but. "I would very much prefer that you find a place to store your trophy as I do not care for the way it seems to look at me."

"Yes, Ma'am."

Mr. Temperance then puts the over-mandibled roach head that he has devised to disengage from his 'mud pounders,' into a large cloth valise.

Passing down a long hallway, we find the rooms of 'Athletique de Rigor', the clubbe suggested to me by de Guaita. I stop to confer with the gentleman of the offices, while Mr. Temperance is inexorably drawn straight through, and out into the open courtyard behind.

"Mademoiselle?" The gentleman is desperately glancing back and forth between me and my impatient friend. He wants to dart after Mr. Temperance, but French chivalry forbids him from any discourtesy. I 'push my advantage,' as Mr. Temperance might say.

"This clubbe has been referred to me under the most glowing references. Monsieur St. Clair said how effective your training methods are; Count Baruzy spoke very highly of the depth of skill shown in this amazing form of honorable combat. Finally I come from Monsieur de Guaita directly." This name snaps the man into supplication modus operandi. "Monsieur de Guaita wishes this man to be extended your every courtesy and assistance."

"Let's hurry after your friend and make sure he is staying out of trouble," says the harried manager,that has introduced himself as Monsieur Lebaeux. "Some of the boys might be a little rough with him. Oui?"

When we catch up to Mr. Temperance, I see that he has begun practicing with the other students.

This school to which we have been directed is one that practices a gentlemanly French defense. It is a civilian, though martial based sporting exercise known as 'Savate', or, 'old shoe.' The primary focus of the exertions is directed to 'hand to hand' combat, or should I say, 'foot to foot'! The strict laws of this country consider striking a man with a clenched fist to be assault with a deadly weapon. To get around this law, many Frenchmen have learned to fight with their feet! This talent has been honed to an art form within this community. Here, we have the best Savate students in Paris to help instruct my friend.

I look to the courtyard to see Mr. Temperance with a large group of young men. I can easily discern that these young French rowdies are not giving Mr. Temperance an easy time of things.

Monsieur Lebaeux informs the aristocratic ruffians that Mr. Temperance is to be shown a few basics as a courtesy, before being sent on his way. Some of these Frenchmen look as if they are happy to apply a few of the basics to this intruder in their personal domain. These rowdier gentlemen give a definite aura of not wanting this foreigner included within the inner sanctum. I am suddenly very concerned for Mr. Temperance's safety!

Mr. Temperance is shown the proper stances, and

balance so as to be able to use one foot or the other.

Standing in a manner that places him sideways to his opponent, Mr. Temperance is shown how to use the leg and foot closest to his foe for some kicks, and the foot further away for other types of kicks. Some of the more subtle attributes are revealed, such as the fact that the foot upon the ground's surface would seem to be as, if not more, important than the leg endeavoring to make contact with its foe. Mr. Temperance is shown how to get a 'snap' out of his ground foot that resonates through his taut body to be released in a devastating climax of energy on the unlucky target. Some kicking techniques even employ a spinning maneuver that develops remarkable torque for uncanny velocity to be unleashed on the unwary enemy. With knees drawn high, tremendously stout blows are practiced on the heavy bags of material hanging about the yard.

Some of the more eager participants are ready to move past basic instruction and begin some light, friendly sparring. I foresee one on one bouts not unlike English fisticuffs. These foot fighting Frenchmen fancy footicuffs.

To my dismay, I see that several of the more aggressive and adept students have begun buffeting Mr. Temperance with blows much harder than practice, however rigorous, usually entails. The kind and trusting nature of Mr. Temperance is taken advantage of by the roughhousing sophisticates. A small moue of disgust crosses my face. I tamp down an urge to go batter the brutes with my parasol in defense of my good hearted friend.

I look to Monsieur Lebeaux for interference, but then I notice that a strange phenomenon has occurred. At first,

Mr. Temperance is like one of the heavy leather punching bags that are hung about the court. His naive gullibility makes him easy sport for what appears to be a gaggle of bullies. I fear that my presence has exacerbated these attacks, as prideful glances are interspersed with appraising looks cast my way. Men again! If these ruffians think that this impresses me, they could not be more wrong. Yet before I can say anything, I see that Mr. Temperance is fast becoming more adept at the spins and kicks of this esoteric fighting art.

He no longer falls for their taunts and tricks as before. He seems to be able to come up with a trick or two of his own!

Before my eyes, I can see the intrepid and persistent young man developing the balance and coordination enjoyed by his fellows. Soon, it is apparent that the determined American has within himself, the grace, balance, and focus that the art of Savate requires. He turns the disadvantage of his smaller size to an advantage as he maneuvers around his larger opponents.

Before long, my fellow adventurer has begun to surpass a few of the less advanced students. I keep silent, wondering. Then, as time passes, I see that he has eliminated most of the lower and middle ranks; now he is matching blow for blow with two students the manager indicates (with some amazement) are among his most advanced pupils. My earlier musings seem confirmed. It is my belief that the Revelatory Comet's effect upon Mr. Temperance is giving him an edge in his training and performance.

I wonder if Mr. Temperance realizes how nonplussed his would-be tormentors are by his phenomenal speed of learning. In my estimation, he has learned several years' worth of Savate techniques, skills, and - what is more - the muscle memory possessed by a very senior Savate student - in a few hours. Frankly, the other men seem a little unnerved, by the ease with which he has acquired this new skill, but because of Mr, Temperance's modest demeanor, they do not feel threatened, and offer him their sincere admiration.

By the time we leave the gymnasium - several hours after we arrived - the other men seem to have accepted Mr. Temperance as one of 'their own,' and we leave with much greater confidence than we arrived. He is now 'Athletique de Rigor, bon homme, Ichabod.' Modest Mr. Temperance does not even seem to notice just how remarkable his quickly-gained prowess has been.

"Bon voyage, Ichabod, oui, oui!"

"Wee, wee, ya'll."

At Mr. Temperance's behest, we stop for luncheon at a small street-side cafe.

"Miss Plumtartt? This might be a good opportunity to analyze our present circumstances and to get a handle on what we are mixed up in. May I make an attempt at roughly sketching out where we stand? Maybe then we can figure out what our next step ought to be."

"Splendid! Hear, hear. Quite so. I agree Mr. Temperance. Let us try to untangle this unfathomable quandary in which we find ourselves entrenched."

"Yes, Ma'am, thank you. Seems to me that your father, a man who felt the effect of the 'Revelatory Comet,' may have set aside his duties as guardian of the Eye of the Forbidden Gate. Instead he used forbidden, occult craft to complete his experiments concerning the harnessing of the Sun's power. Somehow, this use of unclean magic has cracked the barrier between our plane of existence and that of another, a place of horrible monsters. These creatures wish to conquer us and our universe. This ancient relic I carry is what your father used in his foul experiments. It was while conducting these arcane experiments that you were injured in a laboratory accident of some sort and, unbeknown to you, somehow changed. This has enhanced your natural abilities, allowing you to see and sense these inter-dimensional beings. It has even bestowed a power of protection upon you of some sort. Given the continued, mounting attacks against yourself, the working conclusion is that they desire to kill you, Miss Plumtartt. If we listen to the ugly portents that we heard Herr Himmel espousing, we can conclude that you, Miss Plumtartt, are destined to possibly stop these abominations from transgressing our world. This assumes that we are able to keep you safe from the tentacled likes of Herr Himmel. Further, the information we gathered from Monsieur Bin-Jamin indicates that if our goal is to prevent continued atrocities, we must undertake an arduous journey. Our destination to prevent the manifestation of these atrocities is in the most remote wastes on this planet. Beyond the impenetrable mountains of Afghanistan, and into the Himalayan Ranges of Tibet. Our adversaries seem to possess the means to raise monstrous armies on a moment's notice. Forces of dread intent are mounted against us in overwhelming odds. Have I got it about right, Miss Plumtartt?"

"Oh! I say! Well done Mr. Temperance, a succinct

summation. I applaud your intellectual acuity!"

Since I am more familiar than he with Europe and Asia, I take my turn to set forth what I believe to be our best route. Realizing the necessity of haste, I speak quickly:

"I suggest that we start by heading south of the Alpine Range rather than west through Germany and across the lengthy Northern routes of the European Plain, to get to the Asian Steppes. My proposal is to make our ascensions by the Southern accesses. We can go by train to Montpellier. From there, we can take a boat across the Ligurian Sea to Genoa. Perhaps a dirigible across the Adriatic. From there, we will have to figure it out as we go. Perhaps we can sail down the Danube, skirting the Carpathian Mountains. We shall proceed by ship across the Black Sea, to the inland Azoz. This voyage will bear us all the way to Razoz in the Ottomans. We continue East, going North of the Caucuses mountains. We shall cross the Caspian Sea at Baku. At this juncture, I believe that we shall require the hiring of a caravan to cross the endless wastes of the vast, Great Karskum Desert. Pending our survival, the onus would be upon us to then break through the impenetrable fortress of Mountains that are the Hindu Kush. Following the completion of this challenge puts us onto the Tibetan Plateau. A scant, one thousand miles of desolate, uncrossable, terrain, and Bob's your uncle. Of course, we shall be proceeding on the assumption and hope that we will not be harried by inter-dimensional abominations sorely bent on our destruction along the way."

“Oh, good.” says a delighted Mr. Temperance. “I was afraid it might be something difficult. However, I think I may have a shortcut to get us a little jump on this expedition.”

Chapter 25 - Do I Need a Pass Port Too?

Ichabod

"I have one other observation, if I may, Miss Plumtartt?"

"Why of course, Mr. Temperance, and that would be?" {batt, batt, batt}

I momentarily lose my train of thought under the bewildering breeze of Miss Plumtartt's batting lashes.

"Uhb, ... oh yeah! I'm thinkin' these attacks have only occurred at night."

"Great Drake's ghost! You're right, sir! We must make the most of our daytime hours for travel. Let us fly from Paris at once!"

"Yes, Ma'am. That is exactly what I have in mind. I know that a train to Montpellier and a subsequent boat across this corner of the Mediterranean Sea to Genoa are the more obvious routes, but I suggest taking you up on your idea of flying out of Paris."

"Do you mean by way of Zeppelin? I am sorry, Mr. Temperance, but these modern airships are incapable of surmounting the mighty Alps."

"Yes, Ma'am, but I think a balloon might make it."

"Why, Mr. Temperance! How ingenious! I say, a hot air balloon, theoretically, might just be able to clear the Alpine Range. A high altitude trip over the Alps is exactly what is called for under the circumstances. My word, we should be able to shave several days from our journeys."

Just outside of Parisat Bois de Bologne, we secure passage on a festively bannered Montgolfier hot air balloon.

'*Dante's Roter*' sits ready for us and we make a hasty departure from Mother Earth and are soon soaring high above the French countryside. This is my first time to ever leave the ground! It is a little unnerving at first, but I quickly become acclimated. Miss Plumtartt has been in many dirigibles of different size and shape, but this is her first open air balloon ride and she seems to be as pleased as myself at the wonderful conveyance. We are fortunate in that the prevailing winds carry us South to the village of Villeurbanne, on the River Rhone, where we alight and acquire rooms at an inn for the evening. I believe that we have gotten a jump on our adversaries as we enjoy an uneventful overnight stay. We awaken excited at the prospect of an Alpine crossing. This should be a thrilling exercise!

The white capped mountains of the Swiss Alps loom before us. Higher and higher our daring pilot, Monsieur Jamie Palmatier, fearlessly takes us. We are soon bundling up in cold weather gear that Monsieur Palmatier was smart enough to bring along. I am afraid that we may be dashed upon the mountains, but there always seems to be an air current keeping lifting us safely from the tearing rocks. On one particularly difficult mountain crossing, we feel and hear our basket dragging through the snowy fields that top the range.

"Mr. Temperance, please hurry and save us some of that snow, please, sir."

"Yes, Ma'am," I answer and dutifully scoop some of Switzerland's glittering crystallized winter wonder into a depleted sandbag as our basket drags the top of a lofty Alpine peak.

"Superb, sir!" Miss Plumtartt smiles as she produces a bottle of champagne and tucks it into the burlap igloo. Later, Monsieur Palmatier produces champagne glasses, and we uncork and enjoy the chilled bubbly as we descend from our dizzying heights of the mighty Alps and glide into Northern Italy.

I want another weapon with which to fight my foes. I am interested in some sort of direct energy device. The creatures seem to be vulnerable to powerful strikes of concentrated electricity. Miss Plumtartt claims to have a connection with the city of Graz, Austria-Hungary. Her father made a generous donation to the universities there for their advancements in electrical applications.

Returning to Earth in Milan, we make arrangements to travel to the great Austria-Hungarian Empire's city of Graz. We gain passage on a beautiful, Italian Zeppelin, the "*Bella Donna*,"and cross the Adriatic.

As we approach the ancient city, we see the red-tiled roofs and old clock towers. A fairytale castle decorates the landscape, but there are ominous signs that we can plainly see in this medieval town. The castle is missing a turret and slowly weeps smoke from a recent wound. More smoking craters on other buildings can be seen. From our vantage point, high in the air, we see hurried, unusual construction projects around the area. Great spools of wire are being played out across this valley to embankments that are reminiscent of cannon battery emplacements. Miss Plumtartt is familiar with this place and points out that a famous landmark of the area, the Schlossberg clock, has a different appearance than it has had in the past. A latticed, metal tower grows from a hole ripped in its roof.

This area has been in recent battle.

We land in a field designated for aircraft. There is a tinge of anxiety in the air. Much like our train arrivals in Ipswich and Paris, our landing in Graz places us in a city exuding a tangible fearfulness. We disembark our Zeppelin with some trepidation.

No, this is not quite the same as Paris and Ipswich. These people, and this city, though they share the same frantic energies as was felt in England and France, are not blindly fearful and unsure. With a grim resolve, and moving with purpose, the citizens we observe are mobilized for war.

This city is mounting a defense!

Picking one Burghermeister-looking fella, we ascertain there is a meeting of the muckity-mucks at the largest of the six universities in this Bohemian Beehive.

Arriving at the impressive University of Graz, we enter the ornate complex and make out the noise of a multitude in argument. We follow the sound to a double doorway, crowded with men trying to enter an already packed auditorium. Miss Plumtartt cocks her ear, and listens for a moment. Shaking her head in a dubious manner, she explains to me that she can make out several languages being spoken: German, Serbian, Hungarian, and Croatian, among others.

Miss Plumtartt expresses to me, “This area of the world has never been known for its peaceful existence.”

“Do you mean Austria-Hungary?” I rejoin.

“No. Academia.”

Leaving Miss Plumtartt in the hall, I squeeze my way in through the crowded door. Just inside is a large chair. Not built for comfort, or even for sitting in, this chair could double as a throne for Paul Bunyan. I climb up, and placing my pinkies in the corners of my mouth, I give a terrible, ear splitting whistle.

"Achtung! Achtung! Presenting Miss Persephone Plumtartt!"

There are hundreds of gasps, shufflings, and low murmurings. And then, much as the Red Sea parted for Moses, an opening is created through the crowd toward the doorway, revealing the stunning appearance of Miss Plumtartt. She calmly walks down the aisle that has formed for her. I follow in her wake. The incredible beauty of Miss Plumtartt is hungrily devoured by these academic wolves. They act like they've never seen a woman before, with their mouths hanging open and the wiping of spectacles to get a better examination. Her poise and air of serenity acts to soothe the agitated and embattled burghers and scholars. I also get the impression that she and her name are not unfamiliar to this scholarly body.

"Gentlemen," Miss Plumtartt smiles,"it pleases me to no end, seeing you put aside your differences, in order to further your city's defenses."

There is a lot of looking at one's toes and such, as the chagrined scholars sheepishly cow under the gentle remonstration.

A very distinguished gentleman introduces himself as Doctor Noodlz. He appeals to the reproachful young lady.

"Miss Plumtartt! We are honoured to have you here with us, in this time of need. We give our sincere sympathies to you, for the loss of your dear, departed, father, whom we all so admired. As you can see, we are under siege by supernatural forces... For simplicity's sake!" An uproar threatens to derail his plea. "Let me give Miss Plumtartt our situation! We are under siege by ... something. Approximately two weeks ago, we had the first reports of desiccated corpses. Then, reliable witnesses confirmed of these all-but-invisible creatures of frightful power. The murderous horrors have claimed a frightful toll upon our poor citizens. These monsters, for there is no better word to describe them, please forgive my unscientific terminology, we learned to locate by means..."

"*We!?!* I am not "we!" You would take credit for my brilliance!"

Everyone seems to moan and shake their heads. I hear murmurs of, "Kleine Professor."

Forcing his way angrily forward is a fiery youth. He practically has sparks coming out of his eyes. He cannot be more than sixteen years of age, yet he has all the assurance of any man I've ever seen.

"Meet our 'Little Professor', Professor Tesla."

"Would any of *you* have thought of a device that emits a beam of energy, and then measures the time of its echo return from a given object. To construct a window of wonder. A way to see that which cannot be seen by man? You? You? *Any* of you?"

"Professor, please," Doctor Noodlz begs. "We recognize your brilliance in constructing this amazing machine. But we are all trying to achieve a common goal. Did..."

"Common goal? I defend the city, while you take credit for my insight. It was not the University that designed the "Eye of Graz," it was Professor Nikola Tesla of the Graz Polytechnic!"

Choruses of assent and objection collide throughout the auditorium arising from the impassioned participants.

One voice is heard. "We are all working hard, Professor. ...y that devised the 'Voltage Disruptors.'" ...ptors!' A child's toy!" says the feisty little ... ou the ability to see the foul beasts. I have ... g the city with greater efficiency. A huge ... surround the city, it would be a shield ... e a wall of energy, whatever strikes it, the ... back with greater Force."

... this would be a grand defense of the ... ls, "but our present need is more pressing. ... we were able to secure one of the ... lible Sol Furnaces. Without this ability to g... lous amounts of power, we would be powerless against our enemies."

"Gentlemen, please," pleads Miss Plumtartt, "I am eager to investigate this mysterious window, and intriguing Eye. No doubt the Voltage Disruptors are every bit as stimulating as they sound. However, I wish to first introduce you to an inventive friend from the United States of America, a Mr. Ichabod Temperance."

This is no time to be shy. I step forward.

"You gentlemen are probably familiar with the inability to contact the creatures with metal, whether bullet or blade. Powerful bolts of electricity will completely destroy the creatures. I have devised an alternative. The buggers' own juices can be turned against them." There are noises of assent as this avenue of thought passes through the minds of the men assembled there. "Blast them with electricity, and you get no usable fluid."

"We have been able to collect a bit," some say.

"Then you can make these!"

With that I draw my emerald blade, and throw it down into the middle of the table. It sinks into the wood a good two inches with a solid thud. The blade is recognized immediately for what it is, and what it could mean for the city defenses.

"I am in possession of a formula for the hardening of gathered ectoplasm. This can be used to make blades with which to fight your enemies."

A great cheer goes up in the room.

"I have more - behold!" I hold up my 'Green Beauties.' Their remarkable ability is also easy to recognize.

"These goggles will allow you to see your enemies."

"Wait" calls out Professor Tesla. He steps forward and throws a handkerchief over the goggles. "Before you use this man's intellectual property, we must all, by public assent, grant all rights, ownership, and patents of this device, to its inventor, Mr. Ichabod Temperance."

"Ahh-Greeed..." from the assembled Academics.

"Now then," says the fiery young Serbian-born professor, "let's see what we've got!"

Chapter 26 - Devices Of Destruction.

Persephone

As he strides down the wide hall of the incredible University of Graz, an unruly horde of excited scholars stepping on our heels pushing us forward, Professor Tesla gives a status of Graz's situation. To our East, just across the River Mur, stands the unusual feature of a solitary mountain in the center of the city. It is topped by the famous clock tower of Schlossberg. That landmark now has the added feature of a hastily-constructed metal contraption climbing from one scarred side. This untidy tower is capped by a large, slowly spinning, open-topped, metal basket, laid upon its side.

"The Eye of Graz," explains Professor Tesla. The outrageously brilliant sixteen year old engineer tells how he has fashioned a device that projects a beam of energy covering their expansive valley. "It is like a constantly moving broom. When there is a reflection back to the Schlossberg collector in a particular spectrum of light, a notation is made of the speed of its return. Height, direction, and speed can all be extrapolated from this data. A projection of the spot where this reflection took place is displayed in my 'Window of Wonder.'" It is a round window, two feet across. It looks down into the machine. A large cathode tube is the actual window. "The image corresponding to my beam of energy is shown as a line of light that, if I may return to the broom analogy, "sweeps" across the field of artificial light. A reflection resulting from our spectrum search would take the form of a spot of light on the glass."

"These are good for the big creatures, such as the ones that come down out of the Alps, or across the plain, from the Carpathians. It helps a little in finding and helping with the smaller ones. Your "Green Beauties," as you call them, will help greatly with the smaller, hand-to-hand fighting, that has been just as horrific as that of the big emplacements."

"May we examine them now, please?" asks Professor Saugee-Bahtum.

Poor Mr. Temperance. These scientific cads salivate over his prized goggles in the same manner that I was ogled by Herr Doktor Himmel.

"No dismantlement!" he pleads worriedly. "You may examine them, but do not disassemble!"

There is some grumbling, but they take what they can get.

The formula for creating the Ectoplasmic resin, I write down, along with the principles of the "Green Beauties'" design.

Professor Von Stoughen-Shert explains the Disruptors. These are the direct energy devices that Mr. Temperance had hoped to learn to build, already made!

Huge amounts of energy are required to provide power for any kind of effective blast. Before you can have a weapon, a power source is required. This city has an unusually large power source in the Sol Furnace. Only a few are in use throughout the world. Two powerful Ocean Paddlers, great eight-wheelers, luxuriously transporting their elegant passengers are in possession of the only other two furnaces in use. Plowing the Atlantic Ocean is the Sovereign Ship, *Triumph*. Her sister, the *S.S. Victoria*, is just now arriving to her Pacific duties. Yet to be launched, another Furnace resides within the British Lion of a flagship, Her Majesty's Ship, *Dreadefulle*. Three more Sol Furnace-driven wonders are soon to be launched, one each for France, Germany, and Russia. The Furnace here in Graz is the only such land-based energy source.

I interject that it was one of my father's proudest moments, to donate a Sol Furnace to this city of learning. Now it is as if Providence herself had provided the ability to generate inconceivable amounts of energy with the construction of massive generators. Indeed, it is enough power to provide the energy requirements for a hundred universities. Now these generators power devices of remarkable design and terrifying function.

Voltage Disruptors are being manufactured to a single basic design, in three different sizes. Each starts with a long, tubular shaft, surrounded by concentric rings of glass, descending in size and order, from large to small, a dozen in quantity. These are wrapped in electric apparatuses, with steel framing binding the components securely. This is supported by a mass of machinery able to lift and point the device. A fantastic combination of intricate clockwork, and advanced electric theory, the Disruptors are then assembled atop platforms, allowing for ease of rotation, and wide range of fire. In fact, they are on pivots; the operator of this device would have a veritable umbrella of maneuverability. With sufficient electric power, this voltage cannon is able to direct a blast of energy at its target, if enough power is supplied, and the Disruptor is able to contain the charge.

The smallest version consists of a steam powered,

back mounted generator, which provides power for a rifle-style, hand-held Disruptor. They appear to be used in a "from the hip" manner. These are just now being brought into production.

The next size appears to be the one that is most frequently used. A wagon mounted Disruptor, this is fed by one of two means. Either it has access to energies supplied by the Furnace, or, as is so desperately necessary, it is self-supplied with electricity. Teams of wagon-mounted dynamo squads generate power by means of steam furnace, or by manning pump and crank powered models. These can be sent into troublesome spots that the big models cannot defend, due to the damage that happens collaterally. The Disruptors and their generators must be pulled by teams of men, since horses have proven useless in this crisis. Most of the wagon mounted Disruptors are connected by copper wire to their power source of the Sol Furnace.

And now we are brought to the third and largest of Disruptors being built. It is the same weapon, of the same design, but this beautiful device is twenty feet tall and forty feet long. Truly, it is a device that looks as if it came from a future as yet undreamed. An other-worldly aura surrounds this spectacle; it is quite breathtaking in its deadly beauty. To see this frightening weapon discharge its disruptor blast must be an experience both blinding and shocking.

These Voltage Disruptors are absolutely fascinating to behold! Apparently there are only two of the big ones in service. This one in the university is the third gigantic Voltage Disruptor. It is wheeled out of the laboratory on its way for placement. Its destination is North of the city.

The Plabutsch Mountain dominates the plain overlooking the approach from the Alps. This weapon will enjoy miles of open operating space. The other emplacements are to the North-East, and directly East of the City. Mountaintop emplacements face outwards from the city.

"Our troubles started with 'ghosts'," Professor Tesla explains. "It was my own admittedly brilliant use of this cathode tube and projection reading devices that allowed us to look at what was popping up around us. But then, it also showed the approach of other things. We received distant signals of a creature displaying tremendous size. Fortunately, we trusted our instincts, and barely had a weapon of this design prepared in time to stop the beast. We now endure nightly attacks of invisible creatures that drain our citizens of their life force. These newly created creatures of ectoplasmic beasts would seem to manifest as fiendish, invisible, monsters. I sense that the huge creatures from the mountain ranges are something old, something that has slept under the mountains for untold millennia, but has now awoken."

"Excuse me please, Professor Tesla," Mr. Temperance injects, "if I may have access to your manufacturing facilities, I have a few ideas brewing, gentlemen."

"The first idea: Among the weapons for which you should be making forms for your resin are spear and arrow heads, along with daggers and bullets. Exchange your lead and steel bullets for ectoplasmic resin."

"The second idea involves the explosive nature of the

ectoplasm when given the right amount, or frequency of electrical charge. Can the combustible nature of the material be harnessed to our purposes somehow? Have you tried it as a propellant or as an explosive? Is there a way of enhancing the explosive properties?"

"We have done a great deal of experimentation," says eminent engineer, Dr. Chardz-eneize. "It takes a very particular frequency of generated modulation. Not a lot of power is necessary to fire the ectoplasm. It is easy enough, and portable enough, to ignite the ectoplasm with the right equipment. I am unable to convert this to a direct energy device, and send it out in blasts. Hence the Disruptors. We have the technology to use the ectoplasm as a propellant; we just have not had a reason to do so. But I am very excited about your resin bullets."

It takes little time to prepare the molds and come up with our first batch of weaponry.

Oh! I say! Good show! The formula and process are working perfectly! The efforts towards weaponizing the resin appear to be a success! Hurrah!

As I have done all my life, having grown up in and around laboratories (Father said I was his little test tube baby), I am taking copious notes. All of the experiments and technologies I have been exposed to are meticulously chronicled in my private diary. One never knows when this information may prove useful.

Night has fallen and the attacks may start at any time. The scientists and engineers work without acknowledgment of outside conditions, though I am certain that they truly are only all too aware of the nocturnal danger. I grow anxious as night more firmly takes a hold on the landscape, and I know that we enter the operating zone of the foul creatures.

We conduct an experimental firing of the resin bullets. A heavy log is brought in as a test target.

A rifle round has been bullet exchanged, lead for resin.

The log receives a heavy impact from the durable resin. The trial is considered a success and we predict that these resin projectiles will be very effective against our enemies.

However, I sense that Mr. Temperance is not satisfied.

"Mr. Temperance, are you not pleased with our developments? You should be very proud, my American ally."

The shy fellow blushes and traces a circle with his toe before responding.

"Gee, thanks, Miss Plumtartt, but I really gotta give credit to those English chemysts that helped us out. I do, however, have an itch. I want to try a little experiment of my own, if you think they'll let me."

"By all means, sir."

Mr. Temperance loads a rifle cartridge, utilizing recovered, non-resinated ectoplasm as the propellant. The specialized frequency generated modulation device is hooked up in a makeshift laboratory firearm. Essentially, the cartridge is being held in a clamp. It uses a lead bullet with an ectoplasmic propellant. The makeshift firearm is heavily secured. It is fired successfully. The ectoplasm has an explosive, propellant charge comparable to standard gunpowder.

"Please indulge me," Mr. Temperance requests, "for I am hoping the ectoplasm will interact with the resin to 'charge,' one another."

The inventor prepares another round of ecto-ammo,

this one with an ectoplasmic propellant combined with a resin bullet.

The frequency modulation generator has been prepared.

The round is fired.

{{{BUH-WHOOMP. POW! BOOM!!!}}}

Everyone is sitting on the floor, having been thrown there by the unexpectedly powerful blast. The heavily secured makeshift laboratory firearm has disappeared, presumably disintegrated by the ectic-explosion.

"My word!" I exclaim.

How fortunate I am to be cushioned by bustle! The gentlemen around me were not so serendipitously fashioned.

There is a fine cloud of sawdust from the atomized log, and behind that, a gaping hole in the fine old university stone work.

Just then, we hear the bells of the Schlossberg Clock through the newly opened hole in the outside wall. I can tell from the reactions of those around us that they signal the approach of our enemies.

The attacks have begun.

Chapter 27 - The Battle of Graz.

Ichabod

"Mr. Temperance," calls Miss Plumtartt, "are those bells to signal the populace to hurry to their assigned 'general quarters?'"

"They ain't the bells of Saint Mary's, Ma'am."

The bells are still ringing, but they can barely be heard over the tumult of citizenry readying themselves for war. Fighting panic, the defenders desperately try to get the new giant Disruptor, the one we just examined, into place North of the city. Efforts at getting power to the location are still under way.

The bells stop ringing. Silence falls over the anxious city. Being quiet and watchful are the only means of detection other than the "Eye."

Semaphore signals from the clocktower inform us that the "Eye" has revealed something large to the North of the city. We then get signals of what the locals are calling "Daisies." That is, they just sort of "pop up". The "Eye" searches near and far. Semaphore communicate the "Eye's" findings to the rest of the city and valley.

The university's middle sized wagon-mounted Voltage Disruptors operate on the ends of their copper wire leashes that supply their power. More of the powerful devices adorn the roofs of the houses of learning.

Several Voltage Disruptors sit ready to defend the Sol Furnace.

I understand that the independently powered wagons, be they by hand cranked methodology or steam driven dynamos, are stationed throughout the city. I reckon there're about seventeen, or eighteen, altogether. Our biggest obstacle, I believe, lies in our inability to see and locate the beasts. Crews are trained to listen. Currently, ear horns are used to detect the chittering noises the unearthly beasties make. Sharp young boys and girls who have the heart for such work help to look for the fleeting shadows and listen for the disturbing sounds.

Disruptor squads are already busy throughout the city. Someone makes a comment that the attacks have not started this early before. They are popping up with more frequency. We can see a blast of Voltage Disruption! Great Jehoshaphat! I just about jumped out of my skin at the crack of that charge! And it was nearly half a mile away. Two more! There are excited sounds of combat!

Spinning up my "Beauties," I can see a few fluttery batlike creatures, clumsily flapping through the air. Most are way too far away for me to assist. But one darts near and drops. It lands on the head of an unfortunate victim. I am at his side in a flash. With effort, I am able to pull the thing off and kill it with P.E.R.K. before the poor man is seriously injured.

More citizen soldiers jump in to defend with their new resinated weapons.

The Voltage Squads know their business. They have learned how to track and spot an invisible foe. Amazingly, with the combined efforts of many people, monsters are sketchily tracked. It is the operator's decision whether to take the shot. It is always immediately apparent whether the strike hits home; either there is a terrific explosion from the demon, with the monster briefly visible in a stark silhouette before detonation, or the surrounding buildings are hit instead, and they suffer the blast.

KUH-rrR-ACK!!!

That was a Voltage Disruptor at close range! By my eyes, that was powerful!

KUH-rrR-ACK!!!

Distantly, the big gun in the North East has fired on something. Now the emplacement to the East has fired. This Squad weapon is charging up for another strike. It must have a target or it might explode. There! I climb up on the platform and put the goggles over the operator's face. He sees the creature. The concentric glass circles begin to light up in a sequential pattern, faster and faster, until they reach an electric crescendo!

KUH-rrR-ACK!!!

{{{BOOM!}}} (Exploding monster).

Miss Plumtartt is monitoring the semaphore. More large creatures are moving towards us out of the Alps from the North, and from out of the Carpathians, to the East. The two giant Disruptors cast monumental bolts of destruction from the mountaintops. Apparently there has never been an onslaught like tonight's. There is real desperation that the third emplacement will not come in time.

More Disruptor fire is going off all over the city now. Between the University's and Furnace's roof mounted guns, and those around the city of Graz, there is never a moment when the Disruptors are not firing.

One of the few prototype backpack-mounted handheld device operators hurries by. He has one of the few new sets of "Green Beauties" that have been hastily constructed. That backpack looks like it gets pretty hot, really fast.

Oh no! There is a terrible explosion from the big North-East emplacement! Rings of electrically charged flames burst in strangely patterned circles from the vital, big gun. The gigantic battery that is so essential to this city's defense has apparently malfunctioned. Jagged yellow halos of lightning jump in perpendicular, sawtooth-edged orbits from the misfired battery as it erupts in a fiery sparking demise. There is bound to be a great loss of life with this tragedy. I hypothesize an arc was created and jumped inappropriately when a crewman made contact to discharge the weapon. This errant reach of unregulated voltage triggered the initiation process. These devices are devilishly dangerous to operate.

There are attacks all over the city. In an ominous fashion, though, they seem to be getting closer. Moreover, they seem to be heading for us.

A nearby Disruptor blast nearly knocks us off our feet.

Miss Plumtartt and I can see a green glow coming from the north of the city. The only large Disruptor is the one on the eastern range. It apparently has plenty of targets. The one gun we had in the north is destroyed, with, no doubt, tragic result. The desperation to get the new Disruptor into position is palpable. The glow of green to the north beyond the protective mountains is getting more intense.

Disruptor fire all over the city continues unabated. Miss Plumtartt and I are constantly on the move for safety.

There is a crack of Disruptor fire from the north! The

new emplacement made it in time!

Suddenly, there is a flash of light, followed by a deafening explosion, and we are all nearly knocked from our feet. The greatest explosion the world has ever known has just occurred on the other side of the towering Plabutsch Mountain.

I am not one to leave a friend in a bad spot, but I know it is time to get Miss Plumtartt out of Graz. The Voltage squads are all in full fledged fights. The two remaining major Disruptors are unable to regenerate their charges fast enough for the demand. Something with a green glow is approaching from the north and the east. Those unbelievable Disruptors, bigger than large houses, are unable to stop whatever it is that draws near.

Now I have Miss Plumtartt in tow.

We catch the Zeppelin "*Bella Donna*," just before she casts off her mooring lines. The prudent captain, perceiving the danger his ship is in, has made an unscheduled departure. Captain Stromberger is a forceful and competent commander of his ship. With the danger palpable, he has the presence of mind to get the "*Bella Donna*" aloft, plus the goodwill to catch us up, as he departs. Hands reach down for Miss Plumtartt.

I climb a rope.

The majestic airship gracefully leaves the ground and turns her nose westward. I through my beauties and Miss Plumtartt with her ability to see the creatures, watch in horrified fascination, as a grotesque worm, several city blocks in length, squirms past Plabutsch Mountain. The electric gun emplacement is unable to bear on the beast. She elects to focus her fire northward, at other targets.

The colossal grub turns to follow us. I have no doubt that it wants to kill Miss Plumtartt.

I sense that I have barely escaped with Miss Plumtartt's life.

I allow the Captain to view the scene below through my 'Green Beauties.' He is momentarily shocked, but then quickly recovers from the impossible sights revealed, and goes into action, exhorting his crew for more speed. I return my view to the scene below.

The creatures are definitely pursuing the dirigible. The massive Alpine worm rapidly increases its harried pace. Squirming towards us with all of its energy, the horror seems to exude a joyous excitement. It receives several Voltage Disruptor blasts, momentarily displaying its grotesque form in bright green outline around a black reflection. These Disruptor discharges slow, but do not stop, the beast that seems so intent on catching our rising Zeppelin.

Several long-legged insectile monsters scamper up the worm's back and launch themselves in a vain attempt to jump to our airship off of the worm's head. Vainly except for one. By spreading and flapping its carapace shell, this creature has managed to catch and latch onto the steering mechanisms at the rear of the Zeppelin. The over-sized green beetle is a tenacious monster! It resembles an enraged and voracious ladybug, but one with several sets of large pincers. We have no weapon on board to shoot the emerald-carapaced critter. The frantic thrashings of the ectoplasmic passenger clinging to our steerage induces a nauseating wobble to our flight. A Disruptor blast from the ground explodes the devil. That was a generous use of energy, considerately deployed on our behalf. I know that disruptor's stored energies were desperately needed on the ground. Whoever you are, thank you.

Captain Stromberger's ship continues, but with an oddly off-kilter orientation due to her damaged rudder.

Phosphorescent creatures pursue us on the ground, as we fly westward through the night.

The nocturnal horrors seem to burn away, like the morning dew, as daylight breaks.

Once he lands in Milan, Captain Stromberger is able to make the necessary repairs to his craft. The honourable Zeppelin commander wishes us Godspeed, and we continue our flight Westward in another airship, the *Edelweiss*, a marvelously appointed Austrian Zeppelin.

The Continent is too dangerous for us to stay. Our plans are to continue our flight, making for the French port La Rochelle on the English Channel, then from there to gain transport to England.

However, as night falls, our ship's commander, Captain Zachary Cook, after having been introduced to my goggles, continually alters his course southward. There is a lot of phosphorescent activity to the north, toward Paris. Continually being driven south, we eventually see the Spanish Pyrenees blocking further escape in that direction. Our pursuers are gaining on us. They now have flying insect monsters among them. We are beset by the gruesome harpies. The *Edelweiss* has no defenses for the invisible horrors. Our airship is failing as we pass the coast and are forced out over the Atlantic Ocean. We receive screaming reports over the communication tubes of our ship having been boarded and terrible monsters ravaging the great dirigible.

Captain Cook directs Miss Plumtartt and me to an unusual new addition to these modern aircraft, a safety glider. Miss Plumtartt and I are helped into this amazing device of balsa wood and light canvas. With precious little in the way of operating instructions we are launched. After a sickening freefall to gather speed, we level our craft of flight. Swiftly gliding away from the stricken craft, we see the lovely ship being ripped apart by winged gargoyles.

One vandalistic vulture views our departure. The hawk-eyed harpie makes to pursue us!

I aim our little glider out to sea. "Please hold still, Miss Plumtartt! This craft is difficult to manage already!"

Up, down, and side to side, we maneuver our escape glider, but the horrible harpy is stuck to our tail.

I see the lights of a ship at sea. I aim for this thread of hope.

We heavily collide with the boom sail at the stern of the ship. Miss Plumtartt, I, and our glider, go face first into the stiff cloth and our pursuer crashes into us directly behind. We all slide down the canvas and fall to the deck in a tangled heap of bodies and glider wreckage, but I have a hold of the winged devil before we hit the deck. Those wings are strong, and they are beating the heck out of me. The bat-winged gargoyle is in a murderous frenzy and I am in terrific combat with the ghastly monster. This bugger is strong, but his wings are unwieldy at this close range. In a wrestling contest, I've got the edge. I manage to get him in a bind. Once I get a winged arm of that sucker pinned, I draw the P.E.R.K., slashin' and juke'n him for all I'm worth.

I am able to defeat the living Gothic water spout with the ectoplasmic knife as we leave nightmare-infested Europe in our wake.

Chapter 28 - We Make Land, At Sea.

Persephone.

Once more, I am grateful for my bustle. It has proven itself yet again as a comfortable landing device.

I look up from the deck onto which we have fallen, to see we are in a ring of sailors. They are wide-eyed with astonishment as the invisible monster Mr. Temperance was fighting becomes visible to them.

The quick-thinking Mr. Temperance has no time for gawkers.

"Get me a bottle, or a cask, or something to collect this muck in!" he shouts to our audience. One of the seamen, with an air of authority about him, nods, at which several seamen hurry off and return quickly with vessels to collect the evaporating ectoplasmic substance that is necessary for Mr. Temperance's weapon construction.

Ship's crewmen disentangle us from the wrecked glider. "Good evening gentlemen! Ichabod Temperance here." In a smiling and engaging manner, my defender makes our introductions. Mr. Temperance's open and honest face is a striking contrast to the unusual manner of our boarding the clipper. "This is Miss Persephone Plumtartt. We should like to book passage to wherever you are bound."

Every hand on board, including the captain, was witness first to the death of the *Edelweiss* over the coast of France, and then the subsequent crash of our glider.

They saw Mr. Temperance fight an invisible foe, and then saw that foe made visible.

A heavyset man of stern countenance introduces himself as Captain Denver Hale, and the ship, the *Midnight Minnow.*

"Tell us your tale, son. After what we just saw, we're inclined to give credence to what ye say."

"Miss Plumtartt, would you mind laying out our little set of circumstances for these folks?"

"Why of course, Mr. Temperance."

I turn to our seabound hosts.

"Dear Captain Hale, you are truly our most timely savior. Unclean and supernatural forces have chased us to sea. Evil forces threaten the world and we require assistance in championing good over evil. May we please have passage aboard your providentially-sent vessel?"

"Dear child," says the gruff old seaman, his eyes brimming with tears. "Had we not seen that gruesome terror ourselves, we might have doubted ye. But, by my lights, we got a good two quarts of the disgusting creature's remains bottled up! Oh, we'll help ye' both all right with a free passage to Galveston, Texas. A U.S. city on the Gulf Of Mexico."

There is a murmuring of support from the crew that surrounds us.

Wonderful little cabins are made ready for our use. The next day, I am much recovered. The wind, the Sun and the smell of the open Ocean are really quite invigorating and refreshing.

What a lovely craft this *Midnight Minnow* is! She's absolutely beautiful to behold; how she runs before the wind!

"Miss Plumtartt," Mr. Temperance breaks in upon my thoughts in his quiet and bashful way, "perhaps we have rethought our trip to the Tibetan Plateau."

"Why yes, Mr. Temperance. It would seem that we have taken an unexpected detour."

"Yes, Ma'am. We got run out of Europe like a child spittin' watermelon seeds."

"Oh. Yes. Err. Rather. I see."

"Like the way I got run out of that posh French Clubbe."

"Quite."

"Like the way I got run out of the Strand Hotel when I poked Sir Henry Stanley and bent his beak."

"Why, Mr. Temperance! Was that you? Of course it was! The papers had said 'Mad American.' I should have realized!"

"Miss Plumtartt, I forgot myself momentarily, and I am very embarrassed at my uncouth behaviour. It is not my place to instill manners. If I may resume my observations?"

"Why certainly, my dear Mr. Temperance." I feel my heart glow with elation at the thought of my friend breaking that horrible man's nose. I do so hope he hit him hard enough. The papers had mentioned severe damage. Just another bit of joy this funny little fellow has brought me. How delightful!

My unexpected gaiety prompts an impulsive deed. With a gentle caress of his jaw, I hold his cranium stationary long enough to place a delicate kiss upon his bashful cheek.

His face runs quickly to red and then on without slowing down to a deep burgundy. His hazel eyes sparkle with fireworks that indicate great happiness within.

I privately confess, it does enchant my heart to see the dear boy so deeply moved by my simplest affections.

"Well, if the way to Tibet is blocked from this direction, we may need to make an adjustment in our itinerary." My mild-mannered hero explains. He seems to scarcely make contact with the deck of our ship as he is held buoyant at the lift of my simple kiss. "Maybe we should try to slip in the back door. Let's go to the top of the world via the Pacific Ocean."

"At this juncture, I fail to be able to mount an argument. Let us give the Pacific expanses a go then, shall we?"

"Our Skipper, Captain Hale, says the *Midnight Minnow* is bound for Galveston. It's an American port in the State of Texas. From Galveston we can travel overland across the North American Western territories, to the Pacific coast."

"Splendid, Mr. Temperance! A brief train ride, another 'clip' across the Pacific pond, and we are on the back doorstep to our destination. With a quick skip around the Asian Promontory, we shall land on the Asian continent at Calcutta. A swift trip up the Ganges, a portered ride up the slopes, and there we are, neat as a pin."

"Yes, Ma'am, 'neat as a pin.' Let's hope so. We'll need a quick stop over in Galveston. I have a few ideas floatin' for equipping ourselves."

I peruse a Spanish newspaper that the Captain had

recently acquired. The contents are dreadfully lowering.

There is a heartbreaking report that the Plumtartt Factory has been destroyed. Unseen forces smashed the great factory to the ground, some witnesses claim. No satisfactory explanation has been given. There are mounting numbers of "Ghost" attacks and desiccated corpses.

There are reports of "Ghost" attacks in Gibraltar.

Again, in Egypt, and on the Arabian Peninsula, a grisly trail of terror emerges.

To the best of my knowledge, there have been no attacks in the Americas.

I pray that we have left our tormentors in Europe.

CHAPTER 29 - THE GOOD OL' U. S OF A.

Ichabod

Galveston is a busy spot!

The city's harbor is crowded with ships of all description. Her bay teems with schooners, clippers, freighters and even warships of different nations.

Miss Plumtartt comments on the unusual green hue of the sea that is the Gulf of Mexico.

We bid our friends on the *Midnight Minnow* goodbye. If Captain Hale could, I believe he and his crew would be willing to see us through our coming adventures.

Impulsively, Captain Hale and I call to one another.

"Skipper!"

"Little buddy!"

Miss Plumtartt and I secure rooms at a towering edifice, the Beach Hotel on Galveston Island. This structure sails six stories into the air. Ornately laid out, she is the picture of comfort and elegance. The girl looks like a big, wooden cloud. I sure hope a big wind does not come along and blow her away someday.

I accompany Miss Plumtartt into town, where we separate on our different errands. She must shop for clothes, for we left Europe with nothing but what we were wearing and we lost all that we had upon us when we boarded the *Edelweiss*' glider. The poor girl has been without a parasol for weeks!

I am itching to get to a manufacturing shop. I search out various firearms, and hardware stores, in search of the right place to build my device. None are quite what I have in mind. I purchase the supplies I will be requiring at each location.

This world operates on supply and demand. Since the Revelatory Comet's passing, and the steep rise in the inventive community, so too have businesses arisen to provide the productive tinkers with the material of development. Cogs, wheels, pulleys, spindles, rods, chains, ropes, rivet and plate are now easily gained. Electrical components, just an engineer's dream a few short years ago, are now there for any layman to utilize.

I locate an especially industrious blacksmith. His barn is full of interesting devices that he has constructed. He is shoeing a horse, though, when I arrive. He has a good and gentle way with the animal. I appreciate this as I have a strong connection to animals and find that I like people who like animals.

In exchange for some stable boy work, he generously allows me access to his workshop.

In a few hours, I leave with a most astounding new tool in my arsenal. The ammunition was actually trickier to manufacture than the device itself.

When I return to the Beach Hotel, I find Miss Plumtartt on the expansive seaside veranda reading a pile of newspapers.

"Miss Plumtartt!" I excitedly impart. "Please inspect this device I have created."

"My word, Mr. Temperance, but this does appear to be a fearsome creation."

"Yes, Ma'am, I'm hopin' so."

"I am unhappy to report a change in the status of our

circumstances. It would seem by these many newspaper reports, that there has indeed been an infestation of the ghost's despicable presence in the afore-spared Americas. Rio de Janeiro and New York, South and North American cities, respectively, are now describing horrific attacks and sightings indicative of our foe's unclean manifestation."

"The Eastern seaboards of this hemisphere's two great continents are now affected by this pandemic of supernatural activity." Miss Plumtartt knowledgeably informs me.

I resolutely do not allow the wondrous feminine charms of Miss Plumtartt's prettiness distract me from her fact finding researches.

"Why have the abominations chosen these areas? What do they have in common with England and Graz? If their only aim is to find and kill me, or take the scroll, why are they now in the Americas? What is the connection?"

With our fresh kit of clothes and supplies, Miss Plumtartt and I set out across the American Southwest territories.

I should be ashamed of myself. The pride and joy I feel with my new invention at my side is sinful, but I cannot help it, especially with the curious looks that it and my ammunition cartridges on display in the loops of my holster receive. My features dimple a little with pleasure.

With Miss Plumtartt smartly set out in a new dress, bustle, and parasol, we depart our Texan island on the Galveston-Red River Rail Road. It is a heady feeling to be seen with the beautiful Miss Plumtartt. I'm not sure which I am more proud to be seen with, Miss Plumtartt or the fancy new weapon. Naw, I guess it's Miss Plumtartt.

It is a short ride to the mainland, and in Houston, we change lines onto the Greater Mid Texas Concern. This express line takes us to Austin City. I am happy to get Miss Plumtartt out of this crazy city: it is a wild place!

We pass over the Little River before we get to Waco. Riding on the flagship engine of the Cross, Tuttwiler and Polk railroad line, the "*Screaming Eagle*," we fly North, to Fort Graham.

From Chambers Creek, we begin a gradual ascent. This quickly turns to dizzying heights as we enter the first foothills of the Rockies. We skirt Caddo Peak, the train clinging to the hillsides. Vertical drops of hundreds of feet, are visible directly out our windows. The Royal Pass carries us past Bald Ridge and Church Mountain.

Once we are clear of the mountains, we make good time on the Grand Continental Western. Changing trains in Skilling, Texas, we board the Sawyer, Lane, and Taylor's American Consequential, Sunset Unlimited. Affectionately known as '*The Texas Fireball*,' also, '*Maddog's Meteor*,' it is claimed to be one of the fastest trains on the face of the Earth.

We cross the Rios Pecos at Independence Springs, and then rattle on to El Paso, via the Marco Pass. We continue West, across the wide, Mesilla Valley on the Southern Pacific Railway. This is the grand opening of this line, connecting the country from coast to coast, on the southern end of the Rockies. We are taking part in an exciting, historical event!

This opening of the second trans-continental railway line

of America will save us hundreds of miles of train travel north to the ill-fated Donner Pass. Otherwise, we would need to proceed by stagecoach, across dangerous Indian territories.

Unfortunately, when we attempt to purchase tickets on this historic opening, an ill-tempered ticket lady named 'Miss Barb' tells me 'there ain't no tickets to be had.' I inform Miss Plumtartt and she decides to take the procurement of passage into her own hands. An aura of command that I did not know resided within Miss Plumtartt seems to billow up from a depth of concealment. 'Miss Barb,' and her equally truculent cohort, a 'Miss April,' are unequivocally made aware that she requires those tickets and shall not be detoured. With a proprietary composure, she sweeps past the ticket ladies, going over their heads to their supervisor, a tall and meaty boy named Randolph Keith. He is able to make the proper arrangements for Miss Plumtartt. I don't think he noticed me. People don't notice me much, no how, but especially when I'm around Miss Plumtartt. That Miss Plumtartt! If I didn't know better, I'd swear she was flirtin' with that boy to get us fixed up.

Aboard the *Sunset Limited*, we are diverted most charmingly by a handsome man of the cloth, the Right Reverend Alonzo Dolomite. He is a strongly built coloured gentleman with a shaven head, dressed in a clergyman's black frock. We enjoy this leg of our journey due in great part to our meeting this wonderful fellow.

"Reverend Dolomite" pronounced Persephone Plumtartt, "you are quite the raconteur, and you give our spirits a much needed lift! I must say, I suspect that you are one shepherd who would attend to the needs of your flock most assiduously"

"You are a perceptive woman, Persephone. I would be honored if you were to visit me in my new habitat, for I intend to build a church in Los Angelos. I would even allow you to bring Itchy-bod along."

Reverend Dolomite loudly and enthusiastically regales Miss Plumtartt and me with his interesting stories in his high blown evangelical oratorical style. These charming tales are accompanied by frequent injections of an exclamatory "Yes!"(pronounced, ah-yeh-ess-ahhh) punctuating his enthralling tales.

We disembark our train in Tanner, Arizona, to stretch and walk about while the train takes on fuel and water. I am just ruminating upon our fortunate smooth sailing so far - a foolish curse of our luck - when Miss Plumtartt touches the side of her head and appears to suffer from a pain there.

"I find myself in some distress, Mr. Temperance. A headache of quite monumental proportions has seated itself in the front of my cranium. I am becoming as vaporish as my elderly Aunt Matilda with her ubiquitous *sal volatile*." Miss Plumtartt tries to bravely laugh off her discomfort, but I sense it is very troubling to her. "However, I wish for a healthy snifter of Remy Martin to accompany *my* violet compress!"

Miss Plumtartt gives a start with a sharp intake of breath. Looking out to the desert stretching off into infinity to our North, a disturbing blankness of expression comes over her fair features.

"Did you hear that, Mr. Temperance?"

"Ma'am? I didn't hear nothing."

"I am sure I heard a voice call to me."

"Miss Plumtartt? Ma'am? Are you feeling all right?"

Miss Plumtartt gives another sharp inhalation of breath.

"There it is again."

"I didn't hear nothing, Ma'am."

She does not hear me.

"Ma'am? Miss Plumtartt?"

Miss Plumtartt stares out into the desert, North of Tanner.

I move directly into her field of vision.

"Hello? Miss Plumtartt? Are you sure you're feelin' okay?"

The train whistle gives a brisk double toot to signal its imminent departure. Miss Plumtartt does not hear the signal. The girl is mesmerized, unable to hear the train whistle or anything else around her.

"Please Ma'am, wake up, Miss Plumtartt. The train's pulling out and we need to be on it."

Miss Plumtartt starts walking towards the shimmering desert.

The train's engineer sees what's up. He sounds his steam whistle with emphasis and rings the train's bell.

Reverend Dolomite calls to us to return.

Miss Plumtartt walks straight out into the unforgiving wastes.

I am powerless to dissuade her.

Dropping her parasol, she uncharacteristically shambles onto the burning sands.

I have no choice but to follow and waste my breath on unheard pleads for her to stop.

Several minutes later, about a mile behind, I hear the train leave.

We are walking into desolation.

"Miss Plumtartt! Please! This is, I beg your pardon, Ma'am,... intolerable!"

The Tanner Station has long since passed from view. Dusk is upon us and we are still walking straight out into the desert.

Miss Plumtartt is in a trance-like state. Stumbling forward without a look to, or care for, her surroundings. She stares straight ahead, and walks onward steadily.

Fortunately, it is a clear night. The Moon and stars light our way.

Even I start to tire. I know Miss Plumtartt is long past exhaustion, yet somehow she pushes herself on.

I see something. Directly ahead of us is a spark of light. This must be the poor girl's destination. I carry her forward. She slips into unconsciousness in my arms.

I approach a small camp fire. A solitary man is waiting.

I carefully place Miss Plumtartt to the ground.

An Indian is the the campfire's only companion. Even though he is sitting down, I can tell he is a man of immense size. He calmly observes me without a flicker of movement. Sharp, black eyes, from a wizened, though inscrutable face survey me.

Several long moments pass.

I decide to break the ice.

"Good evening, sir. I do hope that we are not intruding upon you. My name is Ichabod Temperance. My resting companion is Miss Plumtartt. It would seem that she finds herself compelled to maintain a rendezvous with you this evening. May we be of service?" I inquire.

His features remain impassive. Nothing can crack that wooden countenance. However, a spark, way down deep in those black eyes, betrays a trace of humour.

"I too, felt compelled," says the imposing Native. "I am Chief Running Blind Thunderpaw. My spirit would not rest without giving this girl my guidance."

Miss Plumtartt stirs. She looks to the big Chief.

"Child of destiny, you must complete a great quest. You require instructions to complete your tasks."

"What are my instructions?" manages Miss Plumtartt.

"I cannot tell you, because I do not know. You must go and seek them on your own."

"How do I do that?" asks the exhausted woman.

"Drink this," says the wizened shaman.

It's been about ten minutes since we drank the elixir the big Indian presented. Miss Plumtartt had already taken a big gulp of the juice before I could stop her.

Big Chief Thunderpaw says that if want to go with her, then I must drink the horrible muck as well. I don't think I've got a choice. I take a big gulp of the rancid tasting, foul smelling brew.

The Medicine Man speaks in a strange manner.

He says that we will go on a journey, but to just sit tight, because the journey will come to us.

The stars are gettin' all squirmy. They twinkle and wane more vividly. They forego their normal positioning to chase one another about.

The Indian is gone.

The desert stretches out into infinity. So too, does my consciousness.

Perfectly laid cartographer's lines stretch out in all directions, mapping a plain, plane. The featureless landscape is bordered in odd, dancing, geometric constructions.

There is a large fox.

A huge rabbit towers over Miss Plumtartt.

More enormous creatures sit quietly around us.

Wolf, hawk, gopher, and lion.

We look into the fire.

YOU MUST COMPLETE YOUR TASKS

No one speaks. No one has spoken. It is just "heard."

TALISMAN
FIND IT
IN YOUR WORLD
YET
NOT OF YOUR WORLD
ORB OF PROTECTION
MUST FIND
MUST NOT FAIL
darkness.

Chapter 30 - Am I Awake Or Dreaming?

Persephone.

I...

must...

go...

to...

him...

I...

must...

must...

go...

...

...

fire...

the man I seek...

magic potion... drink...

acrid, bitter, viscous...

I

descend...

not into darkness..

into some place grey and featureless, except for...

Spirits of our world...

They speak to me...

They burden me...

yes.

The Talisman.

In our world, yet not of our world...

of our world...

yet,...
not in our world...
....
We must...
obtain it...
or all ...
will fall ...
...to the....
DARKNESS.

My head feels as if it is being crushed beneath the keel of a Plumtartt manufactured dreadnought.

Where am I?

"Here ya go, Miss Plumtartt, try and drink a little water, Ma'am."

The lids of my eyes do not want to cooperate with my instructions to part. I am forced to open my eyes manually. I am blinded by the Sun's glare, but I force myself through the thick, hazy curtains of consciousness to gain my bearings: I am recumbent in the arms of a worried Mr. Temperance.

A seemingly endless yellow expanse rolls before me. A sea of sand.

Oh. Yes. The desert. The dream.

That was not a dream!

Mr. Temperance is giving me a drink of water. I try not to sputter and waste the precious liquid. He is covered with tiny particles of sand, even in his eyelashes. To the east, the sun has risen a little less than halfway to its zenith position, yet already, the elements oppress mercilessly.

"I fear we have missed our train, Mr. Temperance."

"Yes, Ma'am."

"I've gotta pretty fair sense of what direction to travel. With any luck, we oughta find some train tracks that'll lead us to somewhere's."

I can only follow, maintaining a facade of stoic resolution, as we wander interminably.

Eventually, we do indeed find the train tracks.

Out of the sand's bright mirror of that oppressive, swollen sun, the light of the settled surrounding rays seems weak, grey. Perhaps that is why I look without seeing, pass without comprehension, as in a daze we continue our trek. It is some time before I come to realize that Mr. Temperance is carrying me.

A soothing coolness envelops my face. I open my eyes to darkness and rough texture. A cool, wet, towel covers my face. I weakly pull this aside to find myself in a hotel's furnished room. Mr. Temperance has delivered me to civilization's care. An exhausted Mr. Temperance sits in a chair, having fallen asleep in a no doubt uncomfortable position as he attempted to watch over me before succumbing to the irresistible pull of sleep.

Only the slightest moan escapes my lips, but it is enough to have the poor man bolt upright and leap to my side.

"Miss Plumtartt! Are you all right?" His pleading eyes reveal many hours of worry.

"Yes, Mr. Temperance, I do believe that I am."

He lets out a genuine gush of relief.

"Gee whiz, I sure am glad to hear that, Ma'am."

"I think you may have the liberty of some rest yourself, sir."

"Yes, Ma'am."

With that he removes his tweed jacket, and sets it on the chair. Then he discards the pistol belt, containing the remarkable pistol and its mysterious ammunition. These are placed on the bureau, next to his derby hat.

"May I remove my boots, Ma'am?"

"Socks and all, Mr. Temperance. Please feel free to strip your feet to the skin. I shall not faint, I assure you."

"Yes, Ma'am."

The removal of the chap's enormous boots is not an enterprise to be entered upon lightly, but he does so with an expectation of pedal alleviation.

With feet disrobed, he rolls his jacket into a tube and uses it as a pillow as he stretches out on the floor across the doorway.

"Are you sure you will be all right there, Mr. Temperance?"

"Yes, Ma'am. If anybody tries to come into the room, they gotta get over me. Good night, Miss Plumtartt."

And with the closing of his eyes the tired boy is immediately fast asleep.

We arise in a few hours to resume our journey. A premonition of danger's return hurries us along.

Somehow, my clever companion obtains seating for us on the next conveyance West; our destination is the small town in California that Reverend Dolomite mentioned. With a couple of additional train changes, we are finally on our way into Los Angelos (this little town in California has sprung up, now that the railroad is open.).

'The City of Angels,' is it? Mr. Temperance and I are

speaking of how we are both looking forward to seeing the West Coast, when I involuntarily burst out with a small cry.

A familiar dread sense of loathing spasms through my frame.

A thud passes through the train as if something heavy has made an unscheduled boarding. This is followed by two more substantial thuds in quick succession. The train continues to sway in its swift travels, with the evening passenger additions that have joined our trip.

It is no Angel that tears through the wood at the rear of the train car.

It is a greenish, phosphorescent horror reminiscent of Dante's Inferno.

Welcome to Hades.

The game is afoot.

CHAPTER 31 - ERROR AND TRIAL.

Ichabod

Pushing Miss Plumtartt ahead of me, I maneuver her to the front of the car, staying between her and whatever has just boarded the train. I put on and spin up the "Beauties."

Loud heavy crashes follow us, getting closer fast. A monster walks straight through the steel parts of the rear of the train. The creature has to force its way through the wooden sections. I have seen this many times, at least, but it never ceases to amaze me, how these creatures pass through metal as if their very atoms slip through the molecules of the steel, yet the wood of the door explodes at their touch. But this is no time for idle intellectual speculation. Given its enormous size and strength, the monster is quite capable of tearing through just about anything.

The brute is rather like the Indian myth of Sasquatch, but this aberration, standing upon its hind legs, is more reptilian. It has an extra set of arms and salivates extraordinary amounts of drool from its immense slathering gate/maw.

It spies Miss Plumtartt. The horrible thing practically bursts with an unnerving laughter, in a most excited twittering, flecking its foul spittle in all directions.

I am a bundle of conflicting emotions:

-Repulsed by the horrible monster.

-Terrified that it could reach and harm Miss Plumtartt.

and,

-Curious as to whether this device I have crafted and have so much hope and pride in will actually work.

{{{BUH-WHOOMP. POW!!!}}}

{{{BOOM!}}}

Four sounds have been created by the dangerous handgun. First, the two-stage charging process, then, the discharge of the weapon, and then, finally, happily, the devastating explosion of the horrible monster - a flash of viridian - the monster and the round of electrified resin detonate as one, disintegrating the entire rear of the train car.

With the blast of the exploding monster having taken out the back of our train car, the rest of the subsequent cars seem to be connected to the front and engine by a thread. The back half of our train car, and the first half of the next, are completely atomized and dispersed in the winds of this speeding train.

Looking back across the gap of the train car's missing spaces, on the remaining roof of the following railcar, I can see two more monsters looking down at me.

One jumps across to our car. It lands on the roof and runs to the front of the cab, over our heads.

I go out the ruined back of the train cab. As I am climbing up, the second creature is leaping across. It clatters across the rooftop, turns to meet me, but trips. Its foot has passed through a steel beam. Its inability to make contact with the metals of our world has finally worked in my favour. Wood splinters fly about as the vaguely saurian monster attempts to free its foot protruding into the train.

I calmly aim the P.G.D.D.

{{{BUH}}}-whirrrr-klik...klik...klik...

The device fails.

Dang!

That is disappointing. I was really counting on that weapon. It worked well the first time.

No time to worry about that. I pull the emerald blade of P.E.R.K., and I am all over that murderous fiend with his foot stuck through the roof of the train.

"Oh, no!" As I deliver the death plunge of my blade, it is caught fast in the rib bones of the monster. His brother, the first creature to leap to our car, comes back to get me while I am weaponless. Until he realizes that he has an opening to get Miss Plumtartt.

I abandon the blade.

I run and leap to meet him with a flying Savate kick. His thoughts of the incomparable Miss Plumtartt have been interrupted. *I kick your face!* The overly large fellow receives a big boot to the mush. And it really is a mushy face.

I remember my Savate training.

Strangely reminiscent of some Russki ballet I saw one time, I run, and jump, but with a spin this time to develop all the torque I can manage, to send a tremendous Mud Pounder-enhanced kick to the freeloading critter.

We both fall to the roof of the train, scrambling to stay atop the swaying conveyance. Just as we get to our feet, I charge the beast and carry us both off the front of the railcar.

We tumble to the coal bin feeder. I hop down to the Engineer's platform, with an idea starting to brew.

The horror dives at me, slinging saliva as he angrily rattles away in an enraged language.

I put a foot up and catch him in the gut, my hands to his paws. Falling backwards to the platform, and using his weight and momentum against him, I kick out with all my might, to propel him up and over my head into the train's roaring coal furnace. He passes through the metal of the train's oven without contact. However, apparently, flames, fire, and coal, are elements of this world with which the creature does interact.

A strange organic smell follows, reminiscent of burning algae.

Its unearthly cries get no pity from me.

Chapter 32 - P.G.D.D.

Persephone.

"It worked, Miss Plumtartt: an unqualified success!"

"I beg your pardon, Mr. Temperance, but I was under the impression that the device had failed you."

We sit at a roadside cafe, not unlike the one in Paris.

By mutual agreement, we thought it best to let the railroad authorities work things out for themselves as to what happened to their train. We have slipped away.

"Well, on the second activation of the device, certainly, but wasn't it thrilling when, on first ignition, the weapon did work?"

"That is true, Mr. Temperance. I confess, there was an impressive retort from the gun. And it was followed by an equally satisfying combustion of the unwanted visitor."

The P.G.D.D.

Pee Gee Double Dee

"My Plasmo-Gasmic Discharge Device."

Involuntarily, I spit a bit of tea in an uncharacteristic sputtering show of shock.

"I beg your pardon!" I blurt with my eyes bursting from their sockets.

"My Plasmo-Gasmic Discharge Device."

"Why do you tremble so, Miss Plumtartt? Are you chewing the inside of your mouth, to keep from laughing? I must confess, Ma'am, I do not always understand women."

I keep my face turned from Mr. Temperance.

"I'm gonna fix it, Ma'am," says my companion, with some consternation, but I hide my face lest it betray my amusement.

"I have the distinct impression that you are having me on, somehow, Ma'am."

"Oh, no, Mr. Temperance, not at all, sir."

"My pistol does not seem to be the only victim of our latest trans-dimensional encounter. Your poor hat is in a terrible state, Ma'am."

"Oh, pooh. So it is. You will be happy to know, however, that it is due to my own brave sacrifice. When the brute with his foot stuck through the roof began to disintegrate, I had no other vessel at hand in which to catch the dripping ichor. I freely donate this chapeau to Earth's defense."

"That was some quick thinkin' there, Miss Plumtartt. We shall secure rooms for the evening and make our subsequent plans in the morning, Ma'am."

"Jolly good, Mr. Temperance."

CHAPTER 33 - RESTLESS.

Ichabod

As we have finally arrived in Los Angelos, we get ourselves safely ensconced in fine accommodations.

"Goodnight, Miss Plumtartt."

"Mr. Temperance."

We retire to our rooms.

However, I find myself unable to rest.

My mind is buzzing with all the excitement I've been thrust into, I guess.

So much is happening so fast.

The city is calling to me.

I've been cooped up in one train after another.

The city is calling to me.

Maybe I'll just step outside to smoke my pipe.

The city is calling to me.

I'll just go for a walk around the building.

The city is calling to me.

I don't want to get too far away from Miss Plumtartt.

The city is calling to me.

The smell of the Pacific is in the air.

The city is calling to me.

I'll stay close by.

The city is calling to me.

I just want to look around a little.

The city is calling to me.

There's such an unusual architecture here in the west. The local building material is something called "adobe." As I branch out into town, it is easy to see where the "old" Los

Angelos ends, and the "new," begins. From the low, wide, structures of some age, I pass into wooden clapboard buildings. This town is as old as dirt in one spot, and green as a cabbage leaf in another. The paint is barely dry on these tall, fancy halls, each one heavily hawked, promising fun and excitement.

They call to me.

That dance hall seems pretty inviting.

It seems to call to me.

I really want to go in there.

It seems to call to me.

"The GoldenBear Emporium" looks like it's a popular place. I manage to get in, though a fierce doorman surveys me closely. Hair and eyes as black as the darkest night, Mr. Herold gives me a good once over. If one does not pass his scrutinizing inspection, one does not enter the Emporium.

This place is a party! It has three stages of acts. On one end, you got a couple of dandies in tuxedos singing in a manner that reminds me of an ocean of molasses. There's a stage full of dancing girls in the middle. Those little ol' cuties are dancing for all their worth, bless their little hearts. And then you got a little stage opposite the crooners. There dances a little Mexican vamp, a "Senorita Bandita" ("She steals your heart.").

The GoldenBear Emporium is packed with men of all description. Men of the sea are mixed in with cattlemen herders. Nowadays folks call 'em "Cowboys." There's high stakes gambling at tables stocked with steely eyed men in fancy duds. Men of Spanish descent from Mexico sit playing with farmers, ranch hands, and lots more assorted fellas of disparate description and unknown background.

Plus the girls!

Lots of pretty girls!

Girls! Girls! Girls!

Dang! They're everywhere! And most of 'em are running around with their fanciest underwear showing! They sure are purty flirty and charming.

There seems to be a lot of traffic on the stairs, concerning the girls, upstairs.

I am drawn towards the stairs.

As I make my way towards the stairs a large woman of Indian descent blocks my path.

"May I help you, sir?"

What a strikingly beautiful, yet fierce woman this is. I can tell that a warrior's blood is flowing just below the surface.

"I want to go upstairs."

"My name is Abigail GoldenBear. I own the GoldenBear Emporium. Why do you want to go upstairs?"

"I want to see Okzana."

Why did I say that?

She snaps into an even more acute examination of my face.

After a few moments of thought, her onyx eyes never blinking, she tells me, "go on up."

Suddenly, I am trepidatious. I don't really want to go upstairs, but something is making me think I do. This whole situation does not feel right, but I seem to be powerless to stop my slow tread up the stairs.

I've never moved so slowly in my life. After a few steps I turn to look back. Miss Abigail GoldenBear is watching me make my tortuous ascent.

I resume my journey up the Stairway to Heck.

Lead weights at the ends of my legs make the climb difficult.

I have a bad feeling.

What am I doing here?

I keep walking. Normally I skip up and down stairs two or three steps at a time, but right now I'm moving slower than molasses going uphill on a cold, January morning.

Why did I leave the hotel?

I feel as if I am walking in deep, thick mud. The clinging suction of the imaginary muck makes every plodding step an eternity.

I should go back. Why don't I turn and leave right now?

I stop in front of a door.

Why did I come to this door?

"Come in." The velvet, feminine command cannot be resisted.

Opening the door, I enter a room, soft in light and soft in its furnishings. The bedchamber is as soft, inviting, and deadly as the welcome sleep that comes in an odourless, gas-filled coal mine.

Taffeta tidings amongst feminine frippery adorn the sumptuous boudoir.

"Good evening, Ich, a, bod," purrs a thick, syrupy, Baltic accent. "I am so happy you have come to see me."

Rising from a vanity, a ... very ... majestically female form is backlit against a lady's dressing screen. With hair piled high, the shapely shadow ever so slowly slinks from behind its place of concealment.

"Great Googly Moogly," I mutter.

She is stunningly beautiful. Such female proportions I

would not have thought possible. Such a form I could not imagine. Her eyes hungrily take me in. With more sensuality than I would have thought possible on the whole planet, she moves to me.

"Ich . a . bod," her Lithuanian accent is incredibly enthralling. With a panther's deadly gait, her tightly corseted, barely dressed body insinuates itself ever closer, slinking like a big cat trying not to frighten its prey.

"You have come to me."

I should not be here. She should not know my name, nor I hers. This is wrong.

"Ichabod," she wraps me in a sheer, black lace embrace.

"Gulp."

"Kiss, . . . me . . . "

"Gulp!"

"Kiss! . Me! . "

"GULP!"

"Gee whiz, Ma'am. I really shouldn't even be here."

"Kiss! Me!"

Her eyes are shining bright. Her mouth searches for me eagerly.

(! ! !)

The door bursts open. Abigail GoldenBear has knocked it off its hinges.

My amorous seductress hisses at Miss GoldenBear.

The door bustin' regal lookin' Indian woman clutches an amulet and begins a low chant.

The seductive, lingerie-wearing vixen shrieks. Something in her face has a slightly non-human look to it.

"Herold! Get Keef and the Irishman!" commands Abigail GoldenBear to her security/doorman who had followed on her heels. He bolts.

Suddenly, the overbuilt, underclad, black haired Baltic Beauty has me by the throat. Good grief! Her grip is unbelievable! I am being choked into unconsciousness.

The owner of the Emporium begins to chant. It's low and slow at first, but now it is rising with intensity.

On hearing the chants from Miss GoldenBear, the vexed voluptuous Latvian vamp vehemently throws me aside as she unleashes an unearthly scream. Gasping for air, I see her give an apparent psychic headbutt to Abigail.

Miss GoldenBear stumbles.

Just then, two men crash into the room. One is a tall, strongly built man of authority. The other is compact, but he has an air of feistiness.

The BeloRussian Bombshell stretches her arms...

and stretches her arms...

and stretches her arms until they split into many squirmy appendages.

A dozen tentacles or so shoot out in four directions. Miss Abigail, I, and the two unfortunate gentlemen that have joined us are clutched by the loathsome limbs, their rubbery intimacy unbound.

I and my would-be rescue team are all being impossibly thrown about the room in a violent manner.

I am held against a wall, while the big man has been swept off his feet. The smaller of the two is being banged up and down against the ceiling. Miss Abigail is being choked and smothered by the hated tentacles. The evil vixen laughs most horridly.

BANG! BANG! BANG! BANG! BANG! BANG!

The upside down fellow on the ceiling has just unloaded a very powerful revolver into the octo-woman.

The horrible girlie is staggered, but quickly rallies.

"Sit down, lady!" roars the big man from the floor, as he pulls the rug out from under her.

This action is enough to loosen the gruesome lady's hold on me. I get to Miss GoldenBear, and cut the offending tentacles with P.E.R.K.

The monstrous would-be temptress does not like having her tentacles cut. She cracks another ear-splitting scream.

But the big man has pulled his weapon and unloads it into the monstrous woman.

She is staggered, but still does not go down.

The two men make to reload, but she strikes, pinning both of them.

I go to renew my attack, but she catches me, as well.

Miss GoldenBear resumes her chant.

The squid/siren lady falters.

Cutting myself free of the suckery limbs, I press my attack.

The blade sinks home.

The concurrently captivating and blood-curdling creature cackles.

"Vhee have already vhun. As soon as you left her alone, Meese Pluhmtar-r-r-tt vhuz ripe for assassination. By now chee is already dead."

The loathsome/lovely Lithuanian's partially gorgeous, partially grotesque form, stiffens, turns green, and melts.

I am bolting from the room to get back to Miss Plumtartt, when I hear a disheartening cry. Scores of horses outside in the street are screaming in mad panic and terror.

I pull up and spin the "Beauties."

A swarm of phosphorescent mosquitoes as big as lobsters fly in through the swinging front doors. Actually, they do kinda look more like lobsters with wings than mosquitoes. I pass the goggles to the little Irishman. He is taken aback, but then passes the goggles to his big friend. His face turns gray. Apparently, Miss GoldenBear is able to perceive the invasion without the aid of my goggles.

"Gimme those!" I say as I snatch the "Green Beauties" back. The disgusting swarm circles the crowd of revelers. The musicians are shushed and stopped from their performance.

All the gambling, drinking, and frisky floor flirtin' comes to a quiet conclusion.

The dancing girls on the stage stop their enthusiastic high stepping as they too sense the strange danger that has entered the saloon.

People can sense - no, they can hear - the swarm. Tiny flickers of half-seen movement almost gives an idea for the position of the buzzing cloud to the naked eye.

A nameless dread holds the room in its cold clutches.

The disturbingly vicious hum of invisible source circles the girls on stage. The barely dressed girlies cling to each other for support. The spinning swarm reaches a howling crescendo and then drops on the hapless ladies.

The dancing girls try to fight off the parasites in blind terror, desperate and harried, moved with primal defenses.

The disgusting monsters sink into their victims.

The girls are seized in a palsied fit.

They settle back down with a look of evil delight on their adorable faces.

The beautiful girls shriek in unison with a blood curdling cackle. They leap from the stage like so many energetic teenagers, supporting their high school sporting team, except that these little heifers mean to bull their way straight through the Emporium.

Trashing tables, chunking chairs, and pitching patrons, the fringe trimmed, underwear wearing, perky stampede charges the hapless crowd in a billowing cloud of drinks, poker chips, and smashed furniture. Senorita Bandita jumps up and down, screaming. The tuxedo cats have disappeared.

The frisky tornadoe makes to cut us off.

Our lot meets theirs at the bottom of the stairs in a full tilt fight.

I hesitate. Truly, it goes against my nature to strike a woman.

With a bright and playful twinkle in her eye, the cutie-pie I engage has no such compunction about hitting me.

Never before have I had an opponent smell so nice, but hit so hard, as this little gal clocks me square in my left eye.

I can't save Miss Plumtartt from a sitting position!

"Sorry, Ma'am!"

I sink a mud pounder deep into her gut, as I cannot bring myself to hit that adorable, little ol' face.

There is a flash of crimson light combined with a loud boom!

Red smoke fills the air.

Miss Abigail GoldenBear stands at the head of the stairs. A more regal posture I have never seen. She chants loudly in a strong voice. The smoke seems to have cleansed the room somehow.

The possessed dancing girls shiver, and fall to the ground.

I stomp the nasty parasites as they crawl out of the girls.

CHAPTER 34 - BAD JUJU.

Persephone.

"No!" I cry, coming awake.

My heart is racing with fear as I feel an immense, and unclean, presence.

"Mr. Temperance!" I call. He is within easy earshot, in the next room.

I gather a robe around me and call out again to my silent defender, as I step through our connecting door, "Mr. Temperance!?"

A man lounges on the bed. Not Mr. Temperance, this man is splendidly dressed.

"Good evening, Mademoiselle Plumtartt," oozes this snaky villain. "So nice to meet you, at last."

He leaps from the bed. Skeletally thin, he simultaneously sweeps off his overly fancy top hat, and his blue-hued spectacles of many function, and bows.

"Jean-Jacques Bhauh-Buuhm," states the instantly unlikable man. "At your service."

"Where is Mr. Temperance?"

"Your champion has abandoned you, Mademoiselle," says the grinning devil. His eyes, sunken deep within their black rimmed sockets, sparkle with fiendish delight.

I am gripped with the deepest despair.

"We can do this the easy way, most delightful. Or we can proceed in the hard way, most distasteful. The choice is entirely up to you."

I am gripped in crippling panic. A sense of wrongness exudes from this man. A foul emanation of evil pours off his thin frame in almost visible waves.

I fall back into my room, shutting the door and throwing the lock.

Monsieur Bhauh-Buuhm viciously stomps in the wooden barrier.

I strike him about the head with my parasol, to no great effect.

He laughs, most disturbingly.

I pull my hat down about his head.

This brings about a great effect!

The leering scoundrel is now howling in pain and frustration! He is unable to dislodge my hat from his face and head, which is causing him great distress and discomfort. Thrash and scream as he might, he is caught in the hat.

It must be the ectoplasm that I retrieved on behalf of Mr. Temperance, back at the train! Of course! My hat is full of the toxic goo, and it really seems to disagree with my uninvited intruder.

My frugal friend's thrifty habits have proven effective once again.

I depart my room for the open hallway. I hear my visitor's cries of pain and anger behind me. He has apparently freed himself.

I fly to the central stairs. Turning at the landing, I am compelled to look back to where my antagonist stands shrieking.

My tormentor has stopped at the balustrade. Making a sign of ill portent with his hands, and uttering the profane words of a lost language, he calls to an unseen evil in a summoning manner.

Outside, I hear the pitiful cries of terrified horses as something responds to his beckoning.

Six disgusting horrors, in the size and shape of aardvarks, but more insectile, scuttle in through the front doors. They seem to get their direction from the despicable Monsieur Bhauh Buuhm.

"Look out! Flee for your lives!" I call.

I get the attention of everyone in the lobby, but they make no sense of my words, as they see nothing to be afraid of.

The abominable bugs make for a group of friends. They briefly, but futilely, fight an unseen foe, before succumbing to their intimate invasion.

They shake.

They levitate.

They give up an ectoplasmic ghost from their depleted corpses.

These ghosts coalesce into monsters.

Six newly formed brutes land in the sumptuous lobby of our hotel. They stand as tall as a man, but they are reptilian of skin and form though viciously avian in manner. They put me in mind of a new theory of the ancient species of Earth.

I believe I have heard them referred to as "Thunder Lizards."

These give a terrible roar. It shakes the entire

structure!

Like grotesque chickadees, they oddly hop about the lobby in my pursuit. Their large heads twisting back and forth in a curiously birdlike manner. The long snouts allow for enormous mouths that bristle with rows of fangs dripping with poison.

"Unh!" something within me gives a sharp twinge.

An electrical current snaps up and down my form.

"Ahh!" I cry as a red beam of light blasts from my palm. A sphere of energy forms to shoot away and envelop a monster. The lizard bird disintegrates in a blast of ecto particles.

"Unh, Ahh!" Another round of red rounded retribution issues forth to dispel another fearsome fiend.

I falter: suddenly I am drained. I can no longer offer resistance.

Four slavering beasts from a time forgotten hesitate, for they do not want to be blasted away like their comrades. Quickly ascertaining that I am defenseless, they rally once again as brave birdies and close upon me.

Bhauh-Buuhm's voice mocks me, "I would have preferred the easy way."

"Please,".."no,"... "have mercy!"

Bhauh-Buuhm is convulsed with a seizure of sinister snickering.

"It is out of my hands, Mademoiselle. You have sealed your own fate."

The fetid breath of these lizard-birds is upon me.

Nothing can save me!

"It was your choice, Mademoiselle. C'est la vie. To you, I bid adieu. To my associates, I say, bon appetit."

CHAPTER 35 - REUNION.

Ichabod.

How did I end up so far from the Hotel?

I am running for all I am worth. I got to get back to the Hotel and save Miss Plumtartt!

Please! Please! Please! Be all right!

Why did I leave? I shall never forgive myself if anything has happened to that dear girl.

Miss GoldenBear's friends, the big man and the little guy, are staying with me. For whatever reason, they have taken an interest.

We fly in the front doors of our hotel. There she is, surrounded by monsters. I never miss a beat. I Savate kick the one trying to take a chunk out of Miss Plumtartt into next week.

"Mr Temperance!"

"You are running with a rough crowd these days, Miss Plumtartt."

I calls back toward the entranceway for my comrades. The tall, and powerfully built man of frightful countenance, and the smaller, but strongly and compactly muscular man, are pretty swift on the uptake as concerns fighting inter-dimensional invisible monsters.

"We got four big ones in here, boys!"

With my amazing goggles, I am able to point out the invisible saurian creatures to my brave/foolhardy companions.

"There. There. There, and there."

In an impressive show of strength, the bigger fellow

uproots a large, potted palm, for use as a weapon.

His partner arms himself with a brass hat stand.

Boy, howdy! We may very well have slobberknocker of a fight on our side, now!

I continue my attack on the beast that nearly took a piece out of Miss Plumtartt, whilst the three remaining lizards turn their reptilian attentions on our new allies.

Attaboy! By swinging the unpotted palm, our friend with the tree cleverly uses the end with the roots to mark the animals with dirt and mud. One creature is no longer invisible to them!

"I got him!"

This comes from the second defender. He swings the hat stand in a 360° arc for murderous momentum.

It is unfortunate that he is unaware of the curious quality these creatures possess: an inability to interact with metals in our dimension.

The brass hat stand passes through the monster lizard without contact, landing a devastating impact upon the tall fellow that is fighting on our side.

"Excuse me! Young man!" Miss Plumtartt calls. "Try something more organic," she encourages. "Also, you should dodge right now. You are about to be bitten."

Using the heavy P.E.R.K., I complete my grisly work with the first six foot snapping turtle, and then join my companions in their dangerous struggle.

The fierce face of our comrade who received the hat stand blow is terrible to behold. His anger at his partner is unleashed upon the poor monsters. Like a spring tornadoe from my home in Alabama, this giant goes into a frenzy, swinging the tropic plant. In short order, he has got dirt and mud on all three of the nasty beasts. I now safely set aside my precious, though now unnecessary, goggles. I am able to rather adroitly, if unpleasantly, dispatch a filthy combatant with the emerald blade. The frustrated, smaller combatant has gained a leg and arm hold upon his creature. Affixed to his back, the chagrined fellow is riding the hopping bird-lizard around the lobby. The big man is apparently trying to force-feed the palm tree to his unlucky recipient.

With my comrades holding the featherless turkeys pinned, I do not have much difficulty in dealing death to these chirping captives. Soon, four green carcases become visible to my fellow victors. The monsters' corpses soon begin to crack, steam, and disintegrate.

"Oh, bother! Mr. Temperance, the man who is responsible for bringing us these horrid creatures has eluded us. Pooh! It is only now that I realize that the despicable Jean-Jacques Bhauh Buuhm, has escaped, sir."

"Sorry, Ma'am."

"Tut, tut, sir, we have things to attend to. Bottle the quickly dissolving remains, Mr. Temperance."

"Yes, Ma'am, Miss Plumtartt."

"Wine bottles, with corks, please, gentlemen." I call to my as yet unnamed comrades.

The duo of dichotomous dimensions do as directed.

We are able to bottle up quite a bit of the useful, if disgusting, material.

"And now for introductions. My name is Ichabod Temperance. My companion, Miss Plumtartt."

"I'm Keefer Smith," says the looming giant. "This is my partner, Joshua O'Hagan. We are of the newly formed Los Angelos Constabulary, and we'd like to know what in the wide world of spooks is going on around here."

Chapter 36 - An Interesting Errand.

Persephone

After he duly collects all available ectoplasm, Mr. Temperance introduces me to his friends. First is a big gentleman, Constable Smith. He possesses a great imposing and authoritative presence and a frightening countenance until he relaxes. He is actually quite pleasant when not engaged in mortal combat, yet he never loses that "edge" that makes me feel quite safe in his presence. As for Officer O'Hagan, I barely get to speak with the charming little Irishman. Once he has ascertained that I am in the company of Mr. Temperance, he is swiftly off to chat up a lone female by the door.

Mr. Temperance, Constable Smith, and I, *sans* an occupied O'Hagan, square our facts to the best of our faculties. It is determined that we need to re-arm. We must find a means of successfully fighting against these creatures. Our formidable "Man of the City" suggests a weapons-making genius friend of his.

We rendezvous first thing in the morning at a magnificent armaments store. The charming, plain clothed Irish policeman thought to bring biscuits! "They're magically delicious," he says.

The sign reads: Johnson's Pistol Paradise and Armament Augmentation Parlour.

'No Rifle will be Stifled. Every Pistol, treated as Crystal. We Shun no Gun. Problem with your Revolver? We'll solve Her. - God Created Man. Sam Colt made them Equal. Mr. Johnson makes them More So.- Specialty items are our Specialty.'

It's a firearms store like none I've ever seen. Rows of counters lie filled with every description of handgun. The walls are equally loaded with long guns. Interesting armaments from around the world hang suspended from the ceiling.

There are many curiosities among Mr. Johnson's dazzling array of firearms, weapons of varied design with which I am not familiar.

"We want access to the factory for a little while, Mr. Johnson," says Constable Smith.

The proprietor is quite determined in his refusal to allow access to his workshop! A powerfully built, coloured gentleman is the proud but wary store owner. I think he may be one who is touched by the Comet, and has trade secrets, and patents to protect. He reminds me of a certain young Serbian professor.

"What did you just say?" He cocks his head, and with incredulity, giving the giant officer an offended look.

"I can't believe you would ask that. You know I don't let anybody in my laboratory, much less the factory. It is my sanctuary. I won't let you, your dangerously unbalanced partner, much less this hick I've never seen before. I won't let my wife in there. My son, if he proves himself worthy, will inherit the key. My own mother would be denied entrance!"

He glares at us with determined eyes, working a big cigar back and forth in his mouth. He chews it in a challenging fashion, daring us to try to coerce him into allowing entrance to his private workshop.

"Aw, come on, Mr. 'J,' please." From the big man.

Mr. Johnson glares harder.

"Come on, Johnson, this doesn't have to be ugly," from the compact Officer O'Hagan.

The gun enthusiast grips his counter top. The stout display case creaks under his oppressive grip.

"Pardon me, Gentlemen," I inject, as I can readily see that our hoped-for assistance is showing little chance of being forthcoming, "might I have a word with Mr. Johnson?"

I wish to convey my very best attributes to Mr. Johnson; therefore I position myself as I sweep forward to allow the morning sun to create a magic light around the auburn hair piled high upon my perfectly erect skull.

"Kind sir. I find myself at wit's end. I am in the most dire need. Forces of the greatest evil, with the most calamitous intent, are even now moving against me. We require special armaments that these good stewards of the public safety feel that you are singularly qualified to help provide us with in this time of dread and need."

I reach to the Man of Armaments.

At my lightest touch, the hard headed gun enthusiast softens his crusty demeanor.

"You *will* help us, kind sir?"

His eyes start to brim up with tears.

In an effort to seal the bond, I batt my blue eyes encouragingly.

Mr. Johnson's brimming eyes flutter, just a little.

{batt, batt, batt}

{flutter,flutter, flutter}

An interior heat source dries the sympathetic moisture from Mr. Johnson's eyes. Tears of understanding evaporate under the dehumidifying force of the armourer's obstreperousness.

"No."

"My word! You impossible man!"

Fiddlesticks! I confess, this difficult man has driven me to be quite put out.

"Excuse me, Mr. Johnson?" Says a soft-spoken Mr. Temperance.

"Yeah?" Says the obstinate store owner.

"Would you like to examine this?" He offers up the P.G.D.D. The electrical apparati that enshroud the Colt .45 bear witness to the fundamental changes that he has wrought in the device. The curious green ectoplasmic charging chamber tempt and seduce the armourer.

Mr. Johnson's face shows scorn at first, but then irresistibly reveals an ounce of curiosity. This helplessly slides into full attention which inevitably leads to his mouth falling open, thus allowing a lit cigar to fall to the floor.

To my own amused chagrin I have to admit that it is Mr. Temperance's own inventions that win our entrance to the stingy store owner's sanctum sanctorum. I confess that I am not surprised; nothing fascinates a comet prodigy so much as the brilliant invention of another.

Mr. Johnson beams at the little Alabamian, "I didn't catch your name, friend."

The Ecto-Plasm from the hotel's lobby lizards gives us material to work with.

Mr. Temperance's treasured Colt .45 cannot be salvaged. A new weapon must be procured.

Mr. Johnson's store provides a wide variety of weaponry from which to choose our devices' platforms. Mr. Temperance had thought his Colt could handle the tremendous force of the Ecto-Plasmic retort, but he had miscalculated.

The California constables quickly make their choices. This I think is not a difficult choice for the lawmen. A very popular rifle's name bursts from the happy shoppers' lips: the 'Winchester' rifle is what these fellows desire. They feature a high capacity of ammunition, a fast rate of fire, and a proven, deadly accuracy. Mr. Johnson has a very unusual design in mind for his own weapon.

It takes a longer interval of time for my young friend to make his decision. The assiduous shopper pores over Mr. Johnson's vast arsenals. There are so many weapons to select among! Hundreds, if not thousands of every sort of pistol, rifle and shaughtte-gun are on display.

Many are antiques, such as a pair of ancient Dutch blunderbusse. Flintlocked, cap and ball firearms of every description fill many long gun cases. These compete for his attention with breech loading rifles from the recent past. Muzzle loading muskets and Kentucky long rifles dating back to this country's founding make this emporium a veritable private museum.

Many new and modern weapons with unique features and incredible qualities are on display.

"Do these Winchester rifles not appeal to you, Mr. Temperance?" I ask. Certainly, the constables made their decisions very quickly.

"Perhaps you would be happier with these fantastic modern designs?"

"I need to be far-sighted, Ma'am," is the patient and courteous reply. "We still gotta long way to go on our journey to distant Tibet. I need to be able to keep my weapon on my person at all times. As much as I am tempted to kit out a Winchester for myself, I think it prudent to fashion a pistol, instead."

"I defer to your better judgment in these matters, sir."

"Thank you, Ma'am."

Most of this fine store's pistols are of the American six-shooter style that is so famously in vogue at this time here in the States. There are double and single action pistols. That is, as the shooter squeezes the trigger, the cylinder containing the ammunition is mechanically rotated, placing the cartridge to be fired into position. Simultaneously, this action cocks the hammer, positioning the firing pin above the freshly placed new munition. Or, he or she may cock the weapon manually with his or her thumb, for an easier trigger pull. These "Six-Shooters" usually come in thirty-two, thirty-eight, forty, and forty-five caliber chamberings. These weapons are fast and reliable. Mr. Temperance obviously mourns the loss of his 'Colt.'

There are some unusual fellows among the newly-developed weaponry. Does the blast of the round power a series of mechanical events, which in turn, loads another round into the breach to be fired? What an amazing process this initiates as the blast of the munition is harnessed for the automatic chambering of a fresh cartridge. I suppose that this would facilitate a very rapid rate of fire. Perhaps it would fire as quickly as the user is able to pull the trigger!

In this display case, our obstreperous host has his collection of pistols from this country's tragic 'War Between The States.' Many are revolvers of large, elegant design. These deadly works of art were highly prized in their time, but sadly, they are obsolete in this day and age. The single action style, where the user is required to cock the hammer manually, is a thing of the quaint past. The firing cap, powder, and ball, are all loaded separately, instead of together, as a single cartridge. Yet still, I can see that he looks upon them as remarkable creations. I wonder what is his fascination with these older model firearms.

"A marvelous collection of antiques, Mr. Temperance. They truly are lovely, in their way. It is unfortunate that they do not accept standard cartridges as is so required in the modern firearm of our day."

"Yes, Ma'am, but of course, I am not firing standard cartridges, either. In fact, what I have in mind, will actually work better as a front of the cylinder loaded semi-cartridge."

I watch the fellow continue his close inspection. It is as if I can see into the back of his head, and watch the machinations of his active design process.

His face, posture and gestures indicate that he has made an exciting discovery.

"Miss Plumtartt! A La Mat!"

"Is that a good thing, Mr. Temperance?"

"Yes, Ma'am, this here's a Confederate legend. The 'La Mat,' is a cavalry soldier's weapon. This is a very interesting pistol of French manufacture with some peculiar characteristics."

Mr. Temperance explains the history, and design features of the lovely revolver; and I can see the first 'tingly sensations' of a plan start to form in his mind.

"Nine long, forty-two caliber rounds rotate within their own cylinder, around a stationary middle tube. This center passage contains a sixteen gauge shaughtte-gun charge. This small shaughtte-gun barrel is perfectly adapted to accept the ectoplasmic charging chamber for the device in mind."

This large, heavy revolver of unusual antiquity will be the platform of his new weapon.

Mr. Johnson disengages the many locks of a heavy iron-bound door and leads our ensemble to the inner sanctuaries of his esoteric digs.

This workshop has furnaces, presses, and dies. Every sort of scientific pursuit is represented including a chemyst's laboratory, complete with bubbling retorts and burning burners.

Unusual electrical apparatuses' sparks give evidence of the dangerous goings on within mysterious cabinetry. Sputtering electrical components try to bite the unwary. Arcs of wandering electricity keep one grounded in caution. From my father's laboratories at Plumtartt Manor, to the universities of Graz, I have spent a considerable amount of time in various laboratories. This is an impressive and noteworthy workshop.

Workbenches are strewn with the detritus of a thousand projects.

Uncountable firearms lie scattered in varied states of completion and construction. Most are practically unfathomable in their potential use.

A drafting table dominates the center of the room.

This is the nexus of firearm creation.

Mr. Temperance explains the construction of his "Green Beauties," P.E.R.K., and P.G.D.D. to Mr. Johnson.

He then explains the devices we intend to create.

"I might just have to build one of these babies for myself," says the excited armament engineer.

Firearms of unheard of ferocity are now in our possession.

Three more sets of "Green Beauties" have been built.

"Edged weapons are frowned upon in the force." This from Officer O'Hagan. "How about an alternative?"

"I might have something, officer."

Borrowing a couple of tools from the two men, he uses the proffered items to quickly form two casting molds. He soon returns to them their old toys, and the delighted constables' new toys are soon at hand.

For Constable Keefer Smith, it's an emerald truncheon.

"I call it a "BillyPUNC," says Mr. Temperance.

Petrified

Ubiquitous

Necrotized

Cudgel

"And for Mr. O'Hagan, his PUNKdusters." says Mr. Temperance with a smile.

Petrified

Unified

Necrotized

Knuckles

Everyone is shopping and getting new things but me! I rap my parasol pointedly on the floor. “Mr. Temperance, might I have some means of defense, as well?”

“I hate the idea of putting you in a position such that armed combat would be necessary, Miss Plumtartt.”

“Well it seems, sir, that I am finding myself in these circumstances whether you and I wish it or not. I am afraid there is no other choice. I insist.”

“Yes, Ma’am.”

“It’s all right, Ichabod,” O’Hagan reassures me. “I think you’ve got a heck of a girl there with a lot of pluck. She can be trusted with a weapon.”

Mr. Temperance’s eyebrows pull together in a knot of concentration, and then they open back into a happy state of relaxed inspiration. With a snap of his fingers and a carbide flash of ingenious light in his eyes, he ideates a personalized weapon especially for me.

When he shortly thereafter presents it to me, I start to protest, but quickly relent.

“I should really like something more substantial, Mr. Temperance, but I must say, this *is* rather darling!”

“Bring on your old, scary monsters,” snarls an impressively armed Mr. Johnson. A cumbersome, though daunting, weapon is obviously very heavy even in the strong hands of Mr. Johnson. “We’re loaded for ecto-grizzly bear!”

Chapter 37 - We Go For A Stroll.

Ichabod.

Dusk catches us in its ominous embrace as we enter into the operating realm of our enemies.

We have left Mr. Johnson's Emporium in high spirits. Such an arsenal is in our possession! For just a brief moment, I cannot imagine what our enemies can throw at us that we cannot handle.

Then I remember the onslaught of Paris and the battle of Graz, the brave captain and crew of the magnificent airship 'Edelweiss.'

I realize that I am foolish to continue our mission while underestimating our enemies, and to forget our good fortune in escaping such close calls.

We had best not waste a second in continuing our flight.

While we were building our weapons, Miss Plumtartt saw to booking our passage upon the fastest Clipper ship headed west.

Our friends provide a heavily armed escort. We hire a carriage to carry us to the docks.

"Oh no!" Miss Plumtartt cries out. "Gentlemen, I feel a horrible presence arising nearby."

We hear the cry of terrified horses. Then we see ahead of us, in the city's gaslights, horses of many wagons and carriages fighting to get out of the area.

Our own brace of horses rear back in their traces. They are turning away from the docks, despite the driver's best efforts to control his charges.

"Everybody out!" Keefer Smith orders. The five of us

scramble out of the wagon just as it breaks away down the street. The entire street and surrounding areas are in similar tumult. We are stuck in the middle of the street clustering together in a protective huddle. Around us horses drag their broken wagon remains or whatever else is still clinging to them as they retreat from unseen horrors in an equine bridled stampede.

We have abandoned our carriage amidst a cacophony of yelling men, madly panicked horses and thundering hooves. Wagons and carriages become entangled. Individually ridden horses rear up and fly from the scene. A horrible sense of foreboding grips the city.

Citizenry pick up on the horses' fear and decide to follow their example; we soon stand alone in an empty street.

In a remarkably short time, we find ourselves the center of a growing diameter of quiet. The horses of this city have fled eastward.

Every living being in the area flees inland.

We catch ourselves holding our breath as an eerie silence replaces the noisy horses' pandemonium.

We stand on Desolation Boulevard.

We turn towards the wharf.

A tumbleweed blows by.

Slowly, we make our way down the center of the street.

Whereas moments before we were almost jubilant, buoyantly riding the euphoric cloud of our wonderful new weaponry, now we feel oppressive trepidation. It lies like a cold stone of misgiving, in the pit of our collective bowels.

In a low growl from Mr. Johnson.

"I got a bad feeling about this."

Five pairs of eyes search for danger in all directions.

It's less than two blocks to the wharf that has our launch. It sits ready to carry us to a waiting clipper. Both are in our sight.

With a sharp intake of breath, Miss Plumtartt starts.

In the uncanny silence that has gripped this normally busy town, we hear the slow, measured, echoing steps of a man's footfalls.

A skeletal figure walks out into the empty street, strategically placing himself directly between us and our aquatic conveyances. This gentleman is as thin as a rail and dressed in high fashion. A long thin mustache inhabits his upper lip.

"That's Jean-Jacques Bhauh Buuhm, the horrid fellow from the hotel I told you of!" Miss Plumtartt hisses.

"You foolishly put your friends in harm's way, Miss Plumtartt. Had you co-operated with my European Counter-part, Herr Doktor Himmel, you might have spared many people much anguish and heartache. You selfish little girl. You are hereby extinguished."

"That's enough!" I roar. It boils my blood to hear Miss Plumtartt spoken to in this fashion. "Stand aside, we're passing through."

"The intrepid Mr. Temperance," sneers this oily poof. "If you could only get beyond your out-dated sense of chivalry, none of these exercises would have been necessary."

I do not care for his inference.

"Wake up, man. This is 1875!" chides the rude cad. "You cling to the moral convictions and integrities of another time. Chivalry is long past, dead."

"Move it, Slim. We have the means to advance our position."

"Too late! Your fate, and the fate of your companions is sealed. We are familiar with your advancements in weaponry." A laughing fit takes the despicable man. "However, I think you must agree, you still lack the capacity to stop the forces I have at hand."

From their darkened cavities, his beady eyes roll backwards into his skull.

He speaks an unclean word.

His hands go through a ritualistic maneuver and perform an obscene gesture.

I feel as strongly as I have ever felt that something bad is about to happen.

A green light begins to glow behind the sinister skeleton.

It comes from the ocean, behind the malevolent man.

The water has a sickly, ghastly, luminescence.

Things crawl up over the pier's railings.

Horrible things.

Things that should not be.

In what should be an unutterable tongue, Jean Jacques Bhauh Buuhm has summoned an unclean horde.

In a few short moments, the sea walls are overflowing with an abominable tide of aberrant bottom feeders.

Nightmarish visions more horrible than an opiate addict

could concoct in his drug addled dreams crest the wharf in a never-ending wave. Creature after creature in greater numbers and mounting speed issue from the waters.

A torrential tide of terror washing a wave of water based wastes in an inbound undertow of unclean unsavoriness assaults our shores.

"Nnnyunhahahahahaha" cackles the horrid man, as his hordes sweep past him in a swarm of slavering shrimps, grotesque grubworms, and prehistoric prawns.

We open fire.

BUH-WHOOMP. POW! (a plasmo-gasmic discharge)

BOOM! (exploding monster)

There is a phosphorescent maelstrom.

BUH-WHOOMP. POW! BOOM!
BUH-WHOOMP. POW! BOOM!
BUH-WHOOMP. POW! BOOM!
BUH-WHOOMP. POW! BOOM!
BUH-WHOOMP .POW! BOOM!
BUH-WHOOMP. POW! BOOM!
BUH-WHOOMP. POW! BOOM!
BUH-WHOOMP. POW! BOOM!
BUH-WHOOMP. POW! BOOM!
BUH-WHOOMP. POW! BOOM!

The discharges are almost as dangerous as the frightful

combustion of the abominations we shoot.

BUH-WHOOMP. POW! BOOM!
BUH-WHOOMP. POW! BOOM!
BUH-WHOOMP. POW! BOOM!
BUH-WHOOMP. POW! BOOM!
BUH-WHOOMP. POW! BOOM!
BUH-WHOOMP. POW! BOOM!
BUH-WHOOMP. POW! BOOM!
BUH-WHOOMP. POW! BOOM!

etcetera...

Big Keef and the Leprechaun show great alacrity in combat.

Mr. Johnson's choice of weapon design has proven providential. Just like I thought back at the Pistol Parlour, I do believe this gentleman has been influenced by the Comet's passing, for his device is quite ingenious. Much like the Henry, or, Winchester, lever-action, repeating rifles we are familiar with, Mr. Johnson has a similarly designed shaught gun. However, it operates by means of a sliding mechanism, instead of a lever, under its twin, opposite side ejecting barrels. Two large canisters of ammunition replace the under barrel tube to supply higher multitudes of destructive reserves. A pistol's grip adds speed and leverage. Plasmogasm enhances the deadly device's destructive powers exponentially.

My La Mat is shocking in its devastation.

Miss Plumtartt's accessory is proving quite effective! She wields it with precision and murderous intent.

The abominations dart about with deadly purpose, their locomotion alone creating a clickety-clackety cacophony, not to mention their shrill analogue to language. The other indefinable aural phenomena they emit are anathema to my senses, a saturation of maddening sounds that was never meant to be heard in our universe.

A steady rain of plasmogasmic fire creates a green storm of deafening blasts. These are followed in quick response with the huge explosion of each creature.

How long does it go on? The barrage is horrific. The carnage is unimaginable. The hordes of our attackers are relentless. No matter how many monsters are destroyed, a continual wave of foul creatures follow the departed.

BUH-WHOOMP. POW! BOOM!
BUH-WHOOMP. POW! BOOM!
BUH-WHOOMP. POW! BOOM!
BUH-WHOOMP. POW! BOOM!
BUH-WHOOMP. POW! BOOM!

...

BUH-WHOOMP. POW! BOOM!

...

BUH-WHOOMP. POW! BOOM!

... ...

BUH-WHOOMP. POW! BOOM!

... ...

...

BUH-WHOOMP. POW! BOOM!

...Our fire begins to wither. ...

BUH-WHOOMP. POW! BOOM! ...

Dang, our firepower seems to be waning as we use up our ammunitions.

The onslaught of craven crawfish is unabated.

I see Miss Plumtartt taken with a shudder. She seems to compulsively shoot a pair of red energy spheres of sorts from her palms. In the resulting two huge explosions, many monsters are destroyed. Unfortunately, more take their place. Miss Plumtartt has a deathly pallor. Swaying on her feet, she nearly collapses.

Our fire dissipates as our munitions are depleted.

I hate to do it. I don't really know what is gonna happen if I discharge the Ectoplasmic chamber in the shaught gun tube of the LaMat.

I don't have a choice.

BUH-WHOOMP. POW!!!

BOOM!BOOM!BOOMITY-BOOM!!!

It worked! But it is about as useful as lips on a chicken, as more monstricized shrimp fill the void of depleted prawn as fast as we can dispatch them.

My stalwart companions and I have exhausted our entire stock of ammunitions.

We resort to our Resinated weapons.

Big Keef clobbers his adversaries with his emerald truncheon.

O'Hagan clocks monsters left and right with blinding speed. His emerald knuckles are a blur of punishment.

Miss Plumtartt regains her resolve and has great effect with the weapon I crafted for her; an emerald-tipped parasol.

I am P.E.R.K.-o'lating.

Mr. Johnson swings his depleted shaught gun at a monster with a mighty blow. The metal barrels pass through the inter-dimensional horror like air. Mr. Johnson spins three times before landing on his backside.

"Use the other end," I encourage.

Muttering curses under his breath, the angry gunsmith flips his scatter-gun, and cracks the closest monster with the wooden stock of the weapon.

"Take that!" rings Miss Plumtartt's clear British voice as

she cracks the head of a nasty bug, with her "R.O.S.E."

"At you!" insists Miss Plumtartt, as she punctures another beastie with her "T.H.O.R.N."

Somehow, I and my companions demand of ourselves the wherewithal to continue.

We fight with what means are left to us.

Valiant though our efforts be, our position has become untenable.

Monstrous forces run our position over.

CHAPTER 38 - NATURAL ENEMIES.

Persephone

No one wishes to be eaten.

We fight to the bitter end.

{{{BOOOM!!!}}}

There is a crushing sonic concussion accompanied by a blinding flash of red light!

Just as we are overwhelmed by the ceaseless tides of abomination, the creatures have broken off their attack! The clouds of smoke accompanying the crimson explosion are an effective diversion for the plasmic prawn.

Hello, what's this?!

In the strangest manner, the attacking swarms have completely lost focus on us. Communicating with an excited, high speed clicking, and sucking intake, they look back to the city.

All eyes are drawn in one direction.

We sense movement on the empty streets.

The unnatural spawn slowly back towards the ocean.

Monsieur Bhauh-Buuhm is beside himself with rage! He screams and exhorts his disgusting minions to kill us, but they look beyond us, down the street.

Several blocks down, a solitary figure steps out into view.

A woman's statuesque figure centers itself in the wide boulevard.

Miss Abigail GoldenBear!

Like a Goddess out of time, the tall, elegant lady comes forth, bathed in a corona of crimson light. Regal and resplendent, she commands the attention of the combative forces.

A big cat walks out into the city street! Approaching from behind her, a large mountain lion walks up to and joins the woman.

It is quickly joined by many more cats. They are not small, domesticated felines, but great two hundred pound big cats from out of the wild.

The undersea denizens get very agitated.

Jean-Jacques appears quite perplexed.

More and more big cats come up behind Miss GoldenBear, drawn into her beaming vitality. Pumas, panthers, mountain lions, and cougars impossibly fill the urban scene.

Miss GoldenBear conducts herself as some sort of shaman. She has cast some kind of powerful spell, that has acted to summon these hordes of heavy felines.

Our unwanted guests from unfriendly dimensions are quite excited about the arrival of the feline herd. These monsters are not happy about the sight of the hungry kitties. The seafood smörgåsbord sees themselves as cat food chowder for the approaching clowder.

First at a walking pace, but steadily gathering speed, scores of big cats start racing down the street. Perhaps there are hundreds, for there is no way to know the numbers of the slinky torrent flowing like a feline river down this broad, commercial street. From each side street they pass, these cats are joined by even more big cats. They race right past us in pursuit of their scrumptious prey.

"My word!" I gasp as Mr. Temperance pulls me to the ground. He shelters me as a stampede of giant cats, of all descriptions, glide over us. We all lie flat as the feline river flows over our heads in a flood of fury. Every big cat in the South-West, Mexican, and American territories must be running down the streets of Los Angelos!

The cats tear into the fearsome crustaceans in a terrible onslaught. The poor monsters are no match for these ferocious felines.

"Ooh, ... oh, ... my..."

Mr. Temperance shields me from the gruesome scenes of carnage, protecting my delicate senses from this horrific sight.

Soon, the cats have slain or devoured all but Monsieur Bhauh-Buuhm. His wretched features are a twisted rictus, as he searches desperately for an avenue of escape.

The cats have no intention of losing their prize.

With a most un-manly display, he lets loose his tentacles out his coat sleeves in a strangely incontinent-al fashion.

CHAPTER 39 - THE *SHOOTING STAR.*

Ichabod.

Looking back over the stern of our launch, we wave goodbye to our adventure mates: Abigail GoldenBear, Big Keefer Smith, Officer O'Hagan, and the indomitable Mr. Johnson.

I sorely miss their brief companionship, already.

"My, how we fly along, Miss Plumtartt."

"Indeed, Mr. Temperance, we seem to be making tremendously good time. I say!"

The Pacific Clipper, "*Shooting Star*," claims to be the fastest ship in the Pacific. I can believe she's the fastest of sailing ships, certainly, but it is yet to be seen if she can match the gigantic *S.S. Victoria* in speed.

"Sea travel has never been my cup of tea, and yet...and yet..." Miss Plumtartt makes flirty eyes at the captain.

The captain makes flirty eyes back at Miss Plumtartt.

"And yet, I find myself enjoying myself immensely on this trip, Captain Edgeworth."

We stand on the deck of this lovely ship, my companion and I. The *Shooting Star* must be the fairest vessel I have yet seen, and her captain, one Adam Edgeworth, is equally gracious and distressingly handsome. He has made a great show of interest in the story of our travels thus far, and he seems fair to bursting with curiosity at my ingenious martial inventions.

The thing is, though, he wants to hear about them from Miss Plumtartt.

"Pray, dear lady, you used this thing in mortal combat?" asks the vivacious seaman.

"Oh, yes." she explains, "It does more than just protect me from the Sun's indelicate emanations."

"And the emerald accouterments?"

"The mace? We call it the R.O.S.E."

Resinated

Offensive

Striking

Ectoplasm

"And the dangerous looking spike that protrudes from the center of the bud?"

T.H.O.R.N.

Tactical

Handheld

Offensive

Resin

Necrotizer

The young officer attempts to remain nonchalant, but he clearly does not know what to think of such oddities.

Much to my relief, the sea wolf withdraws his amorous fangs and decides to act in a friendly manner towards both me and Miss Plumtartt. We enjoy a splendid time on the immense Pacific, relishing the pleasant respite with a lightened heart.

What is more, for the first time in more days than I care to count, I am not engaged in constant combat. This is a peaceful time, and Miss Plumtartt and I feel at ease in casual conversation for the first time in weeks it seems. We are distracted by the fresh fish and exotic fruits so plentiful at the Captain's table. Small joys, yes, but after so many close brushes with death, every little nuance of life is treasured and savored. We converse for a few lazy moments, then we take our rest as the sun sinks into the horizon.

Enjoying a splendid trip across vast Ocean expanses, we eventually come to a chain of volcanoes in the middle of the Pacific, the Ha'wai-ian Islands.

After days of apparent good spirits, Miss Plumtartt seems to falter.

"What is it, Miss Plumtartt?" I ask.

"Upon my word, Mr. Temperance, I cannot say, but as we approached these Ha'wai-ian Isles, I have begun to feel as if my brief happiness has slid once more into distress. Some alien need impels me."

I do not know what to say to the frightened girl.

"I cannot explain it to you, Mr. Temperance; I honestly wish I could, yet I know, as surely as I know my own name, that we must stay in these Islands until I find what I seek."

Miss Plumtartt cannot give me a rational explanation.

She is in a terribly distraught and confused state of mind.

She steadfastly refuses to leave the island.

Moreover, I do not think she is capable of leaving.

The *"Shooting Star"* continues Westward without us.

"Miss Plumtartt?"

She is about to walk out into the ocean, again.

"Oh, Mr. Temperance. I seem to have wandered to the beach."

"Yes, Ma'am."

"I have been sleepwalking again, in the middle of the day, haven't I? Time after time, I have found myself in a trance, wanting to walk into the ocean. This, combined with my disparate moods, leaves me at sixes and sevens. In a sense, I feel elation at being near to something I want, something that wants me. Yet, I vacillate with a feeling of uncontrollable fear."

"Yes, ma'am."

I try to be a pillar of strength and conviction to Miss Plumtartt, but I am powerless to help her shrug this melancholy shroud.

Her clear blue eyes stare out without seeing.

"My mind is like a cottony cloud, unable to see through."

"No, more like a fog."

"A fog of cobwebs. Clinging. Trapped."

"Unable to see,"

....

"or think."

"Despair threatens to engulf me in its bottomless pit."

"Miss Plumtartt?"

"...?..."

"Miss Plumtartt?"

" ..Yes..?... "

"Let's stay on land, until such time as we have a ship, please, ma'am."

Miss Plumtartt has one foot on the dock, and one foot over twenty feet of open air, above the water. For the third time in as many days, Miss Plumtartt has slid into a trance-like state, and wanted to just walk out into the surf.

"Oh! My word! I beg your pardon, Mr. Temperance, I seem to have done it again, haven't I?"

"Yes, Ma'am."

Miss Plumtartt puts up a brave facade, but I know she is worried. She does not understand what is controlling her actions. She cannot bear the idea of leaving on a boat, yet at at the same time, she wants to go into the ocean.

She claims something is calling to her.

She is calling to something.

What can I do?

Too much idle time on my hands makes me itchy. One of my favorite hobbies is to wander through local craftsmen's supply depots that now dot the world's landscape. These Island tinkerers have their own Pacific flair to their ingenious devices.

All that weapon design work back at Mr. Johnson's has my gears turning.

I jot down some ideas I got while at Mr. Johnson's.

I design a one-man operation, based on the Gattling design, but pneumatically powered, and plasmogasmotized.

I continue thinking in a tinkering manner:

-Miss Plumtartt wants to go in the water.

-That means, I go in the water.

-I cannot breathe underwater.

-Fish breathe underwater.

-How do fish breathe underwater?

-They draw the necessary nutrients from the water through their gills.

-

-

- (*! plinck !*)

"Miss Plumtartt!" I call excitedly.

The poor woman sits on the hotel's veranda, but I fear she is almost in a trance.

She slowly seems to show a light of consciousness in her laudanum-like delirium. Miss Plumtartt is usually so bright and vibrant. It scares me to see her have to struggle to bring my presence into focus.

"Hmm? What? Oh. Oh, yes, Mr. Temperance. I seem to have drifted off again there, haven't I?" from my befogged, feminine friend. "My word, Mr. Temperance. You are absolutely beaming, sir."

"Yes, Ma'am. I have a new goggle design that you may be interested in."

Bravely, the girl gathers the will to peruse my creation.

Layers of gauzy curtains lift from Miss Plumtartt's slack expression as she ascertains their purpose.

I can almost see a bright electric carbide lamp burst into ignition above her head.

She snaps into an alertness I have not seen in days. Her brilliance and intelligence bloom to the surface of her consciousness like the sun rising over the sea's horizon.

"Mr. Temperance! You have quite hit upon it! Our salvation! My despair is dispelled, like water from the back of a swan! With a light heart, I feel my spirits soar!"

"Gee, I sure am glad to hear that, Ma'am."

"My word. Mr. Temperance!" as she smiles at me with incredulous admiration."Why, I do believe you have hit upon a solution, once again!"

"Yes, Miss Plumtartt, I hope so. They are an inter-oxygenating lung liaisons, goggled. I think I'm gonna call 'em..."

"Stop there, Mr. Temperance." Her customary sparkle has returned and she teasingly re-assumes her normal bubbly intellectual sensibilities. "I think I am getting the hang of how these things go. You refer to them as:"

"Goggled
Inter-oxygenating
Lung
Liaisons
or, 'G.I.L.L.s'"

"Why as a matter of fact, yes, Miss Plumtartt." I

sheepishly admit. "Am I becoming predictable, Miss Plumtartt?"

"Hardly, Mr. Temperance."

"Does this still feel to be the right heading, Miss Plumtartt?"

Our schooner, the *'Scarlett Queen,'* has been traveling almost due South from the Mid-Pacific island chain.

"Yes Mr. Temperance, but have the crew slow the vessel; I feel as if we are going to pass it by."

The ship is brought to as still a position as we are able to maintain.

"This is the spot!" calls Miss Plumtartt excitedly. "I cannot fathom why, but I feel we have found our destination. Our quest is here, in the middle of the biggest middle of nowhere on the planet."

"You are sure, Miss Plumtartt?"

"Oh, yes. Quite sure, Mr. Temperance."

Our chartered schooner, the *'Scarlett Queen,'* has brought Miss Plumtartt and me to a place that Miss Plumtartt feels compelled to go. I have the captain throw out buoys to mark our position. Mushroom-shaped sea anchors are dropped, as opposed to the pointy kind for dragging the bottom, the bottom being way too far away. All that can be done to have the boat tread water is done.

I climb down a rope ladder into the blue waters. I look up to Miss Plumtartt who anxiously watches me from the rail.

"It is there, Mr. Temperance. Somehow, I know that

what we require is down there. Though we don't know what we seek, you must find it and return with it. That is imperative for there to be a future of this world."

"Don't worry, Miss Plumtartt. I do this kind of thing every day."

I engage the G.I.L.L.s and slip beneath the waves.

Ohhh! Interesting!

Ohhh! Pretty!

Ohhh! Dangerous!

It is another world down here.

I don't want to end up some fishie's dinner, but the sights are marvelous!

Schools of silvery fish dance about faster than I can keep up with.

Dangerous predatory types view me with suspicion.

Crawly, swimmy. and scuttly, there is no end of the amazing life that thrives beneath the waves.

How does one describe an octopus's travels? Squirty?

Plains of fans. Corrals of corals. Oceans of mountains.

Fields of mullosks, mussells, oysters,

...

and

...

clams.

...

Clams.

Giant Clams.

Biggus clamus humungous.

Hundreds of the white shelled creatures blanket the sea floor for as far as I can see. These range in size from the smallest, little fellows, to the truly gigantic. I never dreamed they could grow to such dimensions. I am dwarfed by their enormity.

Somehow, I know.

Somehow I know I am in the right place.

Somehow I know that what I seek is here.

A trace of light reflects from out of a shadow.

Just a flicker of milky luminescence escapes from an especially large fellow.

I swim to him. He lies there immobile. He does not appear to have moved in years.

Deep within, I catch another flicker of light.

Good Heavens, a pearl! It's enormous!

Somehow, I know, this is my quest.

Everything is very still and silent.

Certainly I can just snatch the object, and be on my way.

I find a sturdy piece of driftwood and wedge it into the clam's open shell, just to be safe.

I look around.

No-one here but me.

I quickly swim into the enormous clam. Far to the back sits the lustrous prize. I quickly cut it loose from its muscley moorings.

"rrr"

"Snap!"

"Kuh-Llunngg!!!..ggg...ggg...ggg..."

"Get off of me, you romantic mussel!"

I am trying to ascertain a way out of here, but this dang ol' clam's tongue, muscle, or whatever it is, won't leave me alone. This bivalve behemoth is almost amorous in its pursuit.

It wants to eat me. Come to think of it, maybe it already has.

I give him a couple of pokes with my emerald blade.

He backs off and gives me a moment to think.

This lid is clamped down tight.

I kick at the swervy lips. I pry with the knife. Nothing affects the indifferent koquina. It would take, literally, tons of leverage to crack this determined crustacean. That was a stout piece of wood I had used for a wedge, and this brute snapped it without a bit of trouble. A large pneumatic press would be handy, but it would have to be of the highest strength.

Could I kill this creature?

Probably, but would that avail me my freedom? So far, my attacks have only served to encourage the creature to clamp down with ever increasing pressure. To kill the amazing mollusc could very well decide my own fate, trapping me within.

Think, Ichabod.

Good grief! It would take the hydraulics of the Gods, to open this obstinate shellfish.

This lid will not open, unless the creature wants to open it.

...

How can I make the fishie want to open up?

...

(!)

Fire!

How to create fire in this environment?

...

(!)

Taking a deep breath, I remove the G.I.L.L.s.

I continue to let the mechanisms work.

In a short time, a bubble of air develops at the top of the shell.

I require fuel.

Everything is wet. I cannot burn an article of clothing, unless I can hold it in the bubble of air until it dries out. That might take a week. I do not have the ability to hold my hands over my head that long. Nor provisions for that length of time.

(!)

I do have two things that are water-proofed.

My tinder.

A man should always have an ability to create fire. The meager sparks that I can create with the tinder will not be enough to shock the creature.

I need more.

I need a fuel to burn.

The other thing that I have water-proofed.

My sammich.

A man should always have a sandwich about him at all times. It saved Miss Plumtartt and me in the desert, recently, and now, it might save me again in a different fashion.

I am a peanut butter and jelly man.

I remove my lunch from its special place in my utility belt.

I hold it up, and into the bubble of air. I carefully unwrap its wholesome goodness.

Splitting the two pieces of bread, I consume the jelly side.

Oil is often flammable. Not only petroleum oils such as kerosene can burn, but many other oils, such as whale and corn oils can be ignited as well. Likewise, non-processed peanut butter can burn. The flammability of raw peanut oil can be a life saver in freezing conditions. Perhaps it will provide fuel for my means of escape.

I work the tinder.

The goober paste ignites!

Smoke fills the air bubble.

My surroundings tremble.

"AHH-CHOOO!!!"

I am flung half a league.

I have our prize!

This giant pearl is certainly the Talisman that we seek.

Now to return to our boat and Miss Plumtartt, my task, successfully completed.

"aaahhhaaahhhaaahhhaaahhhaaahhhaaahhhaaahhhaaahhh"

Did I just hear something?

"aaahhhaaahhhaaahhhaaahhhaaahhhaaahhhaaahhhaaah

hh"

I coulda sworn that I just heard a singing kind of music.

"aaahhhaaahhhaaahhhaaahhhaaahhhaaahhhaaah hh"

It had a kind of ethereal quality to it.

It's the pretty music of ladies' voices, singing in an unusual fashion.

"aaahhhaaahhhaaahhhaaahhhaaahhhaaahhhaaah hh"

Strangely... beguiling...

"aaahhhaaahhhaaahhhaaahhhaaahhhaaahhhaaah hh"

I...

I...

I... think... I... must... go... to... them...

"aaahhhaaahhhaaahhhaaahhhaaahhhaaahhhaaah hhaaahhhaahhhaaahhhaaahhhaaahhhaaahhhaaahhha aahhhaaahhhaaahhhaaahhhaaahhhaahhhaaahhhaaah hhaahhhaaahhhaaahhhaaahhhaaahhhaaahhaaahhhaa ahhhaaahhhaahhhaaahhhaahhhaahhhaaahhhaaahhhaaahhha aahhhaaahhh"

"Oh."

"Oh, my," says I.

"Come to us, Ichabod," say they.

"Shouldn't I wait until you girls are dressed?"

Three beautiful ladies gently float in the underwater currents. They smile and lazily swim in fluid, languid figure eight patterns. They beckon to me.

I hesitate for they are only half dressed!

In fact, they're not dressed at all!

They are only half ladies, from the waist up. From the waist down, they have great, fishie tails!

To my great embarrassment, they are most immodestly attired... Not a stitch!

Well, one of the girls has a conch shell, fashioned into a hair brooch, but I don't think that should count.

They are...

very attractive.

"Ichabod..." They beckon to me, arms and tails, working in a hypnotic pattern. In unison, their irresistible chorus sings to me.

"Ichabod..."

"Ichabod... come to us..."

"Ichabod..."

"Ichabod... come to us..."

I go to them.

They circle me, effortlessly swimming in the most lovely spectacle of flight.

I am enchanted.

"You have come to us."

"I have come to you."

"You have brought something."

"I have brought something."

"Something pretty."

"Something pretty."

"We want it."

"You want it."

"Give it to us."

"Give it to you.."

"wait... "

"not.. you."

"Give it to us!"

"It is for Miss Plumtartt!"

"GIVE IT TO US!!!"

Their lovely faces transform into something less lovely.

They attack.

I am forced to defend myself and the prize I have collected.

I am fortunate that they have let down their pretense of beauty and revealed their monstrous, true identity. Otherwise, I would probably have trouble striking a woman.

P.E.R.K. is a lady killer.

Chapter 40 - Search.

Persephone

Wearing his new goggles, designed for the operator to be able to breathe under water, the temeritous Mr. Temperance disappears from our sight beneath the wide Ocean surfaces.

The entire day passes with no sign of Mr. Temperances return. These are the longest hours of my life. Different sensations and fears run through my soul. I feel danger one moment, and relief another.

I can tell that the schooner's captain and crew have long since given up on Mr. Temperance. Several times, the captain has tried to persuade me to face the facts. My intrepid friend is not coming back, he insists. I refuse him, and insist that the craft wait until the return of my companion.

"Begging your pardon, mum, but he's gone. It's time to go."

Captain Xander Stone has been patient and supportive, as have many of the crew, but night is falling and Mr. Temperance has been gone for a long time.

Mr. Temperance, where are you?

"Please, Captain Stone, he is coming back, I am sure of it."

The dark swarthy features of the Pacific sailor attempt to achieve a sympathetic composition.

"We all became fond of him, Miss, but it looks like he's not coming back. I am sorry."

Despair threatens to tug at my heart, but I staunchly refuse to allow it.

"Patience, Xander, my dear. I have the highest confidence in Mr. Temperance. He has not failed me yet."

Captain Stone releases a deep sigh. "As you wish, Persephone." He turns and walks away, shaking his head negatively to his crew. All the ships hands slump a bit and return to wait idly.

The Pacific sun sets into a vast and empty sea.

Please come back to me, Mr. Temperance. Come back to me, Ichabod.

Wait. What is this light feeling I have? He returns; I know it. He is successful; I can feel it.

I smile. I laugh.

"This way, gentlemen!" as I run to the railing.

The disbelieving sailors follow me. We all look, but there is nothing there. The crew exchange dubious glances.

"Look, there!" calls Captain Xander Stone.

An indistinct shape slowly rises from the depths of the clear, blue Pacific.

He carries our prize, and my relief.

The crew of the '*Scarlett Queen*' breaks into a disbelieving roar of cheers and applause at the improbable reappearance of Mr. Temperance.

He smiles broadly, waving to the crew, and then holds up an enormous pearl. It is larger than the head of Mr. Temperance. Undoubtedly, this is the Talisman that we seek!

"Ichabod! I beg your pardon, Mr. Temperance! I am overjoyed at your return and success. Did you have any trouble?"

"Oh, nothin' out of the ordinary, Miss Plumtartt."

"Mr. Temperance," I say, offering my hand.

"Miss Plumtartt," says Mr. Temperance, assisting me aboard the great *S.S. Victoria.*

We have arrived back in Hawaii just in time to go directly to the floating behemoth, just before she departs.

"Isn't she beautiful, Miss Plumtartt?!"

"Indeed, Mr. Temperance."

"Ye Gads! What a ship, Miss Plumtartt!" Mr. Temperance exclaims. "Though I was on her sister ship just a few weeks earlier, she is nonetheless staggering in her size, grace, and functionality."

I am so jubilant! It is as if a great burden is lifted.

I believe my proximity to the "Orb" is responsible for my soaring spirits.

I do as Mr. Temperance instructs me. I have contrived to keep the "Orb", an object as large as a small pumpkin, upon my person at all times.

Once more, I am grateful for my bustle.

I am quite familiar with the *Victoria.* A Sol Furnace powers her eight, great, paddle wheels. I closely supervised her construction. She and her sister ship are the only two ships currently afloat that are driven by these massive furnaces. After having traveled by commercial ship recently, it is refreshing to enjoy the opulence of this luxurious passenger ship.

I am of a light heart, free in mind and spirit. What a treat it is to be among happy travelers. I am eager to visit with new friends and to mingle with some of our shipmates.

These include Gabriel Getty, a tall, well-built young man with a shock of orange-brown hair, and his beautiful bride, Pipi, with whom I play 'whist' every evening. The Gettys are enjoying a Honeymoon tour of the world.

Next, there are Katie and Bella Brown, two sisters who love to argue over everything and everyone, who regale Mr. Temperance and me with stories of their colorful lives in San Francisco.

Finally, there is Bobbye Olsen, a scholarly young woman who in so many ways could be my twin. Late at night, we share our deepest fears and joys over a snifter of Remy. I think I have been so fortunate as to make a close friend for life!

"Gee, Miss Plumtartt, you sure are in fine spirits! I am glad. You had been so uncharacteristically melancholy of late. But now, after having secured this link to our quest, this Talisman, or good luck charm, or whatever it is, it seems to have had a wonderful effect on your spirits, Ma'am."

"I met a family moving to New Zealand, Miss Plumtartt. They're real nice folks. Mike, Theresa, and their precocious scamp of a boy Dustin, DeWitte. The youngling I nicknamed, "DustBunny."

"I am sure he appreciated that, Mr. Temperance."

"Actually, I think he did, Miss Plumtartt."

"I also met a couple of fellows at the bar who invited me to join them in liquid libations. The first is a great bear of a man. His name means, 'he who runs with the wolves,' Wolfgang Metzger. He's got one of those goatees in the 'circle' style, or, 'Van Dyke.' He was talkin' with an irascible fellow, Aloysius Ytefas. Mr. Metzger is an accomplished artist. His medium is the cutting out of silhouettes. He said that he would do one for each of us!"

"How thrilling, Mr. Temperance! I am always eager to enjoy an artist's creation. Mr. Metzger's work will be enchanting, I am sure."

"While strolling the decks, I met a lovely young mother and her son, Wanda and Nigel Turkerville. I seem to attract the children, and can always keep them entertained with stories or displays of gadgets. Mrs. Turkerville is an absolute delight! Her features practically outshine the sun itself, she is so resplendent in wit and sophistication. Her son is equally bright, in an intellectual sense. I suspect that he might be another possible Comet prodigy."

"Fascinating, Mr. Temperance."

"Then I was able to help a lady struggling with some large, specialized baskets. These were determined to be carrying cats. I estimate four to six felines in all. The woman's name is Nancy Farmer. I related to her that I recently had a very good experience concerning cats."

What fantastic fun I am having!

Such wonderful people.

Such a wonderful ship.

I am so happy to have boarded this fateful paddler.

"Unh."

I feel as if someone walked over my grave...

I am sure it is nothing.

"I trust dinner to be to your satisfaction, Mr. Temperance."

"Indubitably, Miss Plumtartt." responds my jubilant friend.

"All is well for you, Miss Plumtartt?"

"Divine, Mr. Temperance."

We have been invited to share Captain Stewart's table! This is very nice indeed.

All the wonderful people that I have met during the day are here.

However, a newcomer has joined our happy group. Beguiling and mysterious, composed and bemused, entrancingly beautiful, she makes her appearance and is announced, but not until deep in the evening.

"Mademoiselle DeeDee Gauzot," the steward intones.

"Bonsoir, Mademoiselle!" from the entire table. (The welcome may be a little more enthusiastic from the males.)

We resume our merry time.

The food.

The company.

...

The music.

A four piece ensemble attempts to entertain the gathered guests; however, they may not be exactly winning new fans.

"Elegance Of Design" bravely carries on. A sophisticated man, blonde hair, elegant features, ably plays the oboe. He is joined by a delight of a young lady. She is a vivacious flautist, and adds both sparkle and charm to the group. So too, does the violinist. A handsome, bearded gentleman, he has a humorous sparkle to his demeanor, despite the distractions of his last two companions, the cellist and the conductor. The cellist is a sad thing. With a great mop of hair on his head and lip, he struggles to maintain his place in this circle of musicians. His task is not made easier by his (tor) mentor. An intense man of fiery temperament, this director of muses valiantly tries to maintain cohesion of his charges, whilst at the same time, threatening the craven cellist with bodily harm.

The dining hall deck is laid out with tables filled with the finest of delicacies. The room is alive with happy revelers, and our company at the Captain's table enjoy convivial conversation.

We enjoy a marvelous time; however, from time to time, I have the most unsetling sensation pass through me, and then it is gone.

In an unusual display, this ship has scores of stewards spread throughout the ship, bearing lit torches. They seem to be in teams, and frantically alert. I cannot fathom why.

Sparkling conversation is enjoyed by the merry group. I put aside my secret misgivings.

The talk of the table turns to recent "Ghost" attacks throughout the world.

There are commotions and disturbances in the hallways. My sense of something being wrong grows more palpable.

There are stewards standing by with torches alight.

"Why all the torches, Captain?" I inquire.

The captain seems flustered for a moment.

"Buh, buh, buh,...It's an old tradition we recently started. buh, buh, buh....er, yes. Harumph."

I smell a peculiar odour.

"What's that smell, Captain? I ask.

"Harumph! ooooh,... What smell? er.. yes,... hmm. Steward!"

Two stewards run up and dispel the vapours with large rattan fans.

"I recently crossed the Atlantic on your sister ship, '*Triumph*,' Captain." Mr. Temperance brightly enjoins Captain Stewart.

"Hmmm? Er, what, yes, what a shame about the old girl."

"Do you mean her recent quarantine?" asks Mike DeWitte.

"No. Her demise."

"What!" cries the entire table at once.

"Oh! Er. Oops. Er. Yes. Harumph."

"What quarantine?" asks Miss Plumtartt.

"Weeeeelll, it seems there were a few reports of "Ghost" stories on board," from the reluctant officer.

Mr. DeWitte helps us out. Apparently, there were actually a great many "Ghost" attacks aboard the "*Triumph*." These escalated to the point that at the end of the last cruise, the crew mutinied. Or, that is, they refused to go back aboard once they had reached England. A few did stay aboard. The only ones of these who survived were the ones who jumped overboard.

There is excitement in the hallway. Several torch-bearing stewards run by.

I am briefly washed with a disturbing pulsation.

"My word!" I exclaim involuntarily.

"Of what demise do you speak, mon Capitain?" asks Mademoiselle Gauzot.

"Weeeell, this is supposed to be very discreet, you understand. It would seem that saboteurs have wrecked the ship. Something about "unseen forces," smashing the "*Triumph*" like a blown up paper bag. Really! Harumph."

There is a high pitched chittering and excited sounds of commotion from the hall.

A burning frizzling sound is followed by an animal scream, but not a sound made by any creature of Earth's bounty.

A steward with a smoke-soot-smeared face pops his head in and gives the captain a thumbs up.

Something definitely stinks.

I sense the presence of unclean beasts on the ship. They form, and are quickly dispatched. I can sense it. I can smell it.

"Let's get this straight." I have to raise my voice over mounting sounds of chaos throughout the ship. These sounds perturb the captain to no end. He very pointedly ignores them. "The Plumtartt factory and shipyards are destroyed by mysterious, unseen forces, following weeks of murderous attacks with gruesome remains left in evidence."

"Harumph."

"The Sol Furnaces! It must be! They must attract these atrocities. Perhaps they open a portal of sorts, a rift, allowing something to slip into our universe. My father's, Professor Plumtartt's, combination of science and the occult helped him attain his goal, the Great Sol Furnace, but at a high price. Unforeseen consequences fall upon an unsuspecting world."

I find myself pausing for dramatic effect.

"The attack at Graz."

"Harumph. Nothing bad happened at Graz. Harumph. That furnace was built on unstable ground, that's all. It must've been underground caverns, that sort of thing. There is bound to be a reasonable explanation for why the Graz Furnace was sucked into the Earth. Er. yes. Right. Harumph."

Our dinner companions listen enthralled as my dark reckoning continues.

"The "Ghost" attacks have followed the "Sol Furnace" driven ships around their global courses."

"We are ambassadors of goodwill, Miss Plumtartt. Harumph."

"The *Victoria* has touched every major port of the Pacific, the *Triumph* every port of the Atlantic. They have become plague ships of a supernatural pandemic. It caught up with the *Triumph* faster than this ship due to her shorter basin of operations."

From the hall we hear the commotion of animalistic clacking, a fiery frizzle, and an unearthly animal's death shriek. These sounds are followed by a terrible stench.

"Nonsense! Balderdash! Er. Harumph." insists the Captain.

I pop up out of my chair as I see a mosquito, but grown to the size of a rook and with the body of a monstrous prawn, fly into the room. None can see it but I. My shipmates are now my audience, watching me watch 'it.' They, too, develop a sense for the thing and so follow the creature's flight.

A group of monster-chasing stewards enters the dining hall. I can see the grotesque monster as it flies about the room. It is in a confused state, not knowing which victim it prefers.

I tightly grip my parasol in a defensive manner. Locking my eyes on this thing unseen by others fly around the room, I continue my summation:

"Your ship is contaminated with monsters, Captain!"

"Ridiculous!" roars the Lord of the ship.

"Shush!" pleads one of the torch-bearing stewards.

We all become perfectly silent. Everyone present holds their breath.

We are then able to detect the sound of an insect's buzz. It mirrors the track that I follow with my eyes.

One of the stewards steps forward, thrusting out with his torch.

An albatross-sized flying nightmare is briefly visible as it burns to death. With a horrible cry of pain in its clicking analog to language, and a nerve shattering shriek, it quickly succumbs to flame in an overpowering stench. The creature is, apparently, quite flammable.

"Well, Er, Yes, Harumph."

"Is the ship in danger, Sir?" asks a cherub-faced Nigel Turkerville.

"This ship in danger?" roars the incredulous captain. "Poppycock!"

The Captain stands.

He draws himself up into a frightfully noble pose, like the portrait of some great British Naval Lord, adorning the walls of Parliament.

"This Ship shall sail for a thousand years."

Within an hour, the ship will be at the bottom of the Ocean, keel broken, all her passengers and crew, lost.

"Note from the bridge, sir."

"Harumph. Yes. Thank you. What's this then? 'strange glow seen to rear of ship?' Harumph. Nonsense."

Mr. Temperance and I exchange a look. "Get to the back of the boat," I command sternly. He bows to my request.

There is definitely a green glow from behind the ship. What's more, I am not the only one able to see it. Everyone can see it.

A horrible sensation runs through me.

I stagger and nearly fall. My stalwart companion catches me.

Such a concentration of malignant horror I have never felt. An overwhelming wave of fear clutches my heart, my soul, my nerves. I lose control of my composure. I tremble violently and almost start to cry.

I feel like a small child, helpless and afraid.

"Mr. Temperance." My voice shakes with uncontrollable fear. "Something big is coming after me."

The decks are alive with excited crew and passengers.

The glow now surrounds the ship. Something seems to be rising from the depths.

"There!" call many people around us, pointing astern.

A great cry goes up from the throngs of passengers that now crowd the decks.

Something has risen from the deepest depths of the Ocean.

Intuitively, I sense this is something ancient, something that should no longer exist in our world.

It is something my own father summoned back into this universe.

Several hundred yards behind the ship, an island has

risen. It is smooth, and featureless, until it pulls back its great lids. Unstoppable, a scream rips from my own lungs as the ghastly thing opens its horribly great eyes!

It looks upon us!

Every set of lungs that has the dubious honor of witnessing those lights fall upon their owner immediately and helplessly begins to scream.

Tentacles of titanic proportions emerge from the water, hover hundreds of feet in the air, and then slam down with devastating force upon the stricken ship.

Thousands of tiny little humans scream in impotent fright, as squid and octopus arms, on a scale that dwarf even this enormous ocean-going behemoth, grip our doomed vessel.

What was moments ago one of the greatest achievements of Man, is now a playtoy next to this inter-dimensional leviathan.

More tentacles descend upon the ship. They begin to constrict.

The Nipponese on board excitedly say a name: "Gojiro."

Many of the crew who were struck dumb, now seem to come to a realization.

"The Kra-Ken!"

The name is taken up throughout the ship.

"Kra-Ken!"

More tentacles encircle the ship.

Lifeboats are lowered and rope ladders are deployed.

Passengers blindly panic as they desperately search for a way to flee this unfortunate boat.

Great, monstrous tentacled arms squeeze the life out

of this poor, proud, ship.

The body of the monster is steadily drawn closer by its many appendages. More of the creature's form is pulled above the surface of the water until its mouth is revealed. Tentacles actually extend from its gaping maw. It seems the monster means to devour the ship. The bow starts to rise, as the stern is supporting the gross weight of the foul beast.

{{{KER-SNAP!!!}}}

A great tremor runs through the ship! I know immediately that *Victoria's* massive steel keel has snapped. There is no saving her. The *Victoria's* fate is sealed. This ship is doomed.

As fast as I am able to reach that conclusion, Mr. Temperance has already swept me up in his arms, and pitched me over the rail into a lifeboat on its way down.

"Hold that woman!" he instructs the passengers.

I see his features harden with grim resolve. A resolute visage locks into place and I know that he is about to act in a reckless manner.

But then he stops. The hard face of determination relaxes into the kind features of my little hero.

His face regains its playful sweetness as he casually tosses me his derby hat.

Time seems to slow as he and I are taken in a temporal aberration, a little bubble of serenity and quiet outside of the tumult around us.

A heartstopping foreboding comes over me.

Mr. Temperance and I are in our own world, outside the panicked maelstrom around us.

He looks at me and smiles.

"I love you, Persephone."

Then he's off!

The moment is broken and the uproar of *Victoria's* tragedy returns, yet all I see is that foolhardy man. Mr. Temperance struggles past passengers fighting one another trying to go in the opposite direction. Once free of the maddened crowd the clear decks allow him to pick up speed. Instincts give him the ability, bordering on premonition, to dodge tentacles the size of subway cars. He leaps deck chairs. The deck of the *Victoria* tilts towards the stern. The downhill slope increases his mad velocity.

Running, vaulting, and dodging awful-tentacled obstacles, he runs directly to the monster. He leaps atop and then kicks himself off the stern railing, propelling himself out and high into open space.

Once again, time seems to slow as my precious Ichabod launches himself high above the monster.

He arcs higher.

He seems to hang in suspension for a moment.

Then he drops, disappearing from view forever.

Our lifeboat is rowed away from the disaster. Despite many kind attempts to console me, I remain wretchedly distraught.

Heavy sobs wrack my body.

I am completely helpless to assist in the rescue efforts.

The poor *Victoria* explodes, bit by bit, under the irresistible constrictions of the monster.

The behemoth drags the broken remains of the *Victoria* to the bottom.

The unbelievable temperatures of the Sol Furnace and her accompanying boilers and engines roar in angry unhappiness at their submergence. Boiling waters and billows of steam mark her descent.

The ship is a composite of building material, a great steel keel and ribs. She carries tons of steel decking and supports for the Furnace and drive engines. But for the most part, the *Victoria* is, rather, *was*, a wooden ship. Fortunately, most of the wood has surfaced, having been squeezed into splinters by the tremendous sea monster, and is providing buoyancy for our... my ... unlucky shipmates.

I look on helplessly as our people are made safe.

The broken wreckage of *Victoria* is lashed into rafts. Captain Stewart is instrumental in directing the efforts. Whereas before he had struck me as ineffectual, he has now shown great prowess at securing the safety of his passengers and crew.

A cabin is swiftly constructed aboard one of the lashed-together rafts. It seems that Mademoiselle Gauzot has a very serious allergy to sunlight, and must protect herself from its dangerous rays.

In short order, we have arrayed quite an elaborate system of rafts and lifeboats. We have stores of potable water in floating barrels, and tinned food sufficient to keep us in reasonable comfort for a time. It is quite remarkable.

While the efforts of my shipmates are to be lauded, mine are not, for I am unable to do anything. I sit in a spot where I am not in their way, and hold Mr.

Temperance's hat thinking of him.

My friends try to make me feel better, but I am inconsolable.

Once more I am gripped by great, painful, sobs, as I mourn my brave friend.

He said he loved me.

And I...

...

I had no chance to reply.

It has been a week now since the disaster, yet still we float.

Many of the rafters have followed Mademoiselle Gauzot's example, and have constructed shelters to escape the Sun. For similar reasons many of the rescued passengers assay to sleep during the day, and convert to a nocturnal schedule.

Our friend Nancy Farmer has arranged a comfortable raft to share with her cats.

Then, not many days later, an island is spotted.

Our ungainly craft makes little headway, but to our great relief, we do drift toward the small island.

We do not spend much time on our tiny island before we are rescued.

A ship from the United States Navy, the *U.S.S. Enterprise*, has been sent to search for us, and found us on our little island. We are returned to Hawaii. From there, the friends that I, or we, made aboard the ship go their separate ways. They encourage me to put all this behind me, to get on with my life. I appreciate their good intentions, but I am unable to shake my sorrow. One by one, on ships bound to the east and west, they all depart.

This bright, colorful, tropical island is a sharp contrast to my bleak despair.

I have never experienced such profound sorrow.

Mr. Temperance!

Ichabod.

Ichabod!

I rest my hand on his silly hat, this funny Derby of which he was so proud.

It is all I have left to remind me of him, his silly hat, and the parasol he constructed for me.

I think of his bravery and his continued resolve.

If only I could have an ounce of his selflessness, perhaps I could muster the courage to continue.

He had the best of intentions for me, and devoted himself to something larger than the two of us, the very safety of our planet.

He gave his life to save me, to save us all.

Oh, how I wish I could be as he! Although he must have felt disheartened and afraid many times during our travails, he never let it affect him, never let it show. He just kept on going, doing what he had to do, no matter how he felt. That is the stuff of heroes, while I...

For too long, I have been like my namesake, the daughter of Demeter, living in a sort of Underworld, leaving destruction in my wake. I have allowed Mr.

Temperance to fight my battles for me, letting fears for my own safety to remain uppermost, when the safety of the entire world is at stake. Enough!

The time for being a genteel, "helpless" lady is over; I must find the strength, resourcefulness, and courage to stand on my own. I must forge a new Persephone Plumtartt; I must transform my sense of guilt and responsibility for these attacks into something useful. Now it is time to follow in Mr. Temperance's footsteps, and to take the battle to the enemy...

"Unh!"

As I sit by a campfire at night on this Hawaiian beach, making plans to be a better person, I feel an unmistakable creeping sensation. Something is here!

When I look around, I see it, headed towards me. A flying insect, glowing green, terrible, and grotesque, is coming towards me down the beach. As it approaches, its flight path is awkward and clumsy, yet I know in my heart that it means to destroy me.

It circles me several times. The little devil sizes me up in a horrible appraisal. I get an impression that it is actually laughing at me!

After all I have been through. After all Mr. Temperance sacrificed!

After all the pain and suffering endured by so many good people, to have this horrid creature defeat our wondrous planet.

I get angry.

I get very angry.

"You filth! You would ridicule the efforts of the most noble man I have ever known!?"

Snatching up a large, burning stick, I whirl upon my

despicable foe with a heretofore unfelt hatred in my heart. I plunge the torch of tribulation into the gnat of nevermore. The fiery thrust brings me as close to happiness as I have been since the *Victoria* tragedy. I allow myself a smug measure of satisfaction against my enemy.

Breathing heavily as I stand above the smoking remains of my would-be assassin, a ringing clarity floods through my emboldened spirit.

"That's for Mr. Temperance," I bellow, a growing sense of defiance growing in my heart, "and what's more, there shall be further displays of violent vengeance visited upon your vile brothers."

"Aloha, Persephone."

My friend, Miss Tracy T'ea-lor, a beautiful island princess, places a lei around my neck and wishes me safe travels. I embrace her, thankful for her companionship and the realization that even in a world rife with danger and sorrow, there are such simple and wholesome joys as true friendship. Now, however, I must return to the tasks set before me, and act as Mr. Temperance would do.

I mean to move in as a direct line as possible.

This ship is bound for Edo, on the east coast of the recently opened-to-trade country, Nippon.

After an uneventful journey I arrive to a country beset by monsters. The only defense these people have is flame. They have come up with novel devices for the projecting and dispersing of fire to combat their monsters; however, the creatures continually grow in strength, night by night.

I share with the Nipponese leaders my experience with these horrors. The detailed notes of weapon construction that I had secured along with the orb in my endlessly useful bustle are now proving to be of provident worth.

There is a new fiend on this Monster Island.

She is a deadly adversary who wastes no time in useless regret or mere intellectual speculation. A creature wholly devoted to the defeat of her enemies comes this new monster.

This creature is Hades' Queen; the Queen of Death.

Her name is Persephone Plumtartt.

Those who would enslave our fair dimension: beware the Bringer of Destruction.

"Don't let it get away!" I roar.

These men do not know my words, but they can very well take my meaning.

A murderous, gargantuan myriapod tries to escape. It is cut down.

We mean to drive straight across the island. For such a short amount of time, we are rather well kitted out.

These gentlemen love their thin, curved, and single edged swords. H

As I have come to expect, however, their folded steel implements have proven to be ineffective against these horrors. The new emerald blades in the hands of these fearless samurai flash a green light of demon destruction.

Spears of ectoplasmic material are formed in the peculiar fashion of this island peoples.

Fearless female warriors exhibit an uncanny speed and accuracy with their unusual Nipponese bow and arrow. The latter, of course, are tipped with ectoplasmic arrowheads.

A hastily constructed Voltage Disruptor is also a part of our growing armory!

With their own ingenious fire-casting implements adding to our arsenal, we are a formidable force.

Our enemies come to us.

I think they know I am here.

As always, they seem to be drawn to me, but when they near they are confronted by my steadily growing contingent of brave warriors.

We are proving to be more than a match for whatever our enemies can throw against us.

We march across the island.

My warriors grow more heartened with each successive victory.

With jubilation, we slay our horrid opponents, until the fourth night after my arrival.

Earth tremors violently throttle the land.

Where we stand, or attempt to stand, facing a broad valley, we see the mountain across from begin to show cracks opening from top to bottom. An orange/red glow shows through the widening fissures that have been reluctantly rent in the surface running up and down the towering mount. The light of molten lava illuminates the night sky.

This volcano does not erupt with liquid rock; rather, it is a worm the size of Yorkshire that pours forth.

The brave soldiers futilely fight the strangely green tinged black silhouette with courage, but to no avail. It comes for me. I gather all my anger and resolve, and I force this thing within me to ignite.

Electricity crackles up and down my form. I feel the energies form into a ball at my fingertips. A crimson sphere, perhaps a yard in diameter, briefly materializes before my palm before flashing away to the hideous giant worm.

The crimson missile explodes with a massive red light, engulfing the mountainous monster's head.

The horrid worm is wholly cast into colossal nothingness.

The army cheers.

I collapse.

We march into Kawanazawa, a victorious army.

Word has spread of our victories.

The harbor city welcomes us in a shower of cherry blossoms. I ride a magnificent stallion, at the head of, and as the leader of, a substantial army. This army, that started as less than two hundred men and women, now has grown to thousands, and continues to grow with ever-swelling numbers.

A ship from China is waiting for us in the harbor.

"Greetings from Monster Island!" I smile to our Asian continental friends.

The Chinese delegation is there to meet me, as their Wu foretold my arrival. They are amazed at the procession I ride in upon, and are confirmed in mind that I am fated in my path.

I leave the reclamation of Nippon to its able commanders, and depart Kawanazawa for Tianjin, a coastal Chinese city.

It is a very different scene in this city.

Tianjin proves to be a somber community struggling to survive against insurmountable enemies. As in Edo, they have only fire to fight with when we arrive, but they have a vast army waiting for us.

The Chinese citizenry are armed to the best of their abilities. Like the Nipponese, they have had to learn to fight without the aid of steel weaponry. Wooden staves and clubs are wielded instead of metal implements. I remember Monsieur Bin-Jamin's remarks about the monsters' inability to interact with our metals; it is as if their atomic structure passes through such elements.

This is a moment for which my singular background and upbringing have prepared me. The Plumtartt laboratories and manufacturing facilities have provided a lifetime of experience for me to prepare my armies. With all the knowledge I possess of factories and manufacture, I set the Chinese factories to work. My organizational skills are on par with anyone's, I dare say. The detailed notes I have kept of Mr. Temperance's amazing devices, and those of others we have encountered, provide the basis of a wide-ranging and effective arsenal.

Mr. Temperance...

Though I refuse to allow myself to indulge in any more sorrow, I still cannot help but grieve.

That was really something of a man. He had such resolve! I witnessed him survive the unsurvivable time and time again. I think the Leviathan that destroyed the *Victoria* would have continued its attack to find me had not Mr. Temperance fought the Beast and driven it under.

If only he had survived the attack on the undersea beast.

...

Could he have survived that suicidal assault?

...

I feel a tiny spark, deep in my soul.

Perhaps it is from his tinder box.

I make a new resolution.

"I shall keep hope alive, Mr. Temperance."

...

"Ichabod."

"We march in three days."

It has been two days since we arrived in Peking. They seem to have been expecting me. Again, the Wu of this Province predicted my coming, confirming in mind to all, the legitimacy of my place to lead the immense and swiftly swelling forces.

Production of our devices begins immediately, on a large scale.

Concurrently, we begin the training of the armies. These able soldiers must learn to fight diabolical monsters, instead of their fellow man.

I send for the Russian Ambassadors. I inform them of my requirements.

They balk. I insist. They agree.

I send for the Indian Ambassadors. I inform them of my requirements.

They balk. I insist. They agree.

A contingent of priests have come to see me. They do not look like any priests that I have ever seen, with their orange robes and shaven pates. They say that I am to receive their guidance and training in hand-to-hand combat as well as in learning to draw power from the Earth to fuel my 'crimson spheres.' I am skeptical of these fellows at first, but they soon win my confidence.

"I say!" There might be something to this priestly business.

Dispatch: The generals must adapt. I will allow one day of rest and manufacture, combined with three days' hard march. That schedule will change next week.

Dispatch: Where is the Siberian shipment?

Dispatch: Our Shaolin advisers suggest an open area for "advanced training." See that their needs are met.

Dispatch: The pachyderms must be at the Zhing pass at their appointed time. Coordination with Disruptor units is vital.

Dispatch: General Rijon's division is falling behind. Find the problem.

Dispatch: Have the dynamos routed through India, as that will end up being a shorter route. They can rendezvous with their units in the field.

Dispatch: Query: Have any creatures been captured alive for examination?

Dispatch: Keep working on the "Eyes." I appreciate the difficulties of manufacture, but these devices are of the greatest importance.

Dispatch: All armies need to prepare for nightly battles. Ancient creatures that have laid buried and dormant for Millennia awaken at our approach. Consider the combat with these creatures to be a part of your soldiers' training.

Dispatch: Our forces are succumbing to psychic assaults. There appear to be no defenses to these crippling assaults other than a determined attack to break the concentration of the larger, more psychically inclined worms.

Dispatch: All armies, from Divisional, down to Battalion and squad levels, must work in coordinated teams. Voltage Disruptors cannot recharge fast enough to hold back a determined legion of foes. Plasmo-Gasmic Discharging battalions must work to protect the Disruptors. Commanders must integrate their disparate troops and instill in them the need to work as cohesive units.

Dispatch: My training with the monks must continue as we march. If necessary, build a traveling platform for my "Gung Fu" practice.

Dispatch: The Disruptors are of three different sizes: small, medium, and large. Attack different sized monsters with appropriately sized weapon.

Dispatch: All Commanders. We are not getting enough ectoplasm to work with. Please discipline your troops to allow their bladed contingents to kill enough creatures to stockpile our Discharging brigades.

Dispatch: Does any Commander have any suggestions

as to how to combat the psychic assaults?

Dispatch: ...

Dispatch: Has the high-output Plasmo-Gasmic Dicharge Device mobile manufacturing caravan begun operation? I want those guns!

Dispatch: All Commanders. We have been visited by a group of Tibetan monks. Their leader is a Holy Man of sorts, a Lama. He claims that his monks, though normally not warlike, are prepared to travel with our units to protect against the psychic assault threat.

Dispatch: Where are my corset designers? I require strengthening across the duodenum.

Dispatch: We receive word that the Siberians are making the pachyderms nervous. I suggest routing cats by Southern pass.

Dispatch: Have General Li slow down his battalions. I appreciate that he and his forces are eager, but we shall need all our armies to converge in coordination.

Dispatch: All commanders: Maintain a semaphore connection between forces. Imperative that your mobile "Eye" units locate our final destination.

Dispatch: Congratulations are in order for all armies. All units are making splendid time. Morale is high and varied brigades are working in a synchronized perfection. All signs point to a critical conflict soon at hand. Have your armies ready. The importance of the consequences of this final battle cannot be over-stated.

Dispatch: ...

CHAPTER 41 - DEVOURED.

Ichabod.

The Kra-Ken roars:

"EEEEEE-AYE-rROARrrreeeeRRR RRRrrrraaaAAAAAaaaauuuUUUU UuuuurrrRRRRRRrrrrrrrrRRRR RRRRRrrrrrRRRRRrrrraaaaaarrrrrRR RRrrraaaaaaAAAAaaaauuuuuuUU UUUuuuuuuUUUUUuuuuuooOOO OOOOOOOOooooooooooOOOOOoo ooooooaaaaaaAAAAAAAAaaaaaaaAAA AAAaaaggGGGHhhhhhhh!!!!!!!!!!!!

I continue to fall.

However, I think that his roaring, stinking breath is actually acting to slow my descent.

I bounce from rubbery walls.

Rubbery puckery sucker cup pods suck with pluck.

I continue my downward plunge, as one with the wreckage of the Victoria.

"Uh, oh."

I catch sight of the mouth.

I should say beak.

I am inexorably being tumbled toward this horrible intake sphincter.

It's more like a circle of layered beaks, actually, but twisty.

The orifice comprises about a dozen beaks around and a dozen deep, working in a mechanical unison.

They are huge.

I am being thrown into them.

I will certainly be crushed!

I draw my Plamo-Gasmic Discharge Device.

{{{BUH-WHOOMP-POW!!!}}}

{BOOMZKIDY!!!}

(exploding beaks)

I pass within.

"Ow."

This is not very comfortable.

For the most part, the best course of action seems to be to just wrap myself up in a ball and roll with the punches.

I am underwater.

I pull on the G.I.L.L.s.

There! At least now, I can breathe.

Strange, the walls seem to glow. As I get sloshed and squirted along, at least I can see what is going on.

Being able to see and breathe does a lot for my morale.

Eventually, the food conveyor belt I seem to be riding slows down. I think I am in the monster's stomach.

The stomach's gastric juices start to make my boots sizzle.

It's time to go.

I use the emerald blade to cut my way out.

Once clear of the burning acids, I can now get to business.

I gotta distract this fella from Miss Plumtartt.

I draw and push the P.G.D.D. back into the acidic stomach.

BUH-WHOOMP-POW!!!

BRRRZZZSS-SS-SS-KK-KK-BRUH-BAH-KUH–R-R-RUUUHHHMMM MZZ-ZZ-ZZ-ZZ!!!

"Uhb..."

Where am I? Oh, yeah, the *Victoria* and the monster. I think I may have been knocked unconscious by that explosion. Yeah, I'm thinkin' maybe I was.

There seems to be a lot of damage to the creature. I do not think I have slain the Beast, but I hope I have taken his attention away from Miss Plumtartt. I don't think I can risk another plasmic explosion, though. I would like to survive this ordeal and tell Miss Plumtartt about it, and another detonation would very likely prove terminal for me.

I am not averse to hard work. That's good, 'cause I got my work cut out for me... literally.

Cutting through the rubbery walls is not easy. They are thick. One thick walled compartment just leads to another. Each"cell" seems to be composed of sea water.

This is a long, slow process. After a while, I realize that I have lost track of time. Have I drifted to sleep? I allow my instinctual sense of direction to guide me.

Cut.

Cut.

Cut.

These cells are different; they have a different texture.

This is different. These are more stringy and ropey.

Nerves, maybe?

This seems to be a major gathering of the monster's nervous system.

Time for some heavy pruning.

"Struck a nerve, did I?"

The behemoth gives a mighty twinge.

I cut into the next set of walls and cells until I find another nerve bundle. After a couple of dozen slashes, I move on.

I can sense a panic in the beast. I have a sensation that we are on the run. It cannot escape me.

I repeat the process, resting occasionally.

More and more, I can tell that it is a war of attrition, and I intend to win.

How long have I been cutting? How long long have I been in here? How long until I am free?

I cannot tell, but I know the monster is failing.

Finally, I reach a wall with an altogether different texture to it. It is especially difficult to cut, very fibrous and resistant.

Hacking my way through this tough hide is a long, time-consuming, ordeal.

But then, I strike...water!

I am newly enthused and invigorated!

I excitedly tear at the tenacious tissue until I can wriggle through.

I am free!

The hulk of the Great Beast slips into the depths, happy to be free of its Alabamic invader.

Fish: I smell fish.

Sunlight: I feel Sunlight on my face.

I sense the rocking of a boat.

I open my eyes. The face of an old Chinese man is about two inches from my nose.

"Ying yang, bing bang, zing zang, cow."

"Yessir."

"Bing zing, ying ling, wakka wakka, meow!"

"Nossir."

He gives up, and goes back to the work of running his boat.

I think I must have gotten tangled in his nets.

He was debating whether to throw me back or not.

I don't think he has made his mind up yet.

Apparently he has decided to ignore me.

We eventually make it back to his fishing village.

The first thing I do is eat. After much food, I am able to ascertain that I am in the Philippines.

The first order of business is to locate Miss Plumtartt.

I manage to work my way through the jungle. From island to island in the huge group, I steadily make my way until I finally reach the capital, Manila. What a grand city! Such elegance in architecture and such industrious, busy peoples!

I am enthralled by the lovely surroundings, until I pass a newspaper stand.

Dozens of headlines scream at me:

"S.S. VICTORIA LOST!!!"

"ALL HANDS DEAD!!!"

"WORST DISASTER IN HISTORY!"

"TRAGIC MYSTERY!"

"NOT A SINGLE SURVIVOR!"

I am stunned and dumbfounded.

I feel as if drain plugs have been opened in my heels, and all my insides have just poured away into the pit of despair opening beneath me.

A couple of those headlines are wrong, for there is a survivor.

"Hey, Joe! You no sit there. Hey, Joe, you gotta move!"

Apparently I have fallen to my knees. I get up, and shuffle along.

I am in a trance.

The Victoria, lost.

All those wonderful people, dead.

Why is it that I live?

Instead of...

Her.

...

Miss Plumtartt.

...

She is the one who was supposed to live!

I cannot get my mind around it.

I cannot believe it.

She cannot be dead.

"She can't be ... dead."

...

"Miss . . . Plum . . . tartt?"

...

I am finding it difficult to breathe. My lungs have turned to lead and are jumping up and down in my chest. My throat is thick and swollen.

Manila fades away into a distant grayness behind a mounting wall of water building in my eyes.

I find myself wrapped in a cocoon of silence, focused inward only on my terrible loss.

A shell of sound rejection encases me in an enclosed egg of solitude.

...

I can tell that I am powerless to stop the loss of my composure in a devastatingly emotional display.

...

I don't know what to do.

...

(The reader is asked to look away.)

...

...

...

Eventually, I come to a stop. I wipe up the tears and snot.

What am I gonna do?

...

What is left to me?

I only have my inventions and this hated artifact.

I know that it is some sort of scroll. I have kept it secured upon my person, ignoring its disturbing presence. It lies inside the lead tube that I constantly keep. It has been undisturbed since we examined it in the rooms of Monsieur Bin-Jamin in Paris, and before that, my transferring it from its little metal chest to this pipe, all that time ago on our desperate flight across the English Channel to France.

What good is it to me?

I promised Miss Plumtartt that I would help her get it to Tibet. If I could have gotten her there, then she would have found the right location for casting some sort of spell, concerning this scroll.

But I failed.

I failed to protect her.

My promise is spent, unfulfilled.

...

Could I complete the task?

I wonder...

No! I would certainly not act in this manner in front of Miss Plumtartt!

"There ain't no, 'could I' ner, 'should I'?" I shout.

"Do or do not, that's the ticket!"

"Miss Plumtartt, I made you a promise."

"I hereby make a re-affirmation."

"I shall complete our task!"

From Manila, I cross a choppy, South China Sea.

I arrive on the the mainland of Asia in a place called Cambodia. Here I pass through steaming jungles, filled with poisonous swarms of insects. These countries are full of snakes as big as hawsers, and bogs of watery mud that will just swallow you up gone, lickety-split.

This oppressive jungle reminds me of being trapped within the Leviathan. Here, there is no sun, only a diffused light, filtered through lush, green leaves. This is reminiscent of the sickly green light I was afforded in the belly of the Beast. This sweltering, moist, inferno is very much like the hated entrails of my former, submersible friend, though he was, obviously, much cooler.

The heavy humidity makes it difficult to breathe. The air is heavy and oppressive. Nothing survives in this jungle. Everything rots, including my clothes and my inventions. The moist atmosphere indiscriminately eats away at cotton, wool, leather, steel, and flesh.

My "Beauties" are deteriorating.

The La Mat, P.G.D.D., has begun to rust.

I am not pursued. Apparently, the horrors were only after Miss Plumtartt. In order to protect them, I pack away the two remaining devices. No need for them to rot away also.

My boots have succumbed. I am afraid that my poor feet may follow them.

I must endure.

Ichabod Temperance.

"She" addressed me as Ichabod once, in Ipswich. I was fighting for her life, when things faded away from my memory, but I have always had the impression that something of importance happened then.

"She" called me Ichabod.

It is painfully frustrating to be unable to call the precious moment to mind.

It's almost there, just at the edge of remembrance, her magical, musical, British-accented voice urgently called my name.

"Ichabod!"

...

Ichabod.

Hebrew for "inglorious."

Yep, that's me all right. I'm about as inglorious a fella as you could ever hope to find.

That ain't all.

Temperance.

Temperance: To eschew alcohol.

Put 'em together, and you still ain't got much.

Ichabod Temperance.

An inglorious teetotaler.

...

Ichabod Temperance,

...

an inglorious teetotaler.

...

I look at my poor feet.

...

I have to look away...

It is not an inglorious teetotaler who will manage to cross this unforgiving, SouthEast Asian swamp.

...

I've got to get a hold of myself.

I need to draw upon my good horse sense.

I need to engage my tinker's mind.

Don't think like an inglorious teetotaler, Ichabod; think like a tinker.

...

I do not have to be an inglorious teetotaler.

I can be more.

Think, Ichabod Temperance, think!

...

Maybe I can tinker a little bit here. Maybe I can re-evaluate my resources.

...

Inglorious is a word that can be reworked.

Ichabod. -Without Glory.

...

Temperance can also mean being tempered by flame.

Temperance. -Hardened through the crucible of ordeal.

...

Without Glory.

Hardened through the crucible of ordeal.

Ichabod Temperance.

I continue my travels across Laos. At least here, I get to ride an elephant for a few miles.

Finally I get to Burma.

I turn more sharply North.

The going is literally uphill from here.

The terrain becomes more mountainous.

Eventually, countries become blurred.

After a certain elevation, there are no borders.

I follow the Salween river valley as far North as it will take me.

The outlying arms of this Southernmost extension of the Himalayas have been my valley. Now I finally climb to their summit.

I follow this line of the mountains.

I unpack, and clean, my 'Beauties.' So too do I prepare the old La Mat.

I enter Tibet.

"Am I glad to see you boys!"

There is a vicious blizzard blowing outside. Zero visibility hides snow drifts as big as mountains and treacherous crevasses of all-but-bottomless depths. This is not good when you are on top of a mountain. I am relieved to find this shelter. It's a commune of sorts. About twenty people of varying ages share a large, round tent.

They are not the most jolly band I have come across, but I am happy for their company, nonetheless.

Despite the language difficulties, we get along pretty well, until I am offered some bread.

I pull my emerald blade to cut the bread. It is not a threatening gesture.

"I'gnu ztok!"

An excited murmur passes through these people.

"I'gnu ztok bure! I'gnu ztok bure! I'gnu ztok bure!"

They grow quiet again, looking at me.

An old woman spits. " I'gnu ztok bure ien! Jaek' Kol hatan!"

With that, she and the whole lot of them run me out the tent flap. "Ein! Ein! Ein!"

I am staggered. I cannot fathom what just happened, but there is no mistake. They want me gone.

I leave.

Over the next few days, I find that no commune will let me enter. I am met at the outskirts of each enclave by angry villagers with pitchforks.

I finally get the story from a kindly man who takes pity on me. He offers me food, and an explanation. There is a man in the mountains. He has all the area in a thrall of fear. His name is Jaek' Kol. The name is synonymous with an ancient Himalayan curse, or legend, meaning, "Snow Devil." This man, this Jaek' Kol, has let it be known that he wants the man with the green knife.

I thank the kindly man and leave.

I press on. I am unsure of my destination. Tibet as a destination point is kinda vague.

I approach the smoldering remains of a small village. No living soul remains. Torn into a sheer rock wall, someone, somehow, has crudely scrawled the words, "I'gnu ztok bure hatan Jaek' Kol."

I now have the ability to loosely translate, "Green Knife Man come to Jaek' Kol."

I look at the tragedy of this little village. This man has shown what he will do if I do not come to him.

Footprints in the snow stretch out in front of me.

I walk across a desolate frozen tundra.

In the distance, I spot a brief spark.

I make for this only sign of a destination. I see it is a flame.

As I approach this camp fire, I see a man.

He backs up in a gesture that indicates a temporary truce, allowing me access to the fire's warmth.

I start to thaw.

I look at him over the wildly blowing flames of the campfire. He is a big man. He steps forward, and throws back his parka's hood.

The first thing I see is his glaring eyes in a fierce face.

His bald pate gleams in the fire's glow.

"I'gnu ztok bure." He says the words slowly, with great distaste, indicating me.

"I am the Green Knife Man," I confirm.

"Jaek' Kol!" He indicates himself. This Himalayan Genghis Kahn resonates with pride, defiance, and threat.

"Snow Devil. Yes. I would say that it was nice to meet

you, but I ain't accustomed to lies."

"Jaek' Kol get land for kill Green Knife Man. Jaek' Kol will be King of mountain,"

...

"when 'They' take over."

...

The heavy clouds that have clung to this snowy land disperse. The stars reveal fields of snow, circled by mountains, here on top of the world.

The Moon casts a bluish light on this scene of cold beauty.

Jaek' Kol looks up at the Moon with a short laugh. He throws away his parka. He no longer seems to feel it necessary. This is his element.

He seems to bask in, and absorb, the Moon's rays, soaking them in.

He jerks and starts to tremble. A slight foam forms at his mouth.

A terrible laugh starts to bubble up from within.

Several deep, wracking, tremors violently shake the huge Mongol.

Then he starts getting hairier.

Am I hallucinating or is he getting taller?

In a few short seconds, he has transformed from a man into a huge, white-haired beast.

A snow man of abomination stands before me.

I draw the P.G.D.D.

BUH-WHOOMP. skrrrrrr-chik.

It fails to fire.

Jaek' Kol roars, and attacks.

I roll away to the side, instincts taking over.

He is too fast for me to react to consciously.

Stout kicks stagger the beast. My Savate training applies itself unbidden.

Enraged, the monster swings with the murderous thought of decapitation in his brutal mind.

I jack his jaw with a whirlwind boot.

Spinning to the side, I draw my P.E.R.K.

We face each other.

Mutual appraisal.

I can still see the face of the man that was, in the monster's features.

Never have I witnessed such rage and frustration.

We resume our battle.

Ours is a struggle of life and death.

He is strength and fury.

I am cunning and danger.

It comes down to a test of attrition, and will.

I am merciless with my emerald blade.

He tears and bites. He tries to crush and break.

We fight.

And we fight.

He manages to throw me aside, causing me to drop the knife.

He picks it up.

Jaek' Kol looks directly at me as he breaks my Emerald Joy.

The monster almost laughs.

He stalks me as I maneuver, attempting to keep the fire between myself and Jaek' Kol.

I am defenseless.

He lunges.

I fall to the side while simultaneously kicking out to grapevine his proffered foot. I trip him up, the way me and my pals used to wrastle back home.

He goes face first into the fire.

My manipulation of his ankle grants me the leverage to hold him there.

Burn, Jaek' Kol!

He's a little gamey, but I am refreshed after a good meal of fresh meat.

...

Though I am weaponless, I still have my task.

...

...

...

I scavenge his supplies for material.

I find a few parcels of food and a small still he used to produce his own, foul, home brew.

There are a few flasks, and a glass bottle in a crude, heavy form.

I shudder when I find some disgusting items he no doubt took from his victims as "trophies..."

...

I can't think of any use for these items.

...

Wait: a small still!

...

...

(*! plinck !*)

I use the femur of the Himalayan Lycanthrope as a frame for my device, the still for a channeling mechanism; the bottle serves as an ectoplasmic charging chamber.

I scavenge the sad remains of my prized La Mat and the contents of my holster's ammunition to complete my project.

With a newly formed weapon in hand, I resume my journey.

...

I...

...

am...

...

cold....

....

hungry...

....

alone....

...

lonely...

...

The blizzard consumes... all...

...

No visibility...

...

cold...

...

hungry...

...

alone...

...

loneliness...

...

Thoughts of Miss Plumtartt...

...

Miss Plumtartt...

...

Ipswich...

...

She spoke my name...

...

'Ichabod'...

...

...

That moment ...

...

in Paris...

To awaken...

'Her'...

I kissed...

my Princess...

Was it real?...

Did it really happen?...

Or did I dream it?...

...

On the '*Midnight Minnow,'* she kissed my cheek.

She was proud of me, maybe more.

...

Miss Plumtartt...

Miss Plumtartt...

...

cold...

...

hungry...

...

alone...

...

"Wake up, you little American Bug!"

I am kicked in the face.

The kick, combined with the Prussian Pillock's accent, snap me out of the funque into which I have slipped.

"Thanks, I needed that, you Creepy Kraut."

I come to my senses on a vast plateau.

A frozen waste.

I grab my weapon and spin up the 'Beauties.'

"MmBwuhahahahaha!"

"Was zur Hölle!?!" Exclaims the Bavarian Bombast.

"Is that some sort of caveman club you have devised,

Herr Munchkin?"

Herr Doktor Himmel relaxes in his outrageously ostentatious and luxuriously appointed monster-pulled sled.

Scores of horrible creatures scuttle over the ridge behind him. Massive horrors surround him. The beastie that just kicked me in the face backs away to afford the Doktor a better view of yours truly.

"Vas ist this you clutch in your dirty human hands? A bone? A bit of tubing? An old glass jar?"

I only have one shot with my improvised device.

I take it.

{{{BUH-WHOOMP-POW!!!}}}

BOOM! BOOM! BOOMITY

BOOM BOOM BUH-BOOM!!!

"Got him!" I whoop.

More than a dozen kritters got fried in that discharge. The P.G.D.D. exploded in my hands and face, but I don't care! This is my first moment of happiness in months. The fancy sled got blown to pieces, and the Dok... No!

Twenty feet back from where he was standing a moment earlier, the Bavarian Dastard sits up from the snow.

Momentarily dazed, he angrily gets to his feet.

Quickly covering the ground to where I had been blown back, the Dirty Deutschman reaches out with his suddenly tentacled limbs, snatching me up.

"Now, you shall pay for your insolence, you insignificant interloper."

I am bound tight by many tentacles. My arms are pinned and I cannot breathe.

"And this, I think, belongs to me," he says, taking the tube containing the ancient scroll.

"Mwuhuhuhuh"

"Mwuhuhuhuh"

"Mwuh"

"Ahahahahahahahahahahahahahahahahahahahaha!"

The Doktor claims his prize, the lead pipe containing the Dread Scroll of Unutterable content.

As he screws the end cap off, the monsters get restless. Hundreds, no, thousands, no, tens of thousands of inter-dimensional horrors claim this Tibetan Plateau. They have gathered to welcome their wrongful poobah of another plane.

As he removes the scroll from its lead shelter, the hordes of horrors begin an excited chittering.

The disgusting Doktor displays the thing to his rapt audience.

They cheer him wildly.

He begins to read aloud an intonement.

The abominable insect speech subsides.

{KUH, -rrrRACK}

The sky makes a noise.

{{KUH, -rrrRACK!!!}}

The sky makes another, even more ominous sound.

The monsters go berserk with joy!

The Doktor continues his terrible spell.

He holds the scroll aloft...

... and it is speared from out of his hand.

The implement of its removal is quivering, where it has plunged into the ground.

The scroll has been punctured by an emerald spike, protruding from an iridescent green ball, affixed to the end of a pink parasol.

CHAPTER 42 – TIMING.

Persephone

"All equipment and personnel, this is it!" I bellow as I charge ahead of my gathered forces.

The horse rears to flee, but with my new-found Gung Fu-trained agility, I merely use this as a propellant, to spin and continue my forward motion.

I top the icy ridge.

It is as I had sensed. Untold thousands of hideous creatures, great and small, fill this vast plain. A glowing sea of phosphorescent abominations writhe before me.

I almost relinquish my pre-battle meal, but manage to control my nausea.

The hordes of creatures are oblivious to me as they are in a terrible state of frenzied excitement.

There! Not too terribly far away are two men. No, it's one man and he is being held by the other fellow's tentacles.

KUH-rrRACK (Says the Sky!)

Herr Himmel is holding my Ichabod!

KUH-rrrRACK!!!

Himmel intones the manifestation!

Seeing my Ichabod draws my hand to his gift for me as it always does when I think of him.

Instinctively I target the foul scroll.

My pink parasotal missile flies from my hand.

Bullseye!
"I say. Good show!"

CHAPTER 43 - A WELCOME SIGHT.

Ichabod.

"Miss..."

"Miss..."

"Miss ... Plumtartt?"

A vision of womanhood, idealized, stands atop the icy ridge.

Indifferent to her harsh surroundings is this figure of legend, a warrior Goddess.

From her boots, (heavily constructed, they follow the form of her strong legs, all the way past her knees) to the top of her head, (incongruously adorned by a familiar gentleman's hat) she exudes confidence, and control.

Around her waist, she wears a skirt. It's quite short, in fact, presumably allowing freedom of movement.

Her bodice is a corset of heavy leathers, firmly strapped into position. The contours of her remarkable form are securely supported.

Bucklers adorn her forearms.

A confident cock of her shapely hips lock out to one side.

A mischievous fire blazes in her eyes.

"Fraulein Sour-tartt! So, you made it after all, ja?"

"That's Plumtartt. Miss Persephone Plumtartt, but you, Herr Doktor, may call me the Bringer of Destruction. Your destruction."

Chapter 44 - The Battle For Planet Earth.

Persephone

"Ahahahahahahaha!"

Herr Doktor Himmel stands amidst an unending sea of writhing and frenzied inter-dimensional horrors. The size of some of the horrors is staggering. My human size is tiny in comparison.

"Really? Do you think you can stop what cannot be stopped? You? You, and whose army, mein Leibchen?"

"*My* army, Herr Doktor!"

Suddenly, pair by pair, thousands of green points of light blink into existence marking the presence of a set of Mr. Temperance's "Green Beauties".

Tens of thousands of well-armed soldiers and their frightening equipment clear the ridge, stretching out for miles.

Thousands of soldiers come into view, armed in Mr. Temperance's prototype he designed while in Hawaii. From their shoulders, a harness is suspended. This is secured around the waist, to support a structure in front of the user. A triangulated point is formed. On this steady platform, a Gattling Gun of sorts is mounted, but it has no crank to rotate its many barrels and feed its ammunition appetite. Instead, it operates by means of compressed air, stored in tanks on the backs of the soldiers. With the freedom gained by not having to manually crank the devices, the gunmen enjoy a two-handed grip on their deadly devices. Two thumbs comfortably rest on a single trigger. A large supply of ammunition is available via two great round magazines, side mounted on the guns. Did I fail to mention? The Gattling Guns are supplemented in their destructive fire power. Each barrel is coupled with a tube of the emerald fury of Mr. Temperance's Plasmo-Gasmic Discharging Devices.

These soldiers so equipped are interspersed with personnel armed with individually-powered Voltage Disruptors.

Thousands of soldiers armed with polearms, and every other fighting blade known on Earth, mix in amongst their well-armed brethren. Instead of steel, though, their weaponry are cast in Ecto-Plasmic Resin. Their cold, emerald fury eagerly anticipates conflict. They support their comrades.

Room is also made for the positioning of wagon-mounted Voltage Disruptor units. Each of these is followed by its own steam-powered generator. Their crews appear eager to let loose their blasts of electric mayhem.

Incendiary brigades, armed with catapults, flaming spears, javelins, and a nozzled weapon with just a bit of flame at the front, wait in the hopes and expectations of getting to ignite a torrent of fiery death.

Mixed in with all units are funny little monks. They are chanting in low choruses of ominous portent.

And then, one by one, the big guns are wheeled in, pulled by their teams of massive elephants. Gigantic Voltage Disruptors have an uncanny, futuristic appearance almost as alien as the disgusting, writhing mass in the frozen meadow below.

"This is our world, Doktor. We shall not relinquish her Sovereignty."

"We shall conquer this puny world, and have you grovel at our feet!" the repugnant Doktor screams.

"rrrRRRRAAAARRRRR!!!!"
(they cry)

"rrrRRRRAAAARRRRR!!!!"
(we respond)

The obscene creatures fling themselves upon the human armies.

**KUH-rrRACK! BOOM!
BUH-WHOOMP-POW! CHITTER!
BOOM! KUH-rrRACK! BOOM!
BUH-WHOOMP-POW! BOOM!
KUH-rrRACK! BOOM! SCREETCH!
BUH-WHOOMP-POW! BOOM!
KUH-rrRACK! BOOM!
HAH-WHOOSH! EEE-AYE-rROARK!
BUH-WHOOMP-POW! BOOM!
KUH-rrRACK! SCREETCH! BOOM!
BUH-WHOOMP-POW! BOOM!
KUH-rrRACK! BOOM!
BUH-WHOOMP-POW! BOOM!
SCREETCH!**

Et cetera.... thousands of times over.

The various Voltage Disruptor crews attack targets of the appropriate size.

Incendiary battalions launch their painful salvos.

Battalions of troops armed with Gattling style, automated, repeating, self-contained, Plasmo-Gasmic Discharge Devices cut a horrific swath through waves of monsters.

These men and women know that the fate of the world hangs in the balance.

They combat unthinking murderous monsters, bent on the enslavement of our planet, and our entire universe. We are the ones who would deny them this precious world.

By my lights, do we give it to them!

Such a display of raw power! The explosive mêlée is devastating in its concussive brutality.

"Those devils mean to escape! Put the cats on them!"

Scores of gigantic Siberian Tigers chase down and slaughter the fleeing demons.

The men of real genius should be proud of their marvelous inventions, and their noble defense of our home planet. Professor Tesla, and the brave scholars of Graz. Mr. Temperance, ... Mr. Temperance!

I look once more to the two individuals on the field below.

Seeing the battle go against him, Doktor Himmel returns to the dreadful scroll.

He utters a few malevolent words.

"Hahahahahahaha"

"He cannot be stopped, now!"

KrrrRRRRRACK-KUH!!!!

The sky....

I'm looking through a hole in the sky.

Chapter 45 - Manifestation.

Ichabod.

"He comes!" roars Doktor Himmel. "Grovel, you worms!"

Something awful is coming into our world.

"Fire on that abomination!" commands Miss Plumtartt.

The Gigantor Voltage Disruptors swing their massive cones upwards to fling their far-flung destructive electrical bolts. They arc ever higher until they are able to aim at the thing in the night sky. It is almost impossible for the human crews to bear to look upon. The soldiers' Tibetan monks help give them the intestinal fortitude to stay with their difficult task. The major batteries start to open fire.

Smaller weapon units take up the slack where the big guns have altered their targeting. These seasoned troops prevail, where any other human army would balk.

The Gigantor units emit blasts of unbelievable energies, yet they are but tiny pinpricks against the hideous horror. They will not stop the inter-dimensional Conquerer.

With the big Disruptors targeting change, the field of battle's dynamic changes. Slowly, the creatures of Earth's destruction begin to gain the upper hand. Great blasts of green energies strike from the Great Beast above our heads. The monster is destroying our Gigantor units! The tide of battle turns against us.

I see Miss Plumtartt holding a translucent white orb up into the air. It is the Pearl! Does every man and beast gasp? Somehow, a ripple seems to flow through the scene of battle as each person notices the shining pearl.

This draws the attention of the incomprehensible horror above our heads, making it aware of Miss Plumtartt.

With a powerful green beam of energy, the uninvited guest to our fair dimension, rudely assaults the Maiden of Destruction. She is momentarily staggered, but quickly rallies. The Pearl, held high above her head, seems to be absorbing the pulsating ray emanating from the horrible thing in the sky. Atta girl! It's working!

Herr Himmel's bug-eyed face jerks back and forth between the two combatants.

"Nein! Fraulein!" roars the treacherous German. He thrusts out an especially long tentacle. He grasps her tender ankle!

"Miss Plumtartt!" I gasp. She falters!

Her concentration is broken! The Talisman fails!

The Doktor smiles, tightening his repulsive grip. The appendage grasping Miss Plumtartt slowly insinuates itself up her leg.

I scramble up, from where Himmel just turned me loose.

I am on him faster than grease through a goose.

It's clobbering time. We are a two-man whirlwind.

Miss Plumtartt recovers and is able to re-assert her self-control.

The wondrous Pearl, wielded by one who is equally pure, collects the unclean energies that are blasted at our beautiful heroine by the Unknowable Abomination. At last it dawns on me why our enemies have tried so hard to divest her of her virtue.

The Talisman glows with a warm light. It starts to vibrate.

Red pulses of light emanate from the natural wonder

from under the sea. Scarlet spheres of luminescence seem to slow time throughout the battlefield as they pulsate outward in successive waves encompassing the frozen plain. Then they start to come faster. Vertical halos flash outward in brief electrical orbits of red light. Faster and faster they illuminate the high plain until reaching a crimson crescendo!

The "Orb" achieves a critical stage.

"At you!" cries the Goddess of War.

Hhhwww-WHOOOMMPP!

{{{**BOOOM!!!**}}}

The Talisman gives a grand release. Spherical bubbles of scarlet energy pulsate from the Talisman in relentless waves pounding the invader back through its inter-dimensional portal, and pummel the doorway shut.

The reflection is a smashing success!

CHAPTER 46 - TOGETHER.

Ichabod and Persephone.

Every creature on the field of battle, human and otherwise alike, has been knocked off their feet by the blast of the Talisman's reflection of the inter-dimensional horrors deadly green beam. The incomprehensible horror retreats. The perilous portal crumbles in upon itself.

However, Herr Himmel is not yet done. "At least I shall have the pleasure of killing you! You little American bug!"

The big German has got me pinned down, strangling me with his hated tentacles.

He gets kneed in the nether regions.

We roll apart. Himmel looks to me, and then Miss Plumtartt. The Doktor grabs his cane and aims it like a rifle at Miss Plumtartt.

I grab Miss Plumtartt's parasol and fling it at Himmel.

He gets the point.

"I believe this belongs to you, Mr. Temperance," she says, tossing a familiar hat into my lap.

"Why, yes. I believe it does, Miss Plumtartt."

Can this be real? I am unsure, until she helps me to my feet.

I hold the blessed contact of her lovely hands.

I take her in a warm embrace.

...

And we live happily ever after.

Chapter 47 - Ichabod and Persephone.

Persephone and Ichabod

My poor bedraggled Ichabod Temperance! To have you in my arms again is more than I could have dreamed of. I suspect a slight teasing will ignite the fires of your soul.

"Mr. Temperance, I believe that you have been terribly rude to me."

"How?" His face is stricken.

"As I recall, at our last meeting, you had the temerity to throw me overboard like a parcel of British Rubbish...and then..."

Is that a tiny flicker of a smile on his face?

"And then you made the most amazing statement, but you left abruptly, without giving me a chance to reply. Most intolerably rude, I must say!"

Somewhere in the depths of those hazel eyes, I see merriment, and hope.

"May I make my reply now, Mr. Temperance?"

"By all means!" he says. His smile is as broad and open as a boy's, but infinitely more promising.

Casting aside the last traces of the properly reticent English lady, I put my arms about him.

"Will this suffice?" I say, and then suddenly, incredibly, we are embracing.

"Ah say! Rah-thuh!" says Mr. Temperance, after some minutes.

"Are you having me on, Mr. Temperance?"

“Call me Ichabod, ... Ma’am.”

We discover that the kiss is not over quite yet. Together, Mr. Temperance, I, and this great blue marble spinning through space seem to use this Tibetan plateau as its axis. We are on top of the world.

After that embrace, I know we shall live *very* happily ever after.

...

The reader is asked to look away.

...

The End.

AFTERWORD

It is with the utmost pleasure that we, Miss Plumtartt and myself, express our heartfelt gratitude for your reading of our humble story.

"Thank you."

More from the world of "A Matter of Temperance":

A World of InTemperance

(Volume Two of The Adventures of Ichabod Temperance)

For the Love of Temperance

(Volume Three of The Adventures of Ichabod Temperance)

available in print and for Amazon Kindle at Amazon.com

and forthcoming

A Study in Temperance

(Volume Four of The Adventures of Ichabod Temperance)

to be available in print and for Amazon Kindle at Amazon.com

Made in the USA
San Bernardino, CA
11 April 2014